Deja Vu

Also by Mary Hardcastle

The Triple

Deja Vu

a novel

Mary Hardcastle

Book cover: *Notes 53* by Artist Stevie Dissinger. She investigates the perception of time and labor through physical manifestations. *Notes 53* records the work of hands. Ink is applied as fingers move through the process of stitching.

ISBN-978-0-9976728-6-2

For my great grandmother

Contents

Introduction

This novel started out as a romantic fantasy about a young woman who travels back through time to the 1800's and discovers herself through a series of adventures. The tale involved a trip down the great Mississippi River on a flatboat from Illinois to New Orleans. Along the way, the young woman meets captivating characters, falls in love with a rugged 19th century man, and is torn between staying in the past and returning to the future. It is an oft used trope for time travel tales.

And then something happened.

As I perused history books, visited museums and camped along the Mississippi River, I realized that I had chosen a time and place for my story that was pivotal for institutionalizing racism in America. I had not learned this in any level of my schooling, not found it in any of my text books. Mark Twain's *Adventures of Huckleberry Finn* was my main cultural association with the river. In school I was taught that the Mississippi River was vital to 19th Century pioneers for the transport of goods and that along its 2300 mile north south route, four great rivers drain into it from the east and west. I was not taught that the Mississippi was also a confluence of human transport, specifically black and brown people forcibly moved. First Nations tribes from the east were marched hundreds of agonizing miles to the Mississippi, loaded on boats, and moved up or downriver then westward to "Indian Territory," later to become the state of Oklahoma. Families of enslaved Blacks from the east coast were separated and re-sold then walked in chains for hundreds of miles to end up on new cotton and sugar plantations in southern land that bordered the Mississippi.

1835 was the height of this method of economic growth, backed by the Indian Removal Act and the discovery that the Mississippi Delta had the richest soil for growing cotton and sugar you can imagine. Americans of European dissent fought or bought their way to the Midwest and solidified the practice of using chattel slavery to exploit it. The Mississippi River was the center of it all.

Prior to writing this book, I would have told you I was "woke" to my white privilege, that I have been conscious of racial injustice and disparity since high school. But I know that many veils still need to be lifted from my eyes. I now see the roots my ancestors planted in the heartland at the expense of First Nations people losing theirs. My roots were infused with a northern version of racism that kept blacks segregated and oppressed.

Don't read this book if you are rolling your eyes at my ignorance. Don't read this book if you are overwhelmed by the pandemic or the heightened focus on systemic racism or the fact that our democracy is falling apart.

The thing is, America has always been falling apart. We built a country on a cruel and faulty foundation. It is past time to rebuild our nation, make it solid, and truly democratic.

My protagonist is white because I am white, so if you decide to read this story, know that I'm still working on ridding myself of racist tendencies. It is the so called "subtle" language and actions that are sometimes the worst. To people of color, they are not subtle at all. If you decide to read this book, I cannot promise that you won't be offended by white ignorance. I can promise you that I am committed to altering my DNA and to action that will change the system. And to writing adventurous love stories that ring true.

A good traveler
has no fixed plans and is not intent on arriving.

Lao Tzu
(870-490 BC)

Chapter One

Faking It

Chicago

Cory breathed in the sour odor of the tangle-haired man sitting next to her on the crowded CTA bus. He drummed a beat on the worn cardboard sign in his lap that stated Will Work for Food and she flashed on herself at age twenty-four, barely three years ago. Her stomach tightened when the man began ranting an epic poem, each verse ending with "it can't get any worse" because she knew full well that it could.

That evening, as she paced her cramped apartment living room eyeing the pack of Marlboros on the coffee table, Shovel & Rope's "Bad Luck" screamed from her Bluetooth speaker. The defiant vocals matched her mood. She grabbed the cigarette pack, crunched it, and tossed it in the wastebasket and then plopped on the couch and started biting her fingernails. Cory wished she could blame her anger on the state of the world and why not? Every time she listened to the news, it pissed her off. Her eyes flew to the wastebasket and she wondered if there was an unbroken smoke in the smashed pack. She growled at herself and felt like such a hypocrite. It was true that the world was screwed up, but she also knew that her outward rage masked the coward inside.

A cell call cut through the music and the "cricket chirp" ringtone meant it was her big sister Jill. Why did she always call when Cory least desired to talk?

"Hey, what's up?"

"Hi, Cory...what the heck?"

"Sorry. Hold on." Cory turned down the Bluetooth volume, put her phone on speaker mode, and tried not to look at Instagram while her sister talked.

"It's very last minute, but it's Michael's birthday on Sunday and I'd like to book an Airbnb in St. Louis for a long weekend. Would you be able to stay with Sam?"

Cory adored her six-year-old nephew Sam. He was worth any time she spent with him so she answered "yes" to her sister's request, even to the favor that she come on Thursday night. It was the perfect escape and she was already texting her boss to request Friday off.

"I'll pick you up at the station," Jill said.

"Okay. I gotta go. Bye." Cory hung up and leaned over to increase the volume on the final refrain and then jumped up and started dancing. Her moves became frenzied in an effort to throw off her angst. When the music ended, she fished a piece of cigarette from the trash, lit it, and took a drag of nicotine relief.

At the close of business on Thursday, Cory handed a stuffed folder to a colleague at the community law center where she worked. Her need to get away outweighed her guilt over not following up with her clients the next day. She Ubered to the bus station and climbed on a Greyhound charter headed south on Interstate 55 to Springfield, Illinois, her hometown.

It was a three-hour trip through pancake-flat farmland and she tried to settle in for the ride. The urban landscape quickly changed to rural, and though a diehard city dweller, she was surprisingly drawn to the vast acres of rich, black earth divided into perfect squares ready for planting. Forsythia dotted the freeway with bright yellow blossoms that popped against the growing darkness. She had completely missed the fact that it was springtime. Her south Chicago neighborhood had few trees and it was still chilly during her commute to and from work. She watched the countryside fly by and blamed her affinity for it on deep roots planted by a forefather who traveled from Kentucky in the 1830's to settle in Illinois. Cory had been a history buff since ninth grade and though she didn't have a living grandparent to recount ancestral tales, her mother had often shared family lineage.

"Your great, great grandfather, Efraim Dowd, was a scout and hunter for wagon trains of pioneers. He finally settled in Sangamon County and began plowing the three hundred acres of prairie he bought for a song."

Cory loved these stories and then one day they abruptly ended and her world turned upside down. When she was eighteen, an oncoming driver had a massive heart attack, crossed the center line and crashed head-on into her parent's Civic, killing them both. It felt like her whole past was wiped out, never mind the two people she adored. After her parents died, she fought her sister's plan to sell her mother's land to the current tenant farmer who was anxious to buy it. Cory knew in her heart it was the right thing to do, but she also knew her mother would never have sold the family farm.

She was starting to feel antsy, but the scheduled rest stop was not due for an hour so she selected tunes on her phone, put in her earbuds, and tried to let the boundless landscape fade her anxious thoughts. Large tracts of the highway were broken only by a brief ride through a small island of commerce resting in a sea of corn and soybeans. The main street was usually bookended by a modest post office and corner dive bar, with a massive concrete grain elevator rising overhead

The bus exited I-55 and pulled into a truck stop for a fifteen-minute break so passengers could visit restrooms and stretch their legs. Cory stood at the edge of the parking lot smoking a cigarette and gazing westward as nightfall spread to the horizon. They were now in the heart of Lincoln land. Every Illinoian grew up learning about Abraham Lincoln's life. He wasn't born in Illinois, but it was where he became an adult and where he transformed himself into a poet and a statesman. In grade school, Cory had read everything ever written about him and he was the reason she wanted to be a lawyer. As an adult, she was not blind to his imperfect record, especially on slavery, but she wanted to believe that in the end, he would have made everything right if he'd had the chance. She also had many women role models for her career, RBG being the giant one, and often wondered why she felt such a strong connection to Lincoln.

The bus pulled into the downtown Springfield station mid-evening and Jill was waiting in her red Prius sedan. When Cory got in, Jill leaned over to give her a hug.

"It's good to see you," she said.

"You, too," Cory answered mechanically.

They headed for suburbia and Cory's childhood home, now occupied by Jill and her family. The drive was filled with chit chat since Cory refused to reveal her angst-ridden thoughts to her sister. Jill was fun-loving, active in her community and adored by the colleagues in her IT division. She was also drop-dead gorgeous with their mother's blue-green eyes, high cheekbones, silky blond hair, and perfectly curved body. Cory favored her father in both looks and temperament. He was quiet to the point of sullen, loved good lyrics, was prone to making puns, responsible at his profession as a dentist, but tended toward laziness at home. She had his tall, rangy build, dark hair and eyes, and tan hued skin. Her parents had often referred to her as their "brown-eyed beauty," but she had never felt attractive next to her older sister.

"Sam is so excited to see you," Jill said.

"I can't wait to see him, too," she answered.

She glanced at her sister and felt the distance between them. The death of their parents should have brought them closer together. Jill, in fact, was constantly reaching out to her. It was Cory who put up a barrier, telling herself they had nothing in common.

When they arrived at Jill's house, Sam attacked Cory with a huge hug and began the non-stop, full engagement kids do. Jill's husband Michael was a hip and caring stay-at-home dad who wore his armfuls of tats with pride, but his excitement to get away made him literally bounce up and down like a kid as he stood ready at the door with their luggage.

"Happy birthday, Michael," Cory saluted as Sam pulled her toward his lego set spread out on the living room floor.

"Thanks, Cory," Michael grinned. Jill blew a last kiss to Sam, grabbed her bag and they flew out the door.

When it was time for bed, Cory and Sam played the marble game that got him upstairs. The game was a tradition and always tickled them both. It involved Cory putting her hands behind her back, slipping a marble into one of her palms, and then holding her closed fists out to Sam who sat on a stairway step. If he guessed the hand with the marble, he moved up a step. Whether he guessed right or wrong, the result made them laugh. When he got pajamas on and teeth brushed, they sat cross-legged facing each other on Sam's bed while she told him the newest adventure of "Sam the Wonder Kid."

"Then Sam jumped off the rock ledge..."

"With his hatchet!" Sam interjected. He was wiggling with delight and his mop of shaggy brown hair swished across his eyes.

"Right!" Cory said. "He landed in front of the little girl and then waved his hatchet and shouted at the grizzly bear! 'Go Away!' The giant bear stood up on its hind legs and roared back at him, but suddenly turned and ran into the woods. The whole town congratulated Sam and the mayor gave him a big medal with an eagle on it that read: To Sam, the bravest kid in the world!"

"Awesome. I wish I lived back then, don't you, Cory?"

"Well, to tell you the truth, I'd miss my iPad and ..."

"Xbox!"

"You don't have an Xbox."

"I know," he frowned.

"Hey, what are we doing tomorrow?" she asked, trying to change the subject.

"School," he answered glumly.

"Well, on Saturday I thought we could go to the hobby shop and get a new airplane model, then I'll take you to lunch..."

"To the Cozy Dog?"

"Sure."

"YES! Mom never takes me there. "Can I have a corn dog and fries?"

"Absolutely. Our secret."

She tucked him into bed.

"I love you, Cory," he said, reaching his arms up to circle her neck.

"I love you, too," she answered and hugged him tightly. "Good night."

"See you later alligator!" he called as Cory left the room.

"When your legs are straighter," she called back.

Cory watched T.V. for a while, but went to bed early so she could get up and get Sam off to school the next morning.

She slept better than usual except for a bizarre dream about a smiling grizzly bear licking her face as she lay pinned to the ground.

To Sam's delight, Cory fixed scrambled eggs, bean dip and tortilla chips for breakfast, and then she drove him to school in Michael's car. They waved good-bye and she watched him walk into the building. He looked adorable with his little backpack and longish hair. She felt a tug in her heart and heard the unwanted tick of her biological clock. She had already decided not to have children.

When she got back to Jill's house, she made a cup of coffee and stepped outside on the back deck. It was a warm, spring day and she sat on the steps and lit a cigarette. Jill's neighbor, Susan, came out her door. She stood on her patio and used her hand like a visor to block the morning sun as she peered over at Cory.

"Cory, is that you?"

"Yup. Hi, Susan."

"I like your doo," she said.

"Thanks, "Cory answered and ran her fingers through her recently cropped, dark brown hair. It was almost as short as when she buzzed it during her "emo" period in high school.

"I wish I was getting away for three days," Susan whined as she swatted away a tiger mosquito that had risen from the grass.

"Maybe on your birthday?" Cory suggested.

"Maybe in my dreams. I hope Jill and Michael have a great time though. Hey, I thought you were going on Sam's field trip," Susan said.

"What do you mean?" Cory asked.

"Our class is going to Honey Creek Farm today," Susan explained. Her daughter Emily and Sam were in the same class. "Jill must have forgotten to tell you. She signed up as one of the chaperone parents and she was going to ask you to go in her place."

"Great. I can't believe 'Super Mom' forgot to tell me. So, what should I do?"

"Oh, they'll have enough parents. Don't worry about it."

But Cory did worry. It was the reason she didn't want to have kids. The first time she saw Sam's fuzzy, infant head in her sister's arms, she felt a pang of maternal instinct and it terrified her.

She stuck her thin wallet in her sweatshirt pocket, grabbed the car keys, and drove back to the school. When she arrived, it was too late to get a seat on the school bus. There were plenty of parents to chaperone. Still, Cory felt compelled to tag along in her car. If the bus had some horrible accident, she would at least be there to help.

It was a beautiful day with a cloudless, blue sky and hints of spring everywhere. Leaf buds were bursting on every tree and purple crocuses bloomed in flower beds beneath them. Cory had to admit it was a perfect day to visit a farm. She relaxed and decided to enjoy it.

The school bus stopped at an intersection on a quiet suburban street. Cory was listening to world music on 91.9 "The X" when she noticed a man step up to the bus and knock on the door. He wore a business suit and carried a newspaper tucked under his arm. His hair was short, straight and neatly combed. He seemed a model of respectability. He also looked vaguely familiar. The bus driver did not open the door and Cory watched the man slip his hand inside the newspaper and draw out a large handgun. He pointed it at a passenger window and shouted something to the bus driver.

Cory froze in shock, gazing out her windshield as if she was watching a horror film. This couldn't be happening. Her heart stopped as the bus door opened and the man disappeared inside, then she watched with sickening dread as the door closed and the bus pulled away.

"Oh, shit, oh shit," she whispered.

Her mind was racing and her breath was short. She dug in her pocket for her cell phone. It wasn't there and her mind shot to the phone sitting on Jill's kitchen counter. She frantically glanced around hoping that someone had seen what happened, but the intersection was deserted. Calm down. Calm down, she told herself. The bus was getting away. She stepped on the gas.

The bus turned at the next corner and drove down a busy street. As they passed a small shopping center, Cory knew she should stop and call 911, but she was terrified of losing the bus. She watched it turn into a gas station ahead and park beside an open payphone. She drove into the station and pulled up to a gas pump.

The door opened and the bus driver climbed out. He glanced right and left, his face ashen as he stepped over to the phone and picked up the receiver. He pushed "zero" for the operator and began talking. The door to the bus remained open.

Cory hesitated a moment as she placed her hand on the car door handle, and then with full abandon, got out and walked straight toward the bus. The driver, still speaking on the phone, watched in fear and awe as she approached. She reached the bus door and looked up at the figure standing at the top of the steps.

The man glared down at her, his face beaded with sweat, the gun gripped tightly in his hand and held at the temple of a child he clutched by the shoulder. It wasn't Sam. It was Susan's daughter, Emily. Cory could hear other children crying in the bus and Emily began to whimper.

"It's okay," Cory whispered, both to Emily and the man.

"Get away," he growled. His face was angry, threatening, and his previously combed, straight hair fell in his face. He jerked his head back to keep his vision clear as he kept his eye on the bus driver.

"Keep talking!" he ordered, then seeing that Cory hadn't made a move, he snarled at her again. "I said get out of here!"

"I can't," she answered truthfully. Her voice sounded wobbly and foreign. "Tell me what you want. Maybe I can help you."

"It's too late," he said as he continued to watch the bus driver on the phone. "They're going to pay for what they did."

"Who?" Cory asked, trying to keep him talking. Her hand hurt where it gripped the metal edge of the doorway.

"They took my job and screwed me forever. I never hurt those kids. I never hurt anybody!" he asserted. "They're not going to get away with this!"

"What are you going to do?" she asked, afraid to hear the answer.

He finally took his eyes off the bus driver and focused them on her. "I want money and I want out of here. This country has gone to shit. You can't do anything without somebody telling you you're wrong. You can't flirt with women. You can't talk to kids. You can't smoke. You can't have a gun." He was making Emily wince as he pinched her shoulder with his anger.

"I can help you get money," Cory said.

"Shut up!" he told her as he saw the bus driver hang up the receiver. "What did they say?" he yelled to him.

"They said they'll bring the money," the driver answered. "They will do anything you want."

He sneered. "Maybe. And maybe they're just saying that. They're all liars. I taught at that school for five years. They all knew me, but they turned me in."

Now Cory realized why he looked familiar. She had seen him on the local TV news the night before. He was a teacher accused of sexually molesting a female middle school student. Givens, Robert Givens was his name.

"My name is Cory. What's yours?" She said.

"None of your business." He said to her and then yelled at the driver. "Come back in the bus!" he ordered. "At least they've gotta be scared. They're scared, right?"

"Yes," the bus driver answered as he stepped back on the bus. He squeezed passed Cory and they exchanged helpless and unsure looks. She took a step up into the bus after him, but Givens didn't seem to notice. He was more interested in the fact that he had gotten the effect he wanted from whoever the bus driver had spoken to. He relaxed his grip on Emily and then he motioned for the driver to sit in a seat across from him.

"How much did you ask for?" Cory inquired.

"Enough to set me up. Two hundred and fifty grand."

She took another step up into the bus. "It wasn't fair what they did to you. I'd like to make up for it. I can get you the money, all of it, now." She glanced down the aisle of the bus and the children quieted when they saw her. "You don't have to go through with this. My family is rich." She spotted Sam in a seat toward the back. He had always been an observer. Their eyes met briefly, but he didn't call out to her. He was very still, listening to every word.

"How rich?" Givens asked.

"My last name is Dupont."

"Like the company?"

"Yes. I'm here visiting a friend for the weekend."

Cory flashed back on all the times she and Jill had joked about having the same name as the famous corporation. She hoped Givens wouldn't ask himself why a Dupont would wear jeans and a hoodie.

"Prove it," he said.

She carefully reached in her pocket, pulled out her wallet, and showed him her driver's license. "Call the corporate office to verify. I'll give you the phone number." Time was ticking away. "If you wait for the school to come, you're asking for trouble. They'll call the police. If you get caught, they'll crucify you. You've got a bus full of kids here. I'm worth a lot more money to you as a hostage than they are. Take me instead. I swear I'll help you."

Givens stared at Cory hard, considering. He scanned the rows of children then eyed her again.

"How would you get the money?"

"I've got that much in two separate accounts. I'll have it wired to the closest bank."

He was quiet, thinking, but not for long. "Let's go," he said quickly. He shoved Emily toward the bus driver and pointed the gun at Cory instead. Without looking toward Sam, she pivoted and stepped off the bus. Givens paused and glared at the bus driver. "You tell the cops anything and this woman is dead, got it?"

The driver nodded and Givens left the bus to follow Cory to her car. She heard a child yelling and glanced back to see Sam running down the aisle of the bus, but the bus driver stopped him and held him tight. Cory turned away and continued toward the car. Luckily, she had the vehicle to back up her story. Michael's car was a new Volvo S-60 sedan.

*

Cory had been driving several blocks before Givens said anything.

"Do you know where you're going?"

"Yes."

"You're driving away from town."

"The closest branch for my bank is up ahead."

She drove another mile.

"There are no banks out this way."

"Oh." They were out of town, heading west into the countryside.

"Turn around."

"No." She drove faster.

"I said turn around!"

Cory put her foot to the peddle instead and sped down the road past a field of ugly stubbles from last year's harvested corn.

Givens put the gun to her head. "Dammit, pull over! Now!"

She tried to decide if she was far enough away. Would they have the children off the bus by now? Was Sam safe? She let her foot off the gas and slowed.

"Pull in up there!" he demanded.

The place he indicated was an entrance to New Salem State Park. Cory turned into the drive and they were immediately hidden by forest. He told her to stop.

"What the hell are you doing!" he shouted.

She didn't answer.

"Jesus Christ! Okay, we're going to turn around! You're going to take me to the fucking bank and get the money, got it?!"

"I can't."

"What do you mean?"

"I lied. I don't have the money. I just said it to get you away from the bus."

"You're a Dupont!"

"Not the Dupont."

"You fuckin' bitch!" He banged down the handle of his door and shoved it open, then he grabbed Cory's arm and jerked her across the seat and out the passenger door. His adrenalin was flowing and he flung her along like a rag doll. She didn't resist as he dragged her over into the pine trees. It was shaded and quiet and she felt the cushion of pine needles beneath her. He had jammed the gun into his belt, so that he had both hands free. He yanked her to her knees, grabbed a clump of her hair and snapped her head back.

It was impossible not to look at his face. She always looked into people's eyes when they talked to her. She barely heard what he said, but she saw the anger. It was much more than just rage at her. It was a lifetime of fury. Cory knew she would never leave those woods unless she did something.

She thrust her body up so her head cracked him hard under the chin. Then she ran. He caught her about a hundred feet away. He gripped her tightly as his other hand raised back and slammed into the side of her face. The pain was overwhelming and shocking.

She had never been hit before, yet the instant it happened, there was something familiar about the terror and hurt, like a deja vu of the worst kind. The whole scene carried a strange familiarity. The trees, the pine smell, the feel of the soft ground and the horrible, intense pain causing everything to turn red and then black. It was as if she had experienced it all before, but when and how? She had never been at that spot in her life. Maybe this was all a dream and she would wake from this nightmare.

Cory lost her vision and fell back, but Givens held her up as he continued to strike her face and head. Then as abruptly as it had started, it stopped. He let go and she hit the ground in silence, blind to the world. It didn't end though. A second later, she felt Givens climb on top of her. He began to tear at her clothes, ripping her shirt and wrenching her jeans down. Her mind was screaming "No!" but she could not move to stop him. She had the odd sensation that she was fading away like a developing photo exposed to light. A humming sound filled her ears and her body felt as if it were being pulled too fast in one direction. The last thing she remembered was hearing a gunshot.

Chapter Two

New Salem

C ory woke with a throbbing headache. Her left eye was tender and swollen and refused to open more than a slit. Her other eye was blurry at first then slowly came into focus on an enormous wolf staring her in the face. She cried out and a woman's voice immediately cut in.

"Rusty, get off the bed!"

Cory felt a huge weight lift off the mattress and spring away. She quickly scanned her surroundings, a small room with log walls. A woman and a large dog stood next to the bed.

"There now, miss, don't worry. It's just our old hound. He don't mean any harm."

Rusty wagged his doggy tail as the woman patted his large head of coarse, grey fur and pointed ears.

"My name is Ellie. You gave us quite a scare. That's a bad lump on your head. I reckon it'll take some time to go down."

Ellie had a kind face with round, ruddy cheeks and flaxen hair pulled back in a bun. Her plain, beige wool dress was buttoned up to her throat.

"You're lucky. The man that attacked you coulda took your life."

Cory tried to remember what happened...the bump on her head...someone hurting her...Givens with the gun...the school bus...Sam. It was all coming back. She panicked and tried to rise, but the world spun before her and she nearly blacked out.

"There, there. You shouldn't try to move. You need to rest," Ellie gently cautioned her. Cory sank back on the pillow and focused on the rafters of the rustic shelter to stop the room from spinning. She wondered if it was a park ranger's cabin and tried to speak, but her voice came out a strangled whisper.

"How... did I get here?"

"Well, our cousin Lucas was hunting near where you were attacked. He heard shouting and when he saw that man trying to...well, he shot him."

"Shot...is he...dead?"

"I don't rightly know. He was still alive when they took him to town."

Cory's throat was dry and she licked her lips. The corner of her mouth was sore and puffy. She slid a hand out from under the sheets and touched her face, then winced. She laid her hand on her chest and felt the rough, coarse fabric of the nightgown she wore.

"He hurt your pretty face, but it will heal," Ellie said. "Where are you from?"

"Chicago."

"Yes, I've heard of it. It's north, right?"

Cory liked her joke. "Yes," she answered, cracking a smile. "What is this place?"

"Well, it's our home, of course! Don't you worry now. You are welcome to stay here. It's just John and me. We ain't been blessed with children yet and seein' as how I'm nearly twenty-five, it don't seem likely I will be."

Cory stared at her in disbelief. The woman was two years younger than her, but looked ten years older.

"I should try to call my family," Cory said in her groggy voice. She tried to sit up again, but her body felt like a sandbag. "They'll be trying to find me. I need to call..."

"You keep sayin' that," the woman chided. "You won't be calling on anyone for a while yet."

"I just need to use your phone," Cory said weakly.

The woman looked at her blankly, but a noise outside the door made her turn.

"That'll be John. I'll just be a minute."

Rusty followed the woman out the door and then Cory heard the murmur of low voices in the other room. She was starting to feel uncomfortable and slightly afraid. The woman came back into the room joined by a man of roughly the same age. He had a long face, small ears, clipped red hair, and a six-inch russet beard. His lips were tight, but his blue eyes were friendly.

"Howdy. I'm John Traughber. How are you feelin'?"

"Okay, I guess."

"Can you tell us your name, miss? Ellie said she ain't learnt it yet."

"Cory. Cory Dupont."

"I hate to bother you about this, Miss Dupont, but did you know the varmint that attacked you?"

"No," she said.

"Lucas gave him every chance to give up, but the danged fool aimed a gun at him. Even so, Lucas only winged him. Believe me, if Lucas had meant to drop him, we'd be diggin' his grave right now. We took him into town, but when the constable went to fetch the doctor, the buzzard stole a horse and run off. When they catch him, he'll swing from a rope sure enough."

As bad as she felt, Cory almost laughed at John's words. He sounded like something out of an old western. Swing from a rope. Right. He must be a capital punishment freak, she mused. He and his wife were a real pair. Cory was feeling a little freaked out.

"I really need to use a phone if I could...please?"

John and Ellie looked at each other then they both gave Cory a blank stare.

She closed her eyes and tried to quell the panic rising inside.

"Maybe we better let her rest, John," Ellie suggested.

Cory heard them close the rough-hewn door behind them as they left. Am I dreaming, she wondered? This had to be a dream. She pinched her leg under the covers, but it only hurt. She hurt all over. This wasn't a dream. Sam. She needed to know if he was okay. She tried to get up again and finally made it to a sitting position. Spots were swimming before her eyes, but she willed her vision to clear then swung her feet over the side of the bed and stood up.

A single candle flickering on the nightstand lighted the room. Every muscle ached and she was afraid to take a step for fear of falling. She felt like a limp puppet with no one holding her strings as she picked up the candlestick and shuffled to an oval mirror over a dresser. Cory peered at her reflection and gasped at her face. One eye was nearly swollen shut and turning an ugly shade of purple. A scab was forming at the corner of her mouth and her left ear was red and tender. A tear escaped her good eye and ran down her cheek. She wiped it away and turned from the mirror. She tried to forget what Givens had done to her and concentrated on Sam. Maybe if she showed them she was okay, they would let her use the phone. She made her way to the door and opened it.

John and Ellie looked up surprised. They were seated at a table in the center of what seemed to be the only other room of the cabin. Another man stood with his back to her at the fireplace and before Cory got a good look at him, she fainted.

*

Like a recurring nightmare, she came to again in the cabin bedroom. She felt the sun on her face from the open window and a fly buzzed around her head. She rose slowly this time and let the dizziness pass before she got out of bed. Her swollen eye had opened a bit, but her face still felt puffy and sore. She avoided the mirror and went straight to the door.

Ellie was at the stove cooking the most delicious smelling food. It was meat and Cory's stomach grumbled noisily. Ellie turned and saw her.

"Landsakes, girl, you should stay in bed!"

"I feel much better," Cory answered in a slurred voice.

Ellie saw her eyeing the iron skillet she was tending over a bank of wood coals in the fireplace. "Hungry?"

"Yes," Cory answered sheepishly.

"Sit down then and I'll set you a plate."

Cory sat on one of the only three chairs in the room, now clustered around a small rectangular dining table. She surveyed the other spare furnishings that included a cupboard with a narrow counter, a tiny work table and a large spinning wheel in the corner. It dawned on her that her hosts might be Amish. She knew there was a large community of Amish in Arthur, Illinois, but that was further east. The massive stone fireplace had a metal crane device that held several hooks of various lengths over the hot coals. A tea kettle hung from one of them and a round iron stew pot dangled from another, the source of the mouth watering aroma. Rusty left his spot by the door and wandered over to lie at Cory's feet. Ellie served her a china plate of cornbread and a slab of bacon along with a cup of coffee.

"Thank you," Cory said.

"You are most welcome," Ellie answered.

The door to the outside opened and John entered. Ellie quickly removed her shawl and settled it around Cory's shoulders. The Amish were also modest.

"Mornin', miss," John said.

"Good morning," Cory answered.

John sat across from her and Ellie set a plate of food in front of him. He immediately began eating and Cory did the same since she was ravished. She noticed how Ellie stayed in the background when John was around, busying herself at the fireplace, but not sitting with them.

"Feelin' better?" John asked.

"I feel much better. Thank you so much for helping me," she said to both John and Ellie.

"Anyone woulda done the same. Anyhow it was really Lucas that done the good deed," John explained.

"Will you thank him for me?"

"You can thank him yerself. He'll be in shortly. Just went to wash up."

In her nightgown and misshapen face, Cory did not want to meet another stranger, but she had no choice. The door swung open and in walked her savior. For some reason, she was expecting someone older, but the man who stood there was young. His light brown hair was tucked behind his ears and hung down to his shoulders. He wore a buckskin jacket over a long flannel shirt and loose-fitting wool trousers that covered the tops of worn, rawhide boots. He reminded her of a Ralph Lauren model except that he was apparently authentic. Rusty immediately trotted over to greet him and he ruffled the dog's ears affectionately.

"This is my cousin, Lucas," John said.

"Hello, miss," Lucas said in a deep, resonant voice. He did not smile and barely glanced at her.

"Hi," she responded.

Ellie jumped in. "Her name is Cory," she said, completing the introduction.

"Thanks for helping me. Really, thank you," Cory added.

"My pleasure." He turned away from her toward John. "I best be gettin' the rest of that wood chopped."

"You won't stay for breakfast?" Ellie offered.

"No, ma'am, but thank you kindly."

Ellie watched with surprise as Lucas turned on his heel and left.

"He's in an awful hurry this mornin'," she remarked.

"Apparently so," John answered.

"I ain't never seen him pass up a meal...ever. He seemed kinda shy, too," Ellie said to John with the slightest hint of a smile.

More like uninterested, Cory thought. Anyway, her stomach was full and she felt well enough to walk. She wanted to get back to Jill's. She prayed that Sam was okay. Jill and Michael would be home by now and must be wondering where the hell she was.

"I really need to get to my sister and her family in Springfield and I don't want to impose on you anymore."

"You ain't imposin'," John answered.

"I forgot to ask you about my car."

"Your what?" John asked.

"Car. Automobile? A black Volvo?"

"I'm sorry, miss. I don't know what yer referrin' to."

Cory was getting irritated. She needed a cigarette.

"Would you mind taking me to Springfield?"

"That's a bit far from us."

Cory was confused. How had she ended up far away from Springfield?

"What is the closest town to you?" she asked.

"That would be New Salem," John said.

The only New Salem Cory knew was the town that Abraham Lincoln lived in during his young adulthood. The town didn't survive economically, but a historic site had been established there with reproductions of the original houses.

She wondered if maybe John and Ellie were part of a tourist attraction, wearing costumes and demonstrating the way people used to live. She had not been to New Salem since a field trip in grade school.

"You mean Abraham Lincoln's New Salem?" she asked.

"You know Abe?" John asked, surprised.

"Well...I mean, doesn't everybody? You can't grow up in Illinois without knowing a lot about Lincoln. Even so, he's one of my favorite figures in hist...". She stopped talking because John and Ellie were looking at her in that strange way again. "I really need to get going," she said quietly. "Do you have my clothes?"

"They were in a sorry state, Cory," Ellie answered. "And kinda unrecognizable," she added. "I have an extra dress I can loan you."

Cory followed her into the bedroom and Ellie opened an old trunk and took out a dress very similar to the one she was wearing.

"It'll probably be big on you."

"It's fine. Thank you."

Ellie stepped out of the room and Cory quickly pulled off her nightgown and pulled on the dress. She was aware of bruises on her arms and legs, but refused to examine them now. The dress hung loose on her thin frame. Her boots were nowhere in sight and she resigned herself to going barefoot. She walked back out into the other room.

"John went to fetch the horse," Ellie explained. "I do hope you get home alright."

Horse? Did she hear horse?

Ellie opened the door for her and Cory stepped outside. The sun was shining and it was another beautiful spring day. She stood on a bare patch of ground outside the cabin and saw a road about twenty yards away, a dirt road. To one side of the cabin were cleared fields and a vegetable garden. On the other side was open prairie as far as she could see. It was waist high grass of a type she had never seen, but only heard about. She felt as if she were seeing a ghost.

"Are you ready, miss?"

She turned, but it was not John who held the horse for her. It was Lucas.

"I told John I'd take you into town or wherever yer hankering to go. Springfield, is it?" he asked.

Cory's uneasiness changed to annoyance. This had to be a joke thinking she would ride a horse. Sarcasm won out over fear.

"I wouldn't want to put you out."

"I need to go into town anyway."

"Oh."

"Here. I'll give you a leg up."

"You really don't drive?"

"No need to hitch up the wagon if you are okay to ride."

Frustrated, Cory didn't know what else to do but step into his offered hand and be boosted onto the horse's back. She nearly sailed over the other side, but grabbed hold of the saddle horn and planted herself in the seat.

"I'm not that used to horses."

"Don't worry."

He swung up behind her and looped his arm around her, keeping the reins in his hand. Cory became rigid, totally on guard. Having a man's body that close to her after the attack was not welcome. Her reaction caused him to scoot back a welcome notch. After a quarter mile or so of Lucas simply reining the horse and sitting still behind her, she began to relax. She had to admit that she was glad for the warmth of his body. The spring air was chilly and she hadn't thought to borrow a shawl. They rode another bit of the way in silence, then he spoke.

"I've never seen such short hair on a woman."

"Excuse me?"

"You seem in a real hurry to git where yer goin'."

"Why do you say that?"

"You look pretty bad to be traveling."

"It's a good thing you're behind me then. You don't have to look at my face."

She felt his body stiffen, and the tension on the horse's flank caused it to break into a trot. "No offense intended, miss," Lucas said as he pulled on the reins and slowed the horse to a walk again. He was silent for a moment. "John said you didn't know the man that attacked you."

"I didn't. Why?"

"I was just curious why you were alone on the prairie with your hair cut like a man and wearin' men's clothes?"

"This isn't the 1800's, you know."

"What do you mean?" he asked innocently.

"What do YOU mean?!" she snapped back.

"Feels like 1835 to me," he snickered.

His attempted joke unsettled her. "Stop. I want to get off."

"Why?"

She twisted around to face him. "Let me off!"

He furrowed his brow in confusion, but stopped the horse, scooted back and helped Cory slide to the ground. She spotted New Salem ahead and strode angrily toward it without looking back at Lucas.

"What a jerk," she mumbled to herself.

The town appeared the same as she remembered it; however, she recalled a big parking lot and visitor's center that supported the historic attraction where Lincoln spent his young adulthood. The parking lot and center were not visible now. She headed toward the largest building on the street with a sign over it reading: Rutledge Tavern.

It was dark inside, with only one window providing natural light to the room. A fire was crackling in a hearth and several men were seated around a square oak table. The air was full of pipe smoke as everyone turned to stare at Cory. She knew she looked a bit wild in her bare feet, large dress and battered face, but it was something else that drew their attention.

"Holy shit, she's been scalped!" a man yelled.

"Even so, she's a pretty little thing, ain't she?" another man responded.

A pot-bellied man with a cauliflower nose got up and walked over to her. "You must be the young woman stayin' with the Traughbers. Can I help you?"

"Yes. May I use your phone?"

Again she was met by a blank stare and she finally lost her cool.

"COULD SOMEONE PLEASE GIVE ME A RIDE?!" she shouted.

The men looked at each other and one man in a tattered hat sniggered and called out.

"Sure darlin'. Right over here!" He patted his lap inviting her.

Cory stormed out of the tavern angry and frustrated, and though she didn't want to admit it, scared. As she fought back tears, she saw Lucas coming toward her.

"I'm going home!" she told him.

He stepped in front of her. "Hold on, okay?"

She tried to push past him, but he grabbed her by the shoulders.

"Let go!" she yelled fiercely.

"I'll help you go wherever you want," he said.

"I'll get there myself," she informed him.

"You don't have to be scared of me," he said and though she felt like a trapped wild animal being soothed, she stopped pushing against him.

"Come on," he said. He took her gently by the elbow and led her to a one-room wooden cabin nearby. When her eyes adjusted to the dim light inside, she saw that it was a grocery store, though nobody was behind the counter. It had the same simple colonial decor with pine shelves and items from

from an earlier century. Lucas offered her a wooden chair near the single front window, and then he walked behind the counter, pulled out a jug, and filled a small glass. When he handed it to her, she took a sip and immediately started coughing. She knew it was whiskey, but she'd never tasted whiskey like that. She took another small sip, then another. The slow burning in her stomach helped settle her nerves.

"Thanks."

"Don't mention it."

Cory took a deep breath. "Tell me the truth. What is today's date?"

"March twenty-fifth."

"And the year?"

"Eighteen thirty-five."

"Right."

He had to be kidding; however, the expression on his face was absolutely serious and more than a bit puzzled. It struck her as comical and Cory began to snicker. The whiskey had gone straight to her head and the weight of all that had happened in the last twenty four hours hit her full force. His joke about the year and date was so ridiculous that she burst out laughing.

"I wasn't making a wisecrack," he said.

"Okay!" she said, but his insistence made her laugh even more and within moments she was doubled over. Lucas stood watching as she held her stomach and tried not to fall on the floor. He pulled the glass of whiskey away and set it on the counter.

"What is so darn funny?" He crossed his arms and creased his brow though he couldn't help but grin at her obvious amusement.

"N...nothing!" She covered her mouth to try and stifle herself as a new eruption threatened. "You must think I'm crazy!" she gasped, attempting to straighten up and suppress her mirth.

"I don't know what to think," he frowned.

"Neither do I!" Cory sputtered, sending her into a new fit of convulsions.

She could not go on laughing forever. Her stomach hurt and she knew how she must appear. She forced herself to calm down and sit quietly in front of him like a child caught playing a prank. But reality was sinking in and the strong whiskey was making her head spin. She suddenly got up, bolted outside and vomited in the street.

This time Lucas handed her a tin cup of water. She sat on a bench outside the store and he quietly stood by.

"Sorry," she said as she took a sip.

"Couldn't be helped. I shouldn't have given you the whiskey."

"No, the whiskey is fine. You shouldn't have told me that stupid joke."

"What joke?"

"About it being 1835. And why 1835? It's so random," she insisted.

"Miss, are you okay? You want me to get Doc Marten?"

She threatened to burst out laughing again, but his somber look stopped her. He believed what he said, which forced her to consider that he was either totally nuts or actually credible. She shook her head slowly in denial, but then every odd thing that had happened since she woke up in the cabin made her begin to think it was true. She had somehow awakened in another time period. Her body went into shock and she began to shake.

Lucas grabbed a blanket from the store shelf and wrapped it around her shoulders. He knelt in front of her and made her look in his eyes.

"Are you okay?"

"So what happens next?" she asked in desperation. She thought of her family, Jill, Michael, and Sam. No. If it was 1835, there was no family. Her ancestors hadn't even arrived in Illinois yet. She had no place to go. She couldn't tell Lucas what had happened. She didn't know him that well and had no idea how he would react. He had already seen her behaving unstable. She didn't know where they put crazy people in 1835, and she didn't want to find out. She desperately wanted a cigarette.

"Lots of things are becoming clear to me now," she said, thinking fast and trying to sound credible even though her voice wavered. "Wow. Um, that bump on my head affected me more than I thought. I was uh...coming from Springfield when I uh...got lost and that man attacked me. Now that I know where I am, I need to get back on the road to Chicago."

"Chicago? That's a long way. You'd do best to go back to John and Ellie's and rest another day or two. They've got room and plenty of food."

"I appreciate that, but I'd like to be on my own."

"A woman on her own isn't safe in these parts."

"I guess women don't smoke either."

"My granny used to smoke a clay pipe now and again."

His sweet, genuine response made her smile and lessened her panic a tiny bit.

*

"You poor thing," Ellie said, shaking her head, but also interested to finally learn what had happened to Cory when she was attacked. "How awful to be lost in the woods and then to run into that terrible man," Ellie added.

"Have you heard anything about him?" Cory asked, shivering at the memory of the assault.

"Seems he clean got away," John answered.

Cory was not anxious to see her kidnapper again, but she also realized that he was her only link to their own time. Where did he go, she wondered?

"John and I got to talking," Ellie continued. "and come to think of it, another woman was attacked last spring in the exact same spot where Lucas found you. She was picking berries and ran across a bear cub. The mother bear attacked and almost killed her. Morgan was the woman's last name, I think."

"Kinda like lightnin' striking twice in the same spot is your point, Ellie, am I right?" John suggested.

"Yes! In any case, she and her family moved on to Missouri after that."

Cory didn't exactly see the connection between a bear attack and attempted rape, but she did get the point that they both involved terror. The memory sent another shudder through her body.

"Ellie, would you mind if I lie down awhile?" Cory asked. "The trip to town tired me out more than I realized."

"Of course. You go on."

Cory started toward the bedroom, then paused. "Where have you and John been sleeping while I've been here?"

"We made up a straw pallet by the fire. Reminds us of when we first settled here. John added on the bedroom later, but that first year in our one-room cabin was one of our happiest times together," she smiled.

"I can't take your bed. Let me sleep out here," Cory insisted.

"Only if you're sure that you're feeling better."

"I'm much better. I just need to rest awhile."

"Use the bed now and tonight you can sleep out here."

Cory didn't object. The minute her cheek touched the pillow, she was sound asleep. She didn't even notice when Rusty jumped up and curled next to her.

Later she bolted awake, certain that someone had called her name. She had dreamt she was at Jill's house and heard Sam calling for her in the night. Cory looked around in the half-light of late afternoon and saw the chinked walls of Ellie and John's cabin. She felt more alone at that moment than she had felt since landing in this alien world. She wished she could tell someone about what happened to her, but she knew that was impossible. She remembered how she had felt in Chicago, restless and anxious. Now, she would give anything to be in her cramped apartment worrying about the state of the world. She had to find a way back.

Chapter Three

HELP

I feel like a hunted animal. She got me into this mess and she's going to get me out. This bullet wound in my shoulder hurts like hell. I haven't had anything to eat except a can of beans I stole from that dirt hole town. This is the craziest damn place. I saw a newspaper today. 1835! I used to bring my students to New Salem on field trips. "Okay, class, now we are going to learn about Young Abe's early years in the town of New Salem." I hate Lincoln. He freed the slaves and his Yankee soldiers killed half of my ancestors. If he's around now, maybe I'll put a bullet in him and save Booth the trouble.

Cory was quiet at the dinner table that evening as John and Ellie discussed their corn crop and news from town over a meal of fried pork and potatoes. Something John said, however, made Cory sit up and listen.

"I hope Abe can push that construction bill through the legislature. Steamships would be a lot more inclined to use the Sangamon River if they could navigate it."

"Excuse me," Cory asked. "Abe?"

"Abe Lincoln," John answered. "He got elected as our delegate to the state legislature and that's one of the projects we hope he can make happen. Did you say before that you knew him?"

"Knew of him. And he lives here in New Salem?"

"Yup. He and Mr. Berry run a store in town, but Abe is out on his surveying job most days now."

Cory was thunderstruck at the thought that she could actually meet him.

"What is he like?" she asked, trying to contain her excitement.

"Abe? Well, he's not much to look at, homely as a mud fence to be truthful, but strong as an ox. Ain't no man in the county can beat him in a rassle. He's a real joker and he knows the best darn stories, but he's also a fine speaker, and there isn't a more fair or honest man in New Salem," John said.

Cory smiled. It was one thing to read a description in a history book. It was another to hear it first hand.

"I think he's going to be famous someday," Ellie added.

"He was tellin' us the other day that he wanted to be like that DeWitt Clinton fella in New York who got the Erie Canal made. If Abe can get some deeper channels dug in the Sangamon River, that'd be mighty fine."

"Steamships could get through easier and bring more trade to town," Ellie explained.

"And I wouldn't have to take my produce downriver on a flatboat," John added.

"John and Lucas are leaving next month," Ellie said, clearly displeased. "It's dangerous on the river and I worry every minute until they get back."

"Do you stay here alone?" Cory asked.

"I do. I've got Rusty here," Ellie said and touched the dog's head lying at her feet. "And the neighbors are good to look out for me."

The news dampened the thrill of hearing about Lincoln. It made her feel frightened. Cory felt safe with Ellie, John and

Lucas, but if the men left, she felt less secure. In her brief time of wondering what to do, she had thought about going to Chicago, but then again, maybe it was best to stay in the place where she came through time.

The next morning she went to find Lucas. Ellie had told her that he worked part-time in town when he wasn't helping John with his crops or splitting wood for other families. The store where he worked was the same one he had taken Cory to after her run-in with the tavern clientele.

As she started off on foot to New Salem, Cory was glad to have Rusty trot along with her. It was a short distance to town, but this land of old growth forest felt so new to her. She walked down the dirt path feeling totally awed and completely like an intruder. Cory's family had not immigrated here yet. She tried to remember details from her history class in high school. She knew of course that Native Americans had lived in the area, but couldn't remember what tribes they were or if they would still be here now. She also remembered that Marquette and Joliet had been the most famous European explorers in the region.

In a darkly shaded section of the trail, Rusty stopped mid-stride, stared into the woods, and emitted a low growl. Cory felt a sudden chill run down her spine. She couldn't see anything through the dense stands of laurel, but she had a distinct impression that she was being watched. She picked up her pace.

"Come on, Rusty," she called. He bounded after her, but a moment later, Cory caught a flicker of movement through the trees off to her side.

Rusty immediately dashed into the bushes, barking fiercely. Cory took off running, hoping to catch sight of New Salem ahead. She rounded a bend and saw buildings at the top of a rise. She sprinted up the hill to the edge of town, then stopped and turned back.

"Rusty!" she called, but the barking had abruptly ended and there was only silence. A moment later, however, the dog came leaping out of the forest and landed at her side. She smiled and patted him.

"Where were you, boy? What'd you see? A bear?"

Cory was more tentative as she entered New Salem this time. She avoided townspeople and went straight to the store where Lucas worked.

He was standing in the doorway, eyes closed and his face raised to the sun. He cut a strong figure with his long hair and rustic garb, and Cory felt awkward standing in front of him in her oversized dress and bare feet.

"Hi."

Lucas opened his eyes and smiled at her. "I can't stand being cooped up in here all day," he said, indicating the store behind him. "How are you feelin'?"

"Okay. Did you mean what you said about helping me get back to Chicago?"

"Yes."

"John and Ellie said you were leaving next month."

"I'm helping John take a flatboat to New Orleans."

"New Orleans? Why so far?"

"Most farmers around here take their produce to New Orleans. It's a long trip to be sure, but there's no way to sell everything here. Everybody has extra and if we get it to New Orleans, they want it and need it. The sale will keep us through the year and pay for supplies like the goods in this store for example."

They were interrupted by shouts coming from a small crowd down the street. A group of townsmen had surrounded a man dressed in a black suit and stovepipe hat. At first, Cory thought it might be Lincoln, but then she saw that he was middle-aged, not the twenty-six year-old Abe would be now.

"Let's take a gander," Lucas said.

They walked down the hard dirt main street and joined the ring of onlookers. Cory saw the man in the center of the crowd clearly now. He wore an elegant black suit over a paisley silk vest and had curly blond hair, bulging eyes and a mustache. Two wooden crates were stacked in front of him for a table and he was performing sleight of hand tricks with playing cards as he challenged the crowd to make bets on his ability to fool them.

"It's a gift, my friends, knowing where each card lies. The hand is quicker than the eye, but if you guess the card right, you win it all!"

Several men shouted their bets only to groan at their loss when the trickster proved his skill.

"I've seen these fellers before," Lucas murmured in Cory's ear. "He'll win just enough so he doesn't get tarred and feathered and run out of town."

The man continued his banter as he moved three, face-down cards around the table. "Keep your eye on the lucky card and with skill, you can win big, my friends. You never know what's in store for you right, gentlemen? Not like my lady friend. She knows the future. She told me about machines that people will ride in the air! A gift I call it. Like mine. The cards move, but I know exactly where your fortune lies." He looked at a man staring intently at the table attempting to follow. "Okay, friend, choose your card!" The man pointed to one, but the con man frowned. "Sorry, friend." He picked up the card next to it, held it up with a flourish and the crowd saw what had eluded them. The man who had chosen wrong slapped his knee in frustration.

"Who's next, gentlemen?" the hustler asked.

Cory stopped watching and thought instead about what the man had said about his friend. She had never believed in fortune tellers, but on the other hand, she had never believed in time travel either. Time travel. The idea was absurd and yet here she was. If this man's friend could see into the future, maybe she could help Cory.

"Ladies and gentlemen, I require a bit of libation," the con man told the crowd. "Could someone direct me to a tavern?"

"As long as you give us a chance to win our money back, mister," one of the men said.

"Of course, sir, of course."

Needing a drink themselves, several men ushered him toward Rutledge Tavern.

Cory stepped in front of him. "Excuse me."

The man stopped and tipped his tall hat. "The name is Johnson, young lady. Allen Johnson. I don't believe I've had the pleasure."

"Cory Dupont. I'm interested in what you said about your friend, the fortune teller."

"Ah! A fine lady she is," Johnson said, catching sight of Lucas standing behind her. "Are you curious about your future, Miss Dupont?"

Cory followed his gaze toward Lucas. She blushed then continued. "Could I meet her?"

"Well, that would depend on if you were willing to travel. I'm afraid my friend lives quite far away."

"Where does she live?"

"In the illustrious and gay city of New Orleans."

"Oh."

"Would you like to join me for a drink, Miss Dupont? We could discuss my friend and various otherworldly topics?"

"No, thanks."

"Very well then, it was a pleasure to meet you." He continued on with the other men to the tavern.

Cory stood in the middle of the dusty road, thinking.

"Mr. Johnson, wait!" she called and caught up to him. Cory's knowledge of her family history in the early 1800's was sketchy. Most of her ancestors were pioneers from

Kentucky, but she didn't know the name of the town. There was one relative that Cory knew the specific whereabouts of in the 1830's. Her great, great grandmother was from New Orleans.

"I have a relative there. In New Orleans."

"Is that so. Perhaps I know him or her. What is the name?" Johnson asked.

"Rebecca McNeely. My uh...my cousin," she answered realizing that her great, great grandmother would be a young woman at this time.

"I'm afraid I have not had the pleasure."

"When are you returning?" she asked, her mental wheels turning.

"I'll be returning by way of Kentucky, then looping south by stagecoach. I plan to be back in the City in three months," Johnson answered.

"Oh," Cory replied, swallowing her request to travel with him. Three months sounded like forever.

"If you visit your cousin, you must allow me to take you both to dine some evening."

"Thank you, yes, I will," she replied.

"Good day, Miss Dupont," Johnson said, anxious to get to the tavern.

"Good-bye," Cory mumbled as she watched him go.

"You sure are full of surprises."

Cory turned to Lucas and frowned.

"Am I really that strange?"

"You're a bit peculiar, but I reckon I could get used to it."

"Good, because I'm going with you."

"Where?"

"To New Orleans."

"What!?"

"On your trip down the river."

"I thought you wanted to return to Chicago?"

"I'm thinking that I might like to visit my cousin. I can't explain why, but I'm not ready to go home yet. And I may never have a chance like this to go to New Orleans."

"I can't take you on a flatboat," Lucas told her.

"Why not?"

"Too dangerous. The Mississippi River is no place for a woman."

"I'm not afraid and I can pull my weight." It was true, but Cory couldn't tell him why. She had always been strong and she visited a gym twice a week. She tried a different approach.

"What if I traveled as a man? You said when you first saw me that I looked like a man."

"That's a crazy idea."

"I wouldn't be in the way, I promise."

"John wouldn't have it."

"I have no money. There's no other way I can get to New Orleans. Please take me with you."

Lucas inspected her. "I have to admit, it would be worth the trouble just to see you try it. You're more stubborn than any woman I've ever met."

She grinned at him. "Do they sell trousers in that store of yours?"

*

Over the next month, they prepared for the twelve hundred mile trip downriver. Cory became more resolved that going to New Orleans might help her find answers about how to return to her time. If Johnson's fortune telling friend couldn't help her, then she could at least meet a family relative, which might prove fruitful in some way. Besides, she was nervous and scared to think about the fact that there might not be a way back to the future. Traveling would keep her occupied and she still needed time to heal from her experience with Givens and the shock of being in another time. She kept herself busy with preparations for the journey. She helped Ellie pack goods and supplies and she watched Lucas construct a flatboat.

The boat building process was not easy and whenever he could take a break from spring planting, John helped Lucas. They cut down two tall, arrow-straight poplar trees and then Lucas cut off the branches until he had two, forty-foot trunks. He hitched them to a neighbor's team of mules and dragged them to the Rutledge Saw Mill powered by a water wheel on the Sangamon River. The logs were milled down to two massive beams, forty inches thick and then he tapered one end of each beam from forty inches down to about twelve. He borrowed the neighbor's mules again to haul the two beams to a river launch site and laid them parallel on the bank about 15 feet apart. The twin beams were the gunwales, the foundation on which the flatboat would be built.

Cory helped Ellie get supplies ready for the trip, grinding pork for packing in barrels and filling other barrels with wheat and corn. But curiosity drove her to visit boat building site often to see the progress. Sometimes she brought lunch for Lucas and sat with him while he ate.

"Where did you learn to make a boat?" she asked one day as they sat on a dry patch of meadow grass near the bank of the Sangamon.

"I was apprenticed to one of Rutledge's mill men," he answered. He had removed his shirt in the midday sun and she saw the strong, compact muscles of his back and abdomen. His skin had begun to tan in the springtime sun.

"John taught me some, too." Lucas continued. "I've built flatboats for the past two years, a new one each time we go," he added as he bit into an apple.

"Why do you have to build a new one each time?"

"We can't paddle a flatboat back up the Mississippi. The current is too strong and these boats can't maneuver very well. They are only good for drifting and steering downriver. We'll break it down in New Orleans and sell the lumber, then take a steamship back or walk back depending on how much we get sellin' our goods."

"Walk back?!" she asked, incredulous.

"Yup. Nuthin' much to it. Just takes longer."

Cory thought about all of the work he had done on the boat so far and the amount that still had to be done. The labor involved was tremendous and yet it seemed completely normal to Lucas.

"Where are your parents?" she asked, wondering where he inherited his fortitude.

"They died of the milk fever when we lived in Kentucky. That's how I come to be here with my cousins. Their mama pretty much raised me from when I was twelve."

"How old are you," she asked.

"Twenty-two." He looked up from his work. "You look about eighteen I gather."

She was floored by his estimate until she remembered how shocked she had been to learn Ellie's age. Cory thought about her 21st Century, thirty-something girlfriends wasting tons of money to look younger. She wondered if they would like knowing they look like teenagers.

"Uh, I'm not as young as you think. Screw it. I'm twenty-seven."

He looked at her in disbelief and she blushed a deep red.

"Well, you shoulda told me you came from a rich family. It accounts for your unmarked skin and lack of..."

"Skills?"

"Rough hands."

She smiled. "I could help you. Show me what to do."

Over the next few days, he let her help and they began to construct the boat's frame. They laid wooden girders spaced between the parallel gunwales, and he taught her how to join each girder to the twin beams with a dovetail mortise. They milled planks at the sawmill and laid those across the girders, parallel to the gunwales. He showed her how to secure each plank with wooden pegs. Cory was awed by the simple but effective wood and metal tools they used. She had always wanted to learn carpentry, but part of that desire was to use power tools. The satisfaction she got from using her own muscle power to cut, plane, and drill wood was something she had never imagined.

The plank-covered bottom of the boat needed to be sealed so Ellie taught Cory how to make the cording used to fill the seams of the planks to make them watertight. They gathered hemp plants, stripped the leaves, cracked open the stems, separated out the fiber, and worked it between their fingers until it was flexible and broken in. Ellie then showed her how to turn the strands into thin lengths of rope. Awkward at first, Cory soon got the hang of twisting and spinning two strips of fiber at just the right tension to transform them into a strong tight piece of rope. She and Ellie helped Lucas hammer the hemp cordage into the seams of the planks and finished the caulking by pouring rosin and hot lard into the crevices as a sealant.

At this point, the boat reminded Cory of an old-fashioned wooden sled with runners as it sat on the muddy bank. It would be her home for two months during the trip down the Mississippi and she wondered how river worthy it would be. She tried to picture the finished product and asked Lucas to describe what it would look like.

"Well, I guess it looks most like a small barge cause ours will only be about forty feet long. It's flat of course, thus the name, but we build a small cabin on it for the cargo and to sleep in if the weather is bad."

Cory imagined something like a houseboat, but obviously without a motor to propel it.

Boatbuilding was hard work and they did it from sunrise to sunset. John came to help from time to time, but most days he and Ellie were in the fields planting crops. Ellie also tended the spring vegetables growing in her kitchen garden, washed everyone's clothes, and kept them all well fed. Ellie's cooking was simple, but the ingredients were so fresh that everything she made was delicious. She was also famous for making the best biscuits and pies in the region. Cory watched her continue working well into the evening, stitching John and Lucas's clothes for the boat trip. From law school, Cory knew that the land and cabin could not be jointly owned by wives for almost another hundred years. Ellie could not vote in any elections either. Despite having no legal rights, Ellie was always telling Cory how lucky she was to be married to John. He treated her well and her biggest fear was that something might happen to him. She felt sorry for Cory being on her own. She also couldn't believe Cory was going downriver with the men. Not only was she skeptical about the venture, but she was also a little sorry Cory wasn't staying to keep her company.

Sometimes Lucas slept at Ellie and John's, camping in a sheltered spot at the edge of the woods near the house. Tired from working all day, Cory usually fell asleep the moment her head hit the pillow on her pallet bed in the cabin, but she often woke later, anxious and scared from nightmares. Memories of the attack by Givens made her body go rigid with fear. The thought of Lucas sleeping nearby calmed her down. She felt safe around him. He had not touched her longer than it took to position her hands on a saw or adjust her body to avoid injury as they worked on the boat. The thought of being touched by a man in a sexual way was still frightening after her attack, but she couldn't deny a certain attraction to Lucas. She had noticed the way he listened to her when they talked and she had caught him watching her work. Despite their growing comfort with each other, she stayed focused on her desire to return home to her time, to her real life, no matter what. New Orleans was the goal. She hoped the journey there would help her find a way back to the future.

The upside-down boat was now at a pivotal stage and help was needed to flip it over. Neighbors arrived one morning knowing exactly what to do and immediately formed two groups. Cory helped a number of men use levers to raise up one gunwale while Lucas's group held down the other side. Ropes were then used to pull the massive frame over and gently lower it until it sat upright in the river. Everyone let out a common hoot of triumph and then held their breath waiting to see if leaks bubbled up as the forty-foot boat bobbed in the water.

After a few minutes, Lucas smiled at Cory with relief.

"No leaks. No repairs needed for a while. We did good."

Cory stood ankle deep on the muddy bank with splatters of dirt across her cheeks. "Now what?" She asked, grinning ear to ear.

"Yup, lots more to do," he replied smiling back.

But the following day, Lucas paused to repair a wagon wheel for a neighbor, and Cory was left to fill a day on her own. Bored and anxious, she wandered about the cabin yard then decided to walk down the road to help Ellie gather reeds at the wetland edge of a small nearby pond. Ellie wanted to use the long stems for making baskets.

Cory decided to wear her borrowed dress for a change and set out down the road barefoot and feeling free. She had not gone very far when she noticed a tall man holding an odd metal instrument up to his eye as he stared across a prairie field. He looked vaguely familiar.

As she approached, the man spotted her out of the corner of his eye and lowered the instrument for a moment.

"Mornin, miss," he offered with a friendly smile.

"Hello," Cory answered, barely pausing.

"Fine day to be out walking," he added.

"Yes," she replied and continued on.

Something made her slow down; however, and look back over her shoulder. The man had not resumed his task. He stood with his hand on his hip, staring at the ground, seemingly deep in thought. His tall, lanky frame and the relaxed way he stood contemplating the ground made her turn and walk back to him. He was wearing trousers too short for his long legs, a weathered canvas jacket over his rumpled shirt, and no hat covering his dark, wavy hair.

"Do you mind if I ask what you are doing?" she asked hesitantly.

"Not at all," he answered with a sheepish grin. "I wonder that myself all the time."

She smiled at his self deprecating humor and began to have an excited feeling in her stomach.

"I took this job as a surveyor and taught myself to use these gadgets, highly technical mind you," he said with obvious sarcasm. "The money helps me climb out of the deep hole of debt I fell into while squandering my time reading too many books, so my friends tell me. One of these days I truly will get serious about making a living; however I don't think surveying is my true calling."

By that point, Cory had become frozen in awe. He noticed her stillness.

"Pardon me, miss. I get to talkin' and all manner of decency escapes me. My name is Abe. Abe Lincoln. Are you new in these parts?"

"Hi...hello. My n...name is Cory Dupont," she stuttered.

"Pleased to meet you, Miss Dupont," he said.

She looked up into his young face with his warm brown eyes framed by his thick, dark hair and large ears, and she suddenly relaxed. He was after all, a living and breathing human being roughly her age, standing on a road, just beginning his long journey to greatness.

"I'm staying with John and Ellie Traughber, " she explained.

"Ah, yes, I recollect hearin' about your ordeal with that scoundrel. They haven't caught him yet, but I hope you find justice in this matter. To be honest though, he may have hightailed it out of these parts and there won't be a chance to rectify the insult he perpetrated on you."

"I kind of hope that he is gone. I should want him to be caught and punished, but right now I just want to stop being afraid. I am about to travel to New Orleans to visit family."

"Being with family will be comforting. New Orleans...been there myself twice."

"I know," she said excitedly, having read pretty much every biography of Lincoln ever written. "Ellie and John said most everyone from New Salem has made a flatboat trip to New Orleans."

"Yes, mine didn't start out so good. Got hung up on the mill dam and nearly sunk my boss's boat."

"What did you do?" she asked even though she knew that story, too.

"Well, for a time I cussed a blue streak of epithets at the river, the boat and myself for taking the dawgone job, but the cargo was gradually sliding down the deck toward the water so there wasn't much time to keep feeling sorry for myself. I got to thinkin' it was probably weight that bogged us down and figured the best thing to do was unload the cargo. I borrowed another boat, brought it alongside, and unloaded all the barrels. Word got out and pretty soon there was a good crowd gawkin' and givin' advice as only the shrewdest of ignorant folks can do. The Cleary boys came along, viewed our plight, and burst out laughin.' I wanted to jump onto the bank and strangle 'em both, but I looked at the boat with its nose down in the Sangamo, folks yellin' and me tryin' to keep barrels from falling overboard, and darned if I didn't bust up laughin' myself."

The memory made him laugh and Cory did, too. He continued his story unable to contain his mirth.

"A jug of corn liquor was produced and from then on the chore was a lot more pleasurable. I drilled a hole in the boat to let the water out and got to tellin' a few tales while the boys helped us reload. Along about two hours later, that boat was on the right side of the dam with the hole re-plugged and we started our journey drunk as skunks. It's a good thing the Sangamo runs so slow 'cause we could barely hold our heads up as we drifted down the river. Don't tell nobody, but pretty much after we got out of sight of townsfolk, we tied up and slept the rest of the afternoon and night!"

"I won't tell," Cory giggled.

As his laughter subsided, he wiped the tears from his eyes with his shirttail and his voice took on a sentimental tone.

"There is nothing so powerful or wondrous as the Mississippi. Both of my trips down the old Miss were full of adventure and New Orleans is an extraordinary city. Those journeys opened my eyes to many things in the world, good and evil."

"The slave markets," Cory said quietly.

His eyes widened in surprise. "Why, yes," he responded. "It was most disturbing and inhumane. Those markets haunt me. So do the sugar plantations in the Delta. I thank God we don't have slavery in these parts."

"Someone needs to stop it. All of it," she said fervently.

"Yes, you are right. Someone with courage...and authority," he answered solemnly. "On your journey south, you will see how strongly slavery is held there. The economy flows on this indecent trade of humans. I fear that it will not end soon or without great resistance."

Cory looked up into his honest, brown eyes. "The world will not be destroyed by those who do evil, but by those who watch them without doing anything," she said.

"Those are very wise words, miss," he replied.

"Not mine," she smiled.

"I will carry those words with me, especially when I go into the next legislative session in December."

Cory fell silent as she held the weight of knowing his future.

"Good luck," was all she could form into words.

"You, too. I'll be envious thinking about your river trip," he said.

She turned to go and then turned back and reached out her hand.

"It was really nice to meet you," she said.

He was surprised by the uncommon gesture, but shook her hand.

"You, too, miss. I will not forget our talk today," he replied.

She turned and quickly walked away, completely overcome with emotion. She broke into a trot and when she was out of his sight, she crouched down in the roadside grass and burst into tears. It was as if everything that had transpired finally sank in. She might never return to her time and yet she knew everything that was going to happen. She feared for herself and for Lincoln and all that he would experience. She knew he suffered from anxiety and depression, or "melancholia" as it was often labeled. She knew what it was like to have dreams of a better life and to worry about the world. Her future was completely unclear now, but she knew what his would be. She wept for all that would come to pass —war and suffering, the loss of his children. Slavery would end, but racism would keep blacks disenfranchised into her time. She just wanted to stay in this spot, crouched in the tall prairie grass, and never move again.

"Cory, are you alright?"

Cory looked up and Ellie was standing bent over her in concern. She swiped away her tears with the back of her hand and quickly stood up.

"I'm okay. I was coming to find you and stubbed my toe really hard on a rock," she lied.

"I did the same last week. I've got some nice plantain salve that will soothe the pain. Cory, I wasn't going to tell John because I didn't want him to worry on the trip, but I don't think I can keep it from him. I'm going to have a baby," she announced, beaming.

"Oh Ellie, I'm so happy for you," Cory said. "John will be so excited," she added.

That evening Ellie made her announcement when they were all sitting around a campfire at the boat launching site. As she feared, John was concerned about leaving her alone.

"Don't be silly," she said. "I'm only a few months along and can take care of myself just fine," she assured him.

"Congratulations, cousin," Lucas said, giving her a kiss on the cheek. He uncorked the whiskey jug and poured everyone a drink. "We'll get this boat finished, go downriver, and be back home lickety split. John, play us a tune. This is cause for celebration!"

John cracked a smile and let his wife see how happy he was about the news. He reached for his fiddle and began playing an upbeat reel. Ellie stood and pulled Lucas up and they danced in the firelight. Cory watched Lucas bust some fairly adept moves as he twirled Ellie to the jaunty tune. She let herself be lulled by the happy strain of music trailing off into the night sky.

*

The boat was basically a raft at that point. It needed walls and a sheltered cargo hold. Over the next few days, Lucas built the shelter. He cut posts and inserted them vertically into mortises carved every few feet in the gunwales. Cory helped him nail planks across the posts to form the walls. They cut slimmer but longer posts and set them every two feet to make a fifteen-foot line along the center of the boat and then connected the side walls with the center posts with rafters. Across the rafters, they laid two-inch thick roofing planks. They spent the following day cutting wooden shingles and then they shingled the whole roof and caulked it to keep out rain from their valuable cargo. The angle of the roof was just steep enough to shed water, but flat enough for a person to walk on it easily. To finish the shelter, they added front and back walls and Lucas cut out a door.

Continually fascinated by the project, Cory realized they were still not finished. The shelter required interior work to protect the cargo. They added ceiling hooks for hanging smoked hams and wall hooks for roping barrels of salt pork down during rough waters. A few inches of clay distributed evenly upon the floor helped seal crevices and absorb moisture to keep bags of grain dry. They would cook outside, with either a small iron brazier in an open sandbox on the deck or a campfire onshore. The boat was sturdy and practical, not meant to be attractive in any sense, but Cory thought is was beautiful.

"Where do you sleep?" Cory asked.

"I usually sleep on the deck, but I'll build you a little platform bed so you can sleep inside the cargo hold," he answered.

"And if it rains?"

"John and I pull our blankets inside the cargo hold and...," he paused when he realized the room would only fit three people if they bunked close together.

"Look, I never had to think about this stuff before. We'll figure it out along the way," he mumbled as he scratched the back of his head and stared down at his feet.

The last task was building the steering equipment. Lucas carved the fifty-foot long oar that he cleated to the stern to function as a rudder. He and John debated whether to make side oars or "sweeps" that were thirty feet long and attached to each side of the eaves so a person could stand on the rooftop and row. It was these oars sticking out of the sides that caused flatboats to be affectionately called "broad horns." Lucas decided that since there were only three people on the boat that they would not use sweeps. They would simply drift with the current and use the long rudder for steering. He also made a much shorter oar for the bow, called a gouger, that helped keep the craft in the deepest part of the water.

On the final days before leaving, they all helped load the cargo—smoked hams, corn in the ear, bags of oats, barrels of pork and sauerkraut, potatoes and beets. They also stored fresh eggs, butter, milk, and bread to eat for as long as it would last.

Their route was simple. Enter the Sangamon River going north, turn west at the Salt Creek, join the Illinois River heading south, and follow the Mississippi for a thousand miles to New Orleans. Simple but not easy.

Cory's only reference for traveling on the Mississippi River was a vague recollection of the passages in Huckleberry Finn describing Huck's adventures with Jim. She read the book in sixth grade and couldn't remember much besides the deep impression Huck and Jim's relationship had made on her. Huck was a dirt poor, white kid running away from an abusive father and Jim was a black man escaping enslavement in Missouri. They bonded in order to protect each other, but it was a complicated relationship, emblematic of white supremacy and racism. This flatboat trip was taking her straight into the deep South at the peak of slavery in America. What would she see? Lucas had made the trip several times. What had he seen? Illinois was a free state, but that did not mean that everyone was against slavery.

She stood on the deck of the boat as the sun was setting. They had finished loading the supplies and were about to drive the wagon back to Ellie and John's for their last night before leaving in the morning. Lucas walked up beside her and watched the orange-pink sky as it faded to darkness.

"Red sky at night, a good sign for tomorrow," he remarked.

"We'll see enslaved people when we go south," she said.

He looked at her, surprised. "Yes."

"Are you okay with it? Slavery I mean?" She held her breath, hoping he was not.

"I don't think it's right, but it is legal. We are a free state, but there are still the Black Laws.

"What do you mean?"

"Illinois passed laws so that free blacks don't have the same rights as everyone else. It is meant to prevent them from settling here. There are only a few families living in this area and mostly people don't enforce the Black Laws...yet."

"I hate all of it. And it will change," she shared.

"You sound really sure."

"Trust me."

"You are an odd woman. In the best way," he added with a smile. "And I trust you."

"I trust you, too."

"Let's get back to John and Ellie's. We need to get an early start tomorrow."

She heard the nervousness in his voice. She knew this trip was a big responsibility for him. Life for him and his relatives depended on a successful outcome. She did not want to cause him additional worry and she swore to herself that she would not be a burden.

She woke the next morning with a headache. It was drizzling and grey, definitely not the "sailor's delight" that the previous night's sky had promised.

Cory hugged Ellie good-bye and Ellie placed an old fedora hat on Cory's head.

"It was my pappy's. It'll keep the sun off your pretty face," she said.

"Thanks, Ellie," Cory said and hugged her again.

Cory had exchanged the men's jeans she had been wearing for a pair of long underwear and a set of denim overalls. Her hair was still short and she imagined that she looked more than a bit like Huckleberry Finn.

Ellie was trying not to cry when they left the cabin and Cory worried about her. It would take over two months to get to New Orleans and steamboat back. At least Ellie had Rusty to keep her company. Neighbors promised to check in on her and John would return in time to plant the summer crops. Still, her tasks were numerous—tending the kitchen garden, feeding the livestock, and sewing clothes for the baby. As they stepped onto the flatboat and unhooked the rope that tethered them to home, Cory felt Ellie and John's heavy hearts.

Chapter Four

The Sangamon

The fucker that shot me has stayed by her side pretty much every second. I'm getting skinnier by the day stealing food and begging from dimwits who don't know I'm the one that tried to kill her. I found out from that con man Johnson that she wants to go to New Orleans to see a relative. What the fuck? Why? Maybe this relative has some idea about how to get back to our time. Anyway, heading south sounds a shit ton better than being stuck in this place. I need to get to the Mississippi River, hitch a ride on a boat, and I'll find her.

With a full cargo and their strong, new flatboat, Cory, John, and Lucas floated along the Sangamon, but the river twisted so often that it seemed like they were going nowhere. White sand bars jutted from the shore every few hundred feet and Cory pictured their path on Google Earth as resembling a curling blue snake with ivory markings. John and Lucas had not spoken for over an hour. Cory was not used to the amount of silence among people in this time. They seemed to listen to the stillness. No street noise, no stereo, no TV. She tried to relax into the quiet, though in fact, the air was only absent of human noises. There were sounds all around them. From the dense forests on each side came a symphony of mating bird songs. She heard the gentle but persistent April wind rustling through newly formed leaves and she swore she could hear the creeper vines renewing their upward spring journey along tree trunks. As they drifted through this wild landscape, it filled her with wonder and fear.

"How many miles do you travel each day?" she blurted out, startling both men.

"We try and make at least fifty miles a day, but that won't happen until we join the Illinois River," Lucas answered. He noticed her anxious look. "It'll be a couple of days til we get there," he added then he got up and jumped to the roof of the shed. He sat and kept his eyes ahead, watching for fallen trees or "snags" in the water and for the ever-present sandbars that could abruptly beach the boat.

Cory sat back against the cabin and was silent. After a while, she fell asleep.

After fourteen miles, they met the Salt Creek and veered west. They entered a narrow, flat valley that caused the river to slow even more as it meandered back and forth in such a way to form little peninsulas. A few miles further, Lucas steered the boat to the water's edge and hopped out to tether the boat to a tree with a thick rope. It was getting dark and overhanging branches made it too dangerous for nighttime travel.

John cooked a meal of eggs and potatoes using the sandbox stove. Cory was feeling shy amongst them and said little. She helped with washing dishes and then climbed inside the cabin to check her sleeping area.

Later, she lay awake on her pallet looking out the door at a blue black cloudless sky. Masses of stars and a waxing half moon shed light on the boat. The surrounding cargo and the importance of this trip felt like a fifty-pound bag of potatoes on her chest. This was real. People's lives depended on getting this boatload of merchandise downriver. Her life depended on it, too. Going to New Orleans was the only thing she could think to do. She would find her relative and try to find the con artist Johnson and his fortune teller friend. Maybe this woman knew some secret that could help her find a way back through time. She thought of her sister Jill, Michael and Sam and remembered the last bedtime story she told Sam. She heard herself describing the adventure to him: "...and then Sam the Wonder Kid jumped down off the ledge!" She was in that adventure. She was in the time of their stories. Cory turned onto her side and imagined that she was sitting on Sam's bed telling him all that had happened, leaving out the bad parts. It gave her the comfort to finally close her eyes and fall asleep.

They spent another day wending slowly along the Salt Creek and Cory began to feel that she could have walked the journey faster. Finally, she noticed that the narrow waterscape was beginning to change. Within another mile, the overhanging branches gave way to open sky and a vast network of marshes and ponds lined with dried cattails and emergent grasses. It reminded Cory of a watercolor painting with drops of blue, brown, and green puddled across the canvas and feathered into a unified terrain. Marsh birds thrived here; red-wing blackbirds, egrets, and an abundance of herons including Great Blues.

"We're in the floodplain of the Illinois River," Lucas said from atop the cabin where he was stationed at the steering pole. "It won't be long 'til we join it."

She didn't ask questions and just waited.

In a nearby pond, she caught sight of a beaver gnawing through the last inches of a birch tree. It sat back as the trunk snapped, fell, and bounced on the spongy ground. Within seconds, it was busy chewing off a branch to add to an impressive lodge nearby. The effort was not unlike building a flatboat. She looked up at Lucas on the roof and he was watching, too. He turned and smiled at her and she guessed he shared the same thought about industry and construction.

Within a mile or two they entered the wide channel of the Illinois River. It dawned on Cory that they were about to navigate the route that Marquette and Joliet had traveled over one hundred and fifty years before, but in the opposite direction. History had been one of her favorite subjects, especially when she developed a mad crush on her high school history teacher who made every time period come alive. She remembered him describing Joliet's vision after canoeing up the Illinois River back to Michigan and then home to Canada.

"Joliet realized that all he needed to secure this territory for France was a short canal connecting the Illinois River to Lake Michigan, through an area that was covered by stinkweed, called 'chicaguoa' by Native Americans. He figured a town in that spot could become a giant center of trade."

He was of course talking about Chicago. Cory remembered Ellie's remark about Chicago and her own chagrin when she realized that in the 1830s, it was a little known town, nowhere close to fulfilling Joliet's dream of becoming the Midwest center of commerce. It would be another fifty years before it lived up to its prophecy as a trade mecca. She also realized that she knew nothing about the indigenous people who had probably named the city she lived in. And where were they now? It began to dawn on her that what Europeans were calling "wilderness" had been somebody's home.

Eight miles downstream on the Illinois, they spotted some rooftops over a bend.

"Beardstown. Should we stop and get supplies?" Lucas asked John.

Cory could hardly imagine a town nearby, but was excited at the prospect.

"I think we should keep going," John answered.

Cory kept silent, not weighing in on the decision. As they passed the village, she could see it was a bustling river port that served as a popular flatboat stop, but she also saw the rowdy boatmen lining the dock sharing bottles of whiskey. She was glad that they decided to pass by.

South of Beardstown, the channel remained wide and straight and Cory was thankful that they could finally travel more swiftly. The open land on both sides of the river felt much like the low Illinois farmland she was familiar with. By mid morning the next day; however, the wide channel narrowed again and the banks on both sides of the river rose up into tall bluffs covered in hardwood forests. She had never seen such high, white-faced cliffs, some rising over four hundred feet above them. She had only known Illinois topography that was flat and humble and she was awed by the majesty of these towering walls.

A mile downriver they spotted the first sign of humans since Beardstown. Cory was surprised to see the empty dock that appeared along the bank below the steep bluffs. She wondered if people lived on the high precipices above, coming down to the shore to receive cargo or engage in river trade. If they did live up there, the view would be spectacular.

Similar docks appeared every ten miles or so. Some villages sat on wider landings under the cliffs and along the water and yet, here too, there were only a few houses and probably not more than a dozen people at each site. These were European "settlers' moving into a "new frontier." But again, Cory's brain told her that there people who had lived here for thousands of years. This was not a frontier. Whites were not pioneers.

Some eighty miles further down the Illinois River, Cory took note that both John and Lucas stood up as if preparing for something. She caught sight of rugged cliffs ahead that appeared like giant sentinels standing shoulder to shoulder facing south, and then she spotted the confluence of waterways ahead. They had arrived at the Mississippi River. She could see that they were actually above it, that the level of the Illinois River was higher than the Mississippi and John and Lucas were moving fast around the boat now.

"Hold on to something nailed down!" Lucas shouted. Cory plopped on the ground cross-legged and grabbed the door frame of the cargo hold.

John was at the long rudder and Lucas grabbed the gouger paddle, bracing himself at the bow of the boat. They were rushing toward the lower flowing Mississippi water and it was almost like approaching the top of a waterfall. They shot into the air as the Illinois blasted them into the big river and drove them toward the other side like a child shoving a toy boat. Lucas pulled on the gouger and Cory could see his back and arm muscles straining to keep the vessel from speeding toward the opposite bank. Finally, the boat turned and Lucas steered them to the center channel of the Mississippi.

"Wahoo!" Lucas shouted with excitement and relief as they followed the great river south.

Cory let out the breath she had been holding and John jumped down from the roof, smiling.

"Father of Waters is what the Indians call it," he said as they settled into the river.

Cory had crossed the Mississippi River many times by car and airplane, but she had never spent any time at the river's edge, never mind traveling on it. All water as far east as the Appalachian Mountains and as far west as the Rockies flowed to the Mississippi. The river's origin was in Minnesota and it ended in Louisiana at the Gulf of Mexico. She also recalled what Lincoln said about it: "There is nothing so powerful or wondrous as the Mississippi."

The Mississippi also signaled something else. Once they entered the river heading south, the land on their right was Missouri, a slave state. Illinois was still on their left, but in another hundred miles, they would be leaving the free north entirely. Cory knew full well that "north" was not equivalent to true equality for blacks or any other people of color during this time, but at least slavery was against the law there. Very soon, both banks of the river would be states that legally enslaved people.

The next few days were filled with long stretches of peaceful water except that John and Lucas were never truly relaxed. They knew not to drift too far from the mid channel and to avoid the eddies that collected near the sand bars that dotted the river every few miles. They maximized speed by staying in the deep trench of the center channel or "thalweg" which leaned to either side when the river curved. Staying in the center channel also kept them away from the friction and debris along the banks. Most surprising to Cory was that the water was crystal clear, not the muddy Mississippi she had always heard about.

Over the next two days, they occasionally saw other flatboats, but not up close. Mostly they passed slow-moving barges, their decks loaded with cargo. By now, they had established routines for daytime travel and evening landings. At dusk, Lucas would jump on shore and secure the lines to tree trunks on the bank. The boat was heavy and he wanted to be the judge of how much slack the cable should have to prevent damage from bumping against the banks. Cory would throw him a rope at the bow and when that was secure, she tossed him a rope from the stern. In the mornings, he untethered by throwing one line onto the deck, pushed the boat away from the shore, and threw the second line as he climbed on board. They made small cooking fires either onshore or in the iron brazier sandbox where John fried up potatoes and pork. They went to sleep when it turned dark and were up at dawn. Other than that, there were hours when nothing much happened as they drifted downriver. Sometimes, John would break out his fiddle and play a tune. Lucas would pat the rhythm on his thigh or join in singing with his deep bass voice. Cory figured the songs were popular ballads. Most of them described love or hardship. One day, Lucas was crooning one of their favorite numbers as he stood at the long pole on the roof of the cabin. The ditty was about a shepherd so lonely he was eyeing a pretty little sheep in the meadow and John was hooting at the man's dilemma. Cory guessed the tune was Top 5 on the local hit parade, which probably stayed current for years since songs only traveled by word of mouth. At moments like this, Cory felt distant from John and Lucas. The songs were not hers. The culture was foreign. She was on a lone quest to find an answer that might not exist. Lucas was in the middle of the song when she stood up and walked to the stern of the boat. The tune ended and Lucas came to her side.

"We didn't mean to offend you," he said.

"You didn't. I was glad you were having fun. I was just sitting too long and needed to stretch my legs."

"It's a long trip. Sometimes there's not much to do on a flatboat but watch out for sand bars and warble foolish songs."

She heard the boredom in his voice and realized that she wasn't the only one who was restless. She smiled to herself and began to sing in a soft voice.

"You ain't nothin but a hound dog, cryin' all the time."

He looked at her curiously. She raised her voice and sang a little louder, adding a twang to her speech.

"You ain't nothin' but a hound dog, cryin' all the time." She let her body begin swaying.

"You ain't never caught a rabbit, and you ain't no friend of mine!"

Lucas smirked and John called out from the roof, "Sing it, girl!

Cory laughed and decided "what the hell?" She belted out at the river.

"Well they said you was high-classed, well, that was just a lie!" She began air playing a guitar and thrusting her hips. *"Yeah, they said you was high-classed, well, that was just a lie! You ain't never caught a rabbit and you ain't no friend of mine!"*

John grabbed his violin and picked up the melody as she repeated the whole first verse. Lucas joined in and when they came to the last line, they drew out the words.

"You ain't never caught a rabbit and you ain't nooo friend of mine!"

Cory air strummed the ending note with a downward flourish and John gave a full-throated "Yee haw!"

"Thank you. Thank you very much," Cory said with her best Elvis impression although she knew full well that Big Mama Thornton had made the tune a blues hit years before Elvis.

They were all laughing and at first, did not hear the sound of a dog barking in the distance, braying actually since it was a hound dog. The coincidence was not lost on the three of them as they looked at each other and then walked to the bow of the boat. They spotted a small island ahead where a man stood on the sandy bank waving to them. A large, spotted hound bounced and barked at his side. As they got closer, the man commanded the dog to sit and be still. Cory noticed a log cabin roof through some trees with smoke climbing from the chimney.

"I've got butter and milk!" the man called out.

Lucas glanced at John. They had run out of their fresh supply of both.

"I've been hankering for a biscuit with butter," John said to Lucas.

"Okay," Lucas replied.

"Keep an eye out though," John warned and touched his right boot where Cory knew he kept a sheathed bowie knife for protection.

John and Lucas steered for the bank and Lucas jumped off to secure them onshore. Before she tossed the rope to Lucas, Cory grabbed her fedora hat and put it on, pulling it low over her brow to hide her face and disguise herself as a male.

Once Lucas anchored them to the beach, the man walked over and shook his hand.

"James Hunter," he said. His speech was slightly muffled by the wad of tobacco in his cheek.

"Lucas McCain. And that's John Traughber and Cory Dupont," Lucas replied thumbing toward the boat.

"Welcome to my island," Hunter smiled with a toothless grin. He was tan, tall, and lean and Cory guessed he was in his forties by the grey at his temples. A jagged scar crossed his right cheek and toned biceps showed that he was prepared to defend his small kingdom.

As they walked along the path toward Hunter's cabin, Cory tried to act boyish. She modeled herself after the teens in her Chicago neighborhood—head down, hunched shoulders, hands in pockets. She stayed behind the three men who were now exchanging information about the river and news from north and south. The island was covered in scrub trees and vines. She saw a couple of beef cattle grazing on a lonely patch of wild grass, and as they approached the cabin, she noticed a fenced paddock with a brown-eyed Jersey cow munching on hay. There was also a pen of black-spotted hogs lying in the sun and a flock of multi-hued chickens foraging under bushes at the edge of the clearing.

Cory gathered from the small talk between the men that Hunter had lived on the island for ten years, providing travelers with fresh meat, milk, and eggs. His personal form of entertainment was wrangling traders into a poker game.

"Interested in a game of cards?"

Lucas looked back toward the shore where they could just spot their flatboat through the tree scrub.

"No time for cards," John answered.

Hunter was obviously disappointed.

"Suit yourself."

"How much for a jug of milk and a dozen eggs?" John asked.

"Two bits," Hunter said then spat some tobacco juice into the dirt at his side.

John and Lucas exchanged a surprised look at the high price.

"Makes a hand of poker a little more appealing," John commented.

"Yup. You might win all the provisions you need," Hunter replied.

John nodded and Lucas turned to Cory.

"Go back to the boat and keep an eye out. We'll be there shortly," Lucas told her.

Cory pivoted and headed back to the shore. She did not look back until she reached the boat, but by then John and Lucas had disappeared, presumably into Hunter's cabin.

She looked upriver, but saw no sign of other boats. The island shore was a sandy beach so she decided to sit down and wait for the men to return. The afternoon sun warmed her back and she hugged her knees and gazed out on the river. She had not slept well the night before. Rustling sounds had kept her awake and she was convinced that rats had climbed onto the boat and were scurrying around in the cabin darkness. Her worst nightmare had to do with a rat climbing onto her leg and crawling up her body.

Cory jolted awake just as a flatboat slid onto the shore. She stood up quickly.

A man jumped down to secure the boat. Another man, burly and bald, carefully but deftly lowered himself onto the ground. Cory noticed his wooden, peg leg. The third man stayed aboard and tossed the landing rope out.

"Sleepin' on the job, huh?" the peg-leg man laughed as he walked toward her.

Cory looked toward Hunter's cabin and kept her head down.

"My name is Beachum," he announced. "I take it the rest of your party is with Hunter in a game of poker?" he asked, making friendly conversation.

Cory nodded, unsure whether she should run or stay with the boat. She wondered where the barking hound dog was and pictured him sound asleep at his owner's feet under a card table.

"I hope your friends are losing or Hunter will be in a sour mood," Beachum added. "We came to trade for some eggs."

The other two men finished securing their flatboat and Cory got a closer look. They both had scruffy beards, one with brown curly hair and the other with straight black hair. She felt the black-haired man eyeing her then she suddenly froze. He was about twenty feet away, but the way his hair hung down across his brow made her stomach clench. It was him. Givens began walking toward her.

Cory stood there stunned and terrified. Beachum noticed and watched as Givens strode up to Cory and knocked her hat off.

"Hey, what'd you do that for?" Beachum shouted.

Givens ignored him. "It is you," he said to Cory. He lifted up his shirt, pulled out his gun, and put it up to her head.

The other two men stared at him in disbelief.

"What's goin' on here?!" Beachum demanded.

Givens grabbed Cory, spun her around, and held her in a chokehold from the back with the gun pressed above her ear as he pulled her toward the flatboat.

He looked at the curly-haired man. "Untie the boat. We're taking off."

Beachum started toward him.

"Stop there, Beachum," Givens commanded.

"I don't know what you are trying to pull, but you are not taking my boat," Beachum replied. "Let the kid go."

"She's not a kid. She's a fucking bitch and I'm taking her with me," Givens growled. He shouted at the curly-haired man. "You help me, Porter, and we'll split the money in New Orleans when we sell Beachum's cargo."

He gripped Cory and pointed the gun at Beachum to stop him from coming closer.

"He's lying!" Cory shouted and dug her heels in the sand, but Givens banged the butt of the gun against the side of her head to shut her up. She cried out in pain and didn't resist as he pulled her toward the boat.

"Gag Beachum and tie him up," Givens ordered Porter.

Porter grabbed a rag from his pocket and walked toward Beachum.

"You son-of-a-bitch, Porter!" Beachum shouted. "When I find the both of you, I'll kill...," Porter cut his words off by stuffing the cloth in his mouth and then tied his wrists behind his back.

"Sorry, boss," Porter answered. "This is my ticket out west."

Porter then quickly unknotted the secure line to Beachum's boat and climbed on board. Givens lifted Cory up and Porter pulled her onto the deck. She wanted to call out, but she didn't want Lucas or John to get hurt.

Porter jumped back down and he and Givens shoved the boat into the water. Cory looked frantically toward Hunter's cabin, but there was no one in sight.

"Get us outta here, fast," Givens told Porter after they hopped back on the boat.

Porter ascended to the covered cargo hold to operate the two long oars or "sweeps" attached. He pulled on the oars as if he was in a row boat and Cory could feel the flatboat instantly glide away from shore. They entered the channel and then swiftly floated down river.

Cory and Beachum exchanged helpless looks from afar as he struggled against his bonds onshore and she drifted away, a captive on his boat.

"Won't the other men come after her?" Porter called from his perch on the cabin.

"They don't have any real connection with her," Givens shouted back. "Worst they will do is stop in the next town and report us to the authority and what are they going to do?"

Cory hated to admit it, but Givens was probably right. John and Lucas could not risk their cargo, their livelihood, to chase after her. If this boat got far enough ahead, it would be difficult to catch. She was not their kin and the risk of danger was exactly why they had not wanted her to come with them in the first place. She had insisted they take her, but this was more than they bargained for.

Givens dragged her over to some rope on deck and tied her hands behind her back.

"Sit down and don't move," he warned.

"We're coming up on the Missouri," Porter called as he looked ahead.

They were approaching the junction of the Missouri River. Cory rose up to her knees to peer over the side and even Givens turned his attention to the tributary on their right that was dumping its contents into the Mississippi. Muddy water full of debris rushed into the river. This was the flotsam and jetsam of cleared forests and eroded topsoil from the western frontier land. Half-burnt logs and whole trees with their branches torn off formed floating islands of timber that swept and whirled along at a furious rate. The refuse immediately changed the color of the Mississippi to an opaque brown and from this point on, travelers had to avoid the sand bars and log jams caused by sediment clogging the river. The dirty, sepia-colored water matched the dark feeling that overwhelmed Cory.

Porter was a skilled riverman. He easily maneuvered them through the rushing water and debris and they continued south.

"Now, how about you tell me why you are going to New Orleans, and more importantly, how you are planning to get back to our time," Givens demanded as they settled into the channel. The river was calm again, but Porter kept an eagle eye out now for refuse in the water and only half-listened to the conversation.

"I don't know how to get back," Cory replied.

"You do, too. You wouldn't go all the fuck way to New Orleans if there wasn't something or somebody there to help you."

"I have a relative there, that's all," she answered.

"I don't believe you, but if it's true then I should just dump you overboard right now," he told her.

"Hey, I ain't gonna be part of no killin'," Porter warned, now alert to the conversation. "What if this relative of hers might pay to get her back," he suggested.

"I don't care about fuckin' money right now," Givens snarled at him and then turned back to Cory. "See, I'm not so dumb as you think just because you pulled that fast one on me with your story about being rich." He stood over her menacingly. "You know, the bad thing about this time in history is everybody knows everybody. I nearly starved to death sneaking around with a bullet wound in my arm trying to steal food from those shitkicker farmers that all knew each other and knew about me. But...," and he stopped to rest his back against the boat railing and sneer at her. "The good thing about this time in history is that everybody knows everybody. I bumped into a gentleman outside of town and we started talking. He tried to entice me into a shell game. Con men are always the same. Same game. Same talk. While he was blabbing away, he told me he met a strange, young woman who was very anxious to get to New Orleans. Which prompted him to tell me that he has a friend there that predicts the future, which the young woman seemed very interested in. It didn't take much to put two and two together."

Cory's heart sank. Finding her relative was her main purpose for going to New Orleans, but she did have a secret hope that the fortune teller might help her figure out how to get back to the future. Givens guessed her secret and now he was going to destroy it.

"If you figured it all out then why do you need me? You can find her yourself," she said.

"Because I don't know exactly how this thing works. We came through time together. Maybe we have to go back together. I'm not taking any chances. You are going with me then we'll settle things," he said.

She knew what "settle things" meant. Givens would use her until he got what he wanted and then...the memory of him attacking her flashed in her mind.

"Nobody is going to save you this time," he said, reading her thoughts as he rubbed his arm where Lucas shot him.

Cory looked up at Porter who was staring out at the water, minding his own business. He had no idea what Givens was talking about nor did he care. She was trapped. Her head was swelling where Givens hit her with the gun and it was making her nauseated and dizzy.

Givens looked at her and laughed.

"Pretty miserable situation, isn't it?" he commented. "Enjoy the ride, baby. I'm keeping you alive, but it won't be pleasant, I guarantee you that. You are going to pay for what you did to me."

She leaned back against the railing wall and closed her eyes from the searing pain in her head. Thankfully, she heard Givens walk away and felt herself slump to the floor as she passed out.

She woke to raindrops hitting her cheek. She had no idea how long she had been asleep. A grey sky masked the time of day and the light rain continued to fall. Neither of the men were visible. She straightened her legs that were tingling with numbness and then she struggled to her knees and peered over the railing. The river was straight and wide and the shores were slightly hilly and covered in forest; however, she could hear sounds in the distance, a sort of constant din that was definitely man-made. Givens and Porter were nowhere in sight and it felt like the boat was drifting without a captain. Then she heard voices inside the cargo hold. The rain shower ended and the sun came out, a western sun, which meant it was afternoon. Givens and Porter emerged from the cargo hold wearing different clothes that were a little cleaner, a little fancier, and a bit too large. Cory quickly sat back down on the deck.

"These were Beachum's French grandpa's," Porter informed Givens as he cinched the belt on his striped pantaloons.

"Not my style," Givens remarked as he walked out in a long-sleeved, black silk shirt and denim trousers. His beard and outfit made him look completely normal in 1835 or 2017.

"You sure you know your way around town?" he asked Porter.

"I've been here a hundred times," Porter boasted. "I'll show you a good time."

"I could use that," Givens responded.

The noise and clamor were growing and Cory recognized the sounds of a city...minus cars and trucks. She also noticed plumes of smoke in the sky. What she couldn't see from her sitting position was the long line of flatboats and larger steamboats lined up along a fairly large urban riverfront. The fog in her head from sleep was compounded by a nauseating headache. Givens pulled her up and she grabbed the rail to steady herself. She saw two-story houses made of brick, stone, or wood in the Spanish style, resembling the old houses of New Orleans she had seen in photographs. Some of the homes had terraced gardens extending toward the river. It didn't seem possible, but she wondered if she had been unconscious for days and they had arrived in New Orleans.

"St. Louis, gateway to the west," Porter announced wistfully, ending Cory's confusion.

St. Louis without the famous giant arch as its landmark. St. Louis, founded by the French and alive with a mix of Franco, Caribbean and Native American cultures.

"This is where my furs will end up when I start trapping in the Rocky Mountains!" Porter said proudly. "But tonight I'm going to get me some Creole lovin' from a Frenchie gal," he announced.

Porter steered them past the long line of flatboats docked upriver. He also passed the steamboats that monopolized the wharves in the center of town. Instead, he maneuvered into a spot on the south side of town below the steamships and away from the long line of flatboats. Cory realized that they were now hidden from the hundred other flatboats docked upriver. Even if by some miracle Lucas and John were looking for her, she was like a needle in a haystack of boats and ships. She guessed that she would not be visible anyway, which was confirmed when Givens shoved her into the cargo hold and tied her to a post.

"I need a drink of water," she said.

"I'll do better than that, baby," he said. "Beachum has a shit ton of whiskey on this boat." He brought over a ceramic jug and held it to her lips. "Here, drink this. It'll make you feel no pain and get you all relaxed. Ready for when I get back tonight if I don't get lucky in town," he told her. "Or even if I do," he added.

He shoved the mouth of the jug between her teeth and forced her to swallow or choke. When she did start to choke he finally pulled the jug away. He gagged her with a dirty piece of cloth and then he quickly got up and left.

Cory was stunned. She was alone in the dark cabin completely helpless. The whiskey warmed her stomach and dulled her senses, but it also made her instantly woozy and she felt both dazed and powerless. She jerked at the ropes binding her wrists, but that only cinched them tighter. Tears blurred her vision and she growled in frustration and anger. Instinct told her to keep fighting, but she wished she could just give up and die.

She had fallen asleep when a loud thump woke her. The only thing worse than Givens returning was the thought that some other stranger with ill intent would come onto the boat.

She remained very still and listened for footsteps. Someone was definitely slinking around the deck. Cory scrunched into a ball ready to kick her legs out with full force if someone approached. That happened a second later when a dark figure filled the doorway and blocked the small amount of light from the moonlit sky. The figure stepped inside.

A man's voice said her name at the same moment that she thrust her legs and made contact with his shins.

"Damn it to hell," he cursed as he tumbled backward and hit the ground.

Cory froze when she recognized the voice.

"Lucas?!" she called frantically.

"Cory!" another voice called back. It was John.

They were here. They did come. They found her. The relief was overwhelming and she promptly fainted.

*

Cory woke to a beautiful, starlit sky. She was on Lucas and John's boat moving downriver. A full moon was directly above, bathing her in the protection of its warmth and brilliance. She felt her body, her breath, and was unbelievably grateful to be alive and free. She didn't want to speak or move or do anything except savor this feeling. She was lying on a pile of blankets with her head cushioned by a pillow pulled from the cargo hold.

"I thought you might want to be outside," Lucas said. She turned her head and saw that he was standing nearby, scanning the water for debris. He and John had risked the danger of traveling at night in order to put distance between them and St. Louis. She saw John at the stern of the boat searching for signs of being followed.

"How did you find me?" she asked.

"Sleep," he urged. "We'll talk in the morning."

"Thank you," she answered and immediately fell back to sleep.

*

"How did you find me?" Cory repeated the next morning after drinking some willow bark tea to soothe the ache she still felt where Givens hit her. Lucas and John were sitting with her on the deck sipping coffee to stay awake after the long night of keeping watch.

"Anybody else on the run would not have stopped in St. Louis, but those two seemed the types that would risk it," Lucas explained. "Beachum was with us and described his boat, but we couldn't find it so we pulled up at the pier and went into town. We figured they would be in the riverfront saloons, not too far from the docks. We spotted them right away. I bribed a dancer to occupy Givens and another one to pull Porter off into a separate room. Beachum and I convinced Porter to tell us where you were."

"I've never seen Lucas persuade anyone quite like that," John noted. "Let's just say that Porter won't be speaking for a few days with his windpipe in the condition it is in right now," he grinned.

"And Givens?" she asked.

"He must have heard the commotion and took off. He's a slippery bastard if I've ever seen one," John said.

"Did he hurt you?" Lucas asked.

"No, but he threatened to as soon as he got back from town," she answered and looked away. "I can't believe you came after me," she said.

"What did you think? We were just going to let him take you?" John asked.

"Well, I knew you had your boat and cargo to think about. It's your livelihood," she said, feeling oddly embarrassed.

"Why does this buzzard want to hurt you, Cory?" John asked.

Before she could answer, Lucas chimed in. "When he attacked you before and I shot him, I thought he didn't know you. But he came after you again. Do you know him?" Lucas asked.

"No! I don't," she said, but they could tell she was hiding something.

"I think you better tell us what is going on," John requested.

She took a long moment trying to think how to explain.

"He was a stranger who was committing a crime because he thought he was being treated unfairly. I stopped him from hurting people by promising to help him. When he found out I was lying, he was furious and tried to kill me. That's all I can tell you that makes any sense."

"So he's after you for revenge?"

"You should let me off at the next town. I don't want you to be in danger."

Lucas scoffed. "We're taking a flatboat twelve hundred miles down the Mississippi. We're in danger every day. Besides, I'm not afraid of Givens."

John seemed a little less confident. She knew he was thinking of Ellie and the baby.

"Let's just hope we never see him again," John said and looked ahead as if willing the boat to move faster.

Chapter Five

SHOT TOWERS

That morning a storm rolled through and it rained heavily. Flooding caused the river to rise and flow more rapidly, which was good for making time, but also treacherous. Every island threatened to split the channel and send them toward the banks where debris and log jams would damage or sink the boat. They finally pulled over to wait out the storm rather than risk a disaster. The three of them sat on the cargo rooftop huddled under a waxed tarp watching the river swell.

The next morning, they continued south and approached a village at the bottom of extremely high bluffs. Cory spotted three large wooden towers protruding from the summit, an odd but awesome sight in the natural landscape.

"What are those?" she asked.

"Shot towers," John answered. "My uncle worked in the lead mines near here during the War of 1812. They melted lead and poured it from the top of those towers. When the liquid lead dropped into a pool of cold water at the bottom of the tower, it splattered and instantly formed balls of shot. The ammo was shipped back east and it helped us win the war." He pointed to a village near the cliffs. "That's

Herculaneum," he noted. "My uncle is buried there," he added.

"Was he killed in the mines?" she asked.

"No, Osage Indians attacked him and his buddies coming out of a mine one day and massacred them all," he answered.

He shifted the pole and walked to the rear of the cabin roof.

Cory was stunned. She looked to Lucas, but he only shook his head as if letting her know to stop asking questions.

As they drifted past the village, Cory recalled something about Herculaneum that a friend had told her. She had always been fascinated by solar eclipses, but had never seen one. A solar eclipse was coming August 21, 2017 and her friend had suggested a place to view it and avoid crowds.

"There's a town in Missouri that probably won't be crowded like other spots," he told her. "It's called Herculaneum and there is supposed to be totality there for at least a few minutes. You wanna go?"

She had Googled the town because the name was so odd. The founder, a guy named Austin, had named it Herculaneum after the ancient Roman town, destroyed by the eruption of Mt. Vesuvius. He was said to have chosen the name because the limestone face of the bluffs resembled the tiered seats of a Roman amphitheater.

She stared at the orange and white ledges named for a place so far away. She wondered what names had been given to these giant cliffs before Austin. Over the millennia, each landmark, each village was named by new inhabitants. She was overwhelmed by a sense of time, by all that had happened and would happen in the future. One simple truth dawned on her now. She had the sinking feeling that she would not witness the eclipse of 2017, only four months away in her time.

Her thoughts were interrupted by the sound of angry shouting ahead. Very quickly they came upon the scene. On the shoreline, two men had subdued a young boy maybe six or seven years-old. One man held the boy by the elbow, as another pointed a rifle at him.

Cory was surprised to see Lucas quickly take the rudder and turn it, pushing them toward the spot where the men held the boy.

"Hello!" he called.

The men turned, their faces hard and unfriendly. They were wearing army uniforms.

"Unless you need help of some sort, you best be moving on," The man with the gun called back.

Cory watched in amazement as Lucas steered them right to the bank instead. As they pulled closer to the shore, Cory could see that the boy was copper-skinned with black hair falling to his shoulders. He wore a calico printed shirt and fawn-colored breeches.

"Is there some kind of trouble?" Lucas asked.

"We've got things under control. This Cherokee boy got away from our transport is all," the gunman answered.

Lucas jumped off the boat and Cory sprang into action, tossing him the line to secure them on the bank. She caught John out of the corner of her eye standing stock still.

Lucas strode up to the men and reached out to shake the hand of the man with the rifle. "I'm Lucas. We come down from Illinois on our way to New Orleans to sell our farm goods. Are you in need of any supplies?"

The man lowered his rifle and shook Lucas's hand.

"Lieutenant Banks of the 8th Regiment, Union Army. I appreciate the offer, but we are well supplied," he answered.

Cory stared at the boy. He was clearly scared, but also sullen and defiant. She noticed the raw bruises on his face.

"Any chance you are selling this boy?" Lucas asked.

Cory was shocked by his question and she glanced at John who was stone-faced.

"We have orders to accompany all bodies to the reservation in the Indian Territory," Banks answered. He looked at the ground for a moment. "This one is trouble though. If you've got a use for him, you can have him. It'll save me a bullet and the headache of what to do with him. The woman he was with, likely his mother, died on the trail yesterday."

Lucas immediately walked over and grabbed the boy by the arm. The boy struggled, but was no match for Lucas who lifted him up and threw him over his shoulder.

"Good luck," Banks said. "Come on, let's get back to the others," he said to his fellow soldier.

The next thing that happened astounded Cory even more. When the soldiers disappeared, Lucas pulled the boy off his shoulder, set him on the ground facing him, and then knelt down and started speaking to him in a non-English dialect.

Cory climbed off the boat at this point and stood watching. John followed her.

Lucas and the boy seemed to be in an argument. Lucas tried to pull him toward the boat, but the boy was very upset and kept pointing in the direction the soldiers had gone. Finally, Lucas nodded and followed him. Cory and John followed, too.

They threaded a path through tall grass, then the boy led them into some woods until they heard sounds close by. It was the distinctive noise of saddle leather creaking, canteens swishing and swords clanking—the vibration of humans moving—lots of them. They quickly hid behind a stand of Laurel and peered through the branches. Cory saw a line of people shuffling along a dirt road, three rows abreast and at least a hundred feet long. They were Native Americans being forced to keep moving by Union soldiers carrying rifles fixed with bayonets. Bent heads, persistent coughing, and trudging feet told the story of people that had been walking for many days. The boy watched intently and Cory saw that he was torn. He was poised to break away from Lucas and run to his people yet he stayed motionless. Lucas whispered to him and he shook his head. Lucas spoke to him again and the boy finally nodded. They turned away from the scene and Lucas led the boy back towards the boat.

Cory took a last look at the line of people as it slowly disappeared around a bend. John touched her arm and motioned for her to follow him. They joined Lucas and the boy, climbed aboard the boat, and silently pushed away from the shore.

As they floated downriver, Lucas offered the boy some water and a piece of jerky, but he shook his head and stood at the rail watching the land they were leaving behind.

Lucas pointed to himself.

"Lucas," he said.

"Dustu," the boy murmured, barely audible.

"Dustu," Lucas repeated pronouncing it DOO-stoo.

The boy nodded, but hearing his name made him turn away. He said no more and continued to stare out at the river.

Cory looked at Dustu and thought of Sam. She stepped over to the rail and stood quietly next to him looking at the water. After a few moments, he turned his head and looked up at her. His dark brown eyes were filled with loneliness and distrust. She placed her hand on her heart to try and show him that she felt sad for his loss. He saw the gesture, but turned away to stoically watch the river again.

Lucas and John were talking in low voices and Cory tried to listen, but couldn't quite hear. She had so many questions. What were they doing with the boy? How did Lucas know the language? Why did he take him? John's uncle had been killed by Native Americans. How did John feel about the boy?

Dustu sank down on the deck with his arms circling his knees and his forehead pressed against them. His posture was so familiar to Cory. She thought back to the many times when she, too, sat in a huddled ball on her bedroom floor after her parents died. The pain had been unbearable, but she had been a senior in high school, not Dustu's young age. Even at 17, the loss spiraled Cory into years of risky behavior. She hadn't visited those memories for a long time, but they swept vividly into her thoughts now. She recalled one night in particular when she showed up drunk at her sister's house and Lou called her a "slut."

"I hate you!" Cory screamed at her sister as she knocked over a lamp and stumbled out the door.

She eventually took charge of her life, but there was always that hollow place inside that kept her anxious and wary. Seeing Dustu's curled up figure made Cory realize that she was still a victim of loss and heartache, a victim of the past. She sat down next to him and he lifted his head. She opened her palms and beckoned, and he slowly crawled into her lap. She wrapped her arms around him and for once, she had no thoughts about what lay ahead. For this moment at least, she was in the present and that was all that mattered.

Chapter Six

MEMPHIS

They floated past landmarks—Tower Rock, Cape Girardeau, and odd mounds of earth rising up in the distance. Lucas informed Cory they were ancient tribal burial pyramids. Dustu was watching the sights, too, and Lucas repeated the information in Cherokee.

"How do you know how to speak Cherokee?" Cory asked.

"When my parents died of the fever, my father's brother took me in. He used to beat me a lot and one day I ran away and got lost in the woods. A Cherokee hunting party found me and took me to their village. My uncle didn't care enough to find me and the Cherokee kept me. My mother's people found me after two years. I didn't want to leave, but my aunt, John's mother, insisted and took me away. After a while, I was okay being with her. She was nice and she taught me to read and John was like a brother. I missed my Cherokee family though. When I got older, I visited them a lot until we moved to Illinois. When I heard about the Indian removal, I was hoping that it wouldn't happen to my family since they have a large farm, but white settlers want land and President Jackson told them to take it."

Take it they did. Cory was familiar with the Indian Removal Act from law school. President Andrew Jackson invoked the order in 1830.

Lucas continued. "Dustu's people must come from a place that white men wanted really bad, maybe land in north Georgia where prospectors discovered gold."

"They walked from Georgia?" she asked.

"It looks like it," he answered. "The boy said that when the soldiers came, they had to leave everything behind. They could only take the clothes they were wearing. The soldiers burned their houses. It's a thousand miles from Georgia to the Indian Territory where they will live. That's six months walking. I don't understand," he said, shaking his head. "The Cherokee are mostly farmers and they adopted many of the white man's ways, but the government is still making them leave. Nobody cares what happens to people who have lived here for hundreds of generations."

Cory was more worried about the present moment. "What are you planning to do with Dustu?" she asked.

"I don't know yet," he answered.

It rained again that night. Dustu had not eaten at all, but when they took cover in the cabin, he laid next to Cory and slept soundly.

In the morning, they approached the Ohio River confluence. John and Lucas prepared, knowing that the new volume of water from the Ohio could send the boat into a spin. Fortunately, because of the rain, the Mississippi was higher than the Ohio. They flowed over the torrent of clear water rushing in from the Ohio and shot down the now enlarged Mississippi.

That evening, Dustu finally accepted food, and Cory watched him gobble down his dinner of pork and potatoes that John fried on the small iron brazier.

Over the next few days, Dustu became more comfortable on the boat. He followed Lucas around as he either worked the gouger at the bow to keep them in the channel or used the long rudder from the roof to keep them away from debris and shoals. He became such a shadow behind him that Lucas finally stopped and grabbed a piece of wood from their cooking kindling, a small knife from his pocket, and gave them both to Dustu. Cory was surprised that Lucas gave a real knife to such a young boy until she saw Dustu plop down on the deck and deftly begin whittling.

John avoided contact with Dustu and seemed annoyed by the boy. It was so contrary to his normally kind nature and it bothered Cory when John frowned at Dustu or waved him away when he came near.

That evening, when Lucas and John jumped ashore to make a bathroom trip in the woods, Cory saw them arguing when they returned. Later, as John was busy writing Ellie a letter at the back of the boat by candlelight, Cory found Lucas at the bow.

"Is John upset about Dustu?" she asked. "Because of what happened to his uncle?"

Lucas looked over his shoulder towards John as he kept his voice low.

"He's not pleased about Dustu, but it's not what you think. It is not because his uncle was killed by Indians, but because of what happened afterward," he told her.

"What happened?" she asked.

"He was just a boy, but his father brought John with him when he went to Herculaneum to collect his uncle's remains. When they arrived, some soldiers were heading out to hunt down the clan that killed the miners. His father volunteered to go with them. They found the Osage village and massacred every one of them—men, women, and children. He brought John to the site to show him how he had avenged his kin. John was twelve years old. He was in shock. He still has nightmares and won't tolerate any talk from people who want to kill Indians. It is hard for him to be around Dustu because he feels guilty about what his father did." He looked at Cory. "The Indians can and will make war on European invaders. They will kill innocent people, too. They are fighting to protect their hunting grounds and farms, but it is a war they will not win."

Cory knew that fact better than Lucas. 21st Century America still hadn't atoned for the genocide perpetrated on Native Americans during the country's founding and westward expansion. She felt angry and ashamed. It dawned on her for the first time that her mother's family farm was likely land that had been taken from Indigenous people. Whether they were conscious of it or not, her immigrant forefathers had reaped the benefits of people forced from their homeland.

As he followed Lucas around during the day, Dustu began to share more about his family. His older brother had actually escaped the soldiers during the "removal" by hiding out in the woods and so he was still in northern Georgia. Others stayed back, too, but Dustu couldn't say how many. His eight-year-old sister was with his aunt on the march to the Indian Territory. The soldiers had caught him stealing an army blanket for his sister, a crime punishable by death.

Cory learned some Cherokee words from Dustu and he encouraged her to use them though he giggled when she had trouble getting the pronunciation correct. She laughed with him, and in her inability to do much more than express herself with face and hand gestures, she tried to just be there for him, calm and relaxed in his presence. It was one of the hardest things she had ever done. She was used to constantly trying to entertain her nephew Sam and keep up with his energy. Now she was guided by Dustu's different way of being. He was active to be sure, but he was not like the kids in her time that were antsy and bored a lot. Mostly, he spent the days quietly moving around the boat watching the landscape or trying to help Lucas. He often sat for hours working on his wood carving.

One morning, Dustu was whittling and suddenly cried out. He held up his thumb and Cory could see the large splinter lodged in his skin. She also saw John hop up from his seat on the roof and jump down next to Dustu who immediately shrank back and became still. John gently held out his hand toward Dustu.

"It's okay, I'm not going to hurt you. Let me see that thumb," he said.

Dustu slowly reached out his hand and John carefully took it in his.

"That's a whopper," John said calmly as he examined the splinter.

Dustu relaxed a little and with some expert prodding, John lifted the splinter from Dustu's skin. He chucked it into the water and Dustu smiled at him shyly. John put the knife back in Dustu's hands and walked away.

That afternoon, they approached a crowded landing with a small town sitting on a bluff. The number of cabins barely outnumbered New Salem. Cory noticed a small, crudely made wooden sign that announced the town's name, "Memphis." Founded only ten or so years before, Memphis was just beginning to develop its reputation as a center of cotton trade.

There was something odd in the air here, something that made a chill run down Cory's spine. It would be nearly one hundred years before B.B. King, Elvis Presley and dozens of other hometown musicians made Memphis famous for the blues, but something made her feel a deep sense of despair at the present moment.

She spotted a flatboat pulling away from the landing with about thirty people crowded together and sitting on the deck...in chains. Nothing could have prepared her for this experience, not watching the TV series "Roots," not reading Twenty Years a Slave or Beloved, not hearing Billie Holiday singing Strange Fruit. As deeply wrenching as these artistic works were, she was now physically present to the horror of slavery.

The people were barefooted and scantily clothed in tattered dresses or trousers. It was the look on their faces however that made her stop breathing. Some were despondent and exhausted, others angry and proud. She watched a woman gesture to her mouth for a drink of water and saw a guard with a billy club approach and threaten to hit her. Cory's stomach clenched and she stepped to the railing of the flatboat and vomited over the side. She broke out in a sweat as she gulped for air.

John and Lucas were watching the slave boat, too. There were only three men with guns standing over the group of people, but it was easy to see how a few men could keep the group subdued. On every enslaved man's neck was a collar with chains that ran to wrist and ankle bracelets. Rebellion was impossible.

It was like a deja vu of the worst kind. Like the Cherokee transport, Cory was again witnessing people of color being forced to move against their will. She had never thought of the Mississippi River in this way, but she was realizing now that the river was more than a junction of tributaries. It was a confluence of bodies, Native Americans and enslaved Africans, being moved for the convenience of white, European settlers driven by a manifest destiny of the U.S. government. She was incensed.

The outrage was so visible on her face that Lucas grabbed her arm.

"Don't," he said, guessing that she was about to shout something at the boat.

They watched as the boat pivoted out of the landing and drifted downriver. It met a steamboat coming into the Memphis dock loaded with cotton bales. The passing ships were a perfect metaphor for what was happening socially and economically in 1835 America. Re-sell a million enslaved blacks from mid-Atlantic plantations to new farmers in the Mississippi Delta. Get a lifetime of free labor to grow cotton and sugar. Reap enormous profits. So simple. No wonder the American economy was booming. Ever since they landed in America, Europeans had forced indigenous peoples off their land and imported enslaved people to extract resources and accumulate wealth. She had traveled back in time to the pinnacle of nation-building, and the Mississippi River was the epicenter for transporting goods and labor.

Dustu was watching the boat, too, and Cory saw his face go blank as if he was deliberately wiping away emotion and trauma. They waited as the boat drifted out of view. They were not eager to follow it. Cory began to dread going further south.

"We best be moving on," John said, but she heard the reluctance in his voice, too.

*

As they left Memphis, Cory noticed how the landscape rapidly changed. On the right were the vast virgin forests of Arkansas, and on the left was wooded swampland made rich with sediment from the river and slowly being cleared to become the cotton fields of the Mississippi Delta.

Something else made travel different than before. Eddies that normally accumulated deadly tree trunks were free of debris. Logjams were less and much of the vegetation that hung over the banks was gone. Also gone were fallen trees that got stuck upright in the river bottom as if they had been planted there. Similarly absent were the more loosely burrowed dead trees popping up and down through the surface of the water like a see-saw. These "planters" and "sawyers" made travel treacherous. Cory wondered why these obstacles had suddenly disappeared.

"Will you look at that," John remarked.

A steamboat was parked along the shoreline loaded with a massive array of metal equipment and large ropes. Men on board were pulling up a large tree snag from the water. A system of pulleys and hooks allowed them to lift the wood and load it onto an open surface of the boat.

"That changes things quite a lot," Lucas replied.

With less debris, they were able to travel more swiftly with less risk, but they still had to be watchful pilots since the river had changed in another way, too. It meandered more broadly in some areas, but not in others. It required John and Lucas to steer from point to point because they could not see any farther than that.

With each passing mile along this wandering stretch, John had grown quieter. When he did respond, his words were irritable and edged with impatience. Cory and Lucas guessed what was causing his anxious mood.

Cory finally approached Lucas at a moment when they were alone.

"Could we handle the boat ourselves if John went home?" she asked in a low voice.

Lucas stared out at the water and shook his head "No."

After two days, the topography changed again from flat and open floodplain, back to high bluffs and hilltop communities. They drifted past Vicksburg and Cory thought about the Civil War battles that would make it famous in another thirty years. Now it was simply another small village breaking the natural landscape along their way. South of Vicksburg was apparently a notorious river pirate area. They had been warned against being lured to the banks by someone waving them down appearing to need help.

That night as they sat on deck around the sandbox stove, John told tales he had heard about pirates. Cory felt like she was at summer camp hearing ghost stories, only these stories were real.

"I heard of pirates that would put a young girl on the bank to call out as if she was in trouble. When a boat came to help her, they nabbed the crew." John embellished his story with gestures and Dustu watched him wide-eyed, grasping the tale without understanding the words. "One famous gang of Pirates led by a family named Mason robbed their captives, murdered them and hurled them off a cliff. They call that place the Devil's Punchbowl. Where we're headed are two spots for accosting travelers since you can grab people on the river or along the Trace."

"The Trace?" Cory asked.

Lucas chimed in. "Yup. The Natchez Trace. It's an old path made by migrating animals and the Natchez Indians. They used it to travel north and south. It ends near the town on the river called Natchez."

"Pirates have plenty of chances to wreak havoc," John chuckled menacingly, which made a shiver run down Cory's spine. John noticed her reaction.

"You didn't know it, but we coulda met pirates anywhere along the river from the very start," he said.

"Thanks for not telling me," she said and meant it

Chapter Seven

FORKS IN THE ROAD

The next town they encountered was dramatically different than the small rustic villages they had passed the last two days. Resting on a bluff were tall brick buildings with columns and porticos shaded by trees. Below was a typical riverfront that Cory had seen many times now—a series of wooden shacks hosting taverns, trading supplies, and brothels. They decided to pull into the dock and see if they could trade produce for some eggs and milk.

They had barely tied up when a man approached their boat. Cory noticed that he was eyeing Lucas in particular. The man was dressed in a fine, white cloth shirt, houndstooth vest, dark grey trousers, and a topcoat. He looked more like a businessman than a riverman or farmer. His long silver hair was tied neatly in a ponytail and his plump cheeks and protruding belly also signaled that he was not a laborer of any type. He called out to Lucas who was busy collecting a bag of produce to take into town.

"Hello! You there, young man. Would you be interested in earning a little extra money chopping wood for my home?"

"Is this Natchez?" John asked before Lucas could answer the man's request.

"It certainly is, sir! Capital of the state of Mississippi. Welcome!" he answered John and then looked to Lucas for a reply.

"I can do it. Can you pay us in some fresh milk and eggs?" Lucas asked.

"Why, yes, that would work just fine as we keep a fine flock of chickens and a milking cow on our property," he answered.

John and Lucas climbed off the boat and approached the man. They introduced themselves and learned that the man's name was Robertson and that he managed a bank in Natchez. Cory and Dustu watched from the boat, but then decided to join Lucas and John to venture into town. Dustu stayed close to Lucas.

Robertson led them from the wharf up a winding road to the town above. This was the first time they had left the docks to walk into a city. The warm southern air and sunshine felt good on Cory's face as she felt her legs adjusting to walking on solid ground.

Natchez up close matched what they had viewed from the river. It was a charming and quaint city, the largest they had seen on the Mississippi outside of St. Louis. Robertson led them to Main Street and the location of the bank he managed. The bank was a Greek Revival building, one-story tall with a marble facade and four Ionic columns. Cory noticed the house attached to the back, a two-story Colonial red brick structure with a covered front porch and a large yard. The whole complex encompassed a city block and included a small stable and chicken coop.

Robertson brought them around to the yard and Lucas saw the pile of oak stumps that needed chopping into kindling. Satisfied that the source of payment was visible nearby in the form of a dairy cow and a flock of hens, Lucas picked up the maul and iron wedge and began working. Cory watched for a bit as he split a round section of tree stump into pieces and then chopped those into stove size kindling. He stopped for a moment to wipe his brow.

"Why don't you go for a walk and see the sights," he said.

Cory had been thinking the same thing and motioned to Dustu to join her. He shook his head, deciding to stay with Lucas so she took off on her own to stroll through the village. It was the first time she had been around townspeople since New Salem. It was a beautiful spring day and Natchez was utterly charming with its Antebellum style homes lining the streets. Newly planted oak trees added to a warm and inviting atmosphere. She was wearing her hat and men's clothes, and though her appearance was scruffy, most people smiled and offered a friendly, southern-style greeting. She widened her exploration beyond the main streets of town. It felt so good to walk on land and stretch her legs. As she approached a fork in the road, she heard a man's voice calling out the same phrase over and over like a street vendor, but she couldn't quite catch the words.

She arrived at the fork, which was actually a junction for five roads, not just two. At one of the forks, she noticed a group of plain, narrow buildings, long and low. The belting voice was coming from a man standing in a dirt yard outside one of the low buildings. The yard appeared to be functioning like a showplace. People were being marched in circles in front of the shack. Black people.

"Slaves for sale!" the man shouted to the white farmers standing and watching the parade of people. The words were now clear in her ears and Cory was terrified. She froze in her tracks.

Her first instinct was to turn and run because the atmosphere felt so dangerous. Her heart was racing, but something told her that she must witness this with all of her being so that it was burned in her soul forever. A man was handing out sheets of paper and she took one without reading it as she walked toward the low buildings.

Unlike the enslaved persons she had seen on the flatboat in Memphis, the people on display were dressed in nice, clean clothes. The women wore homespun, calico dresses with white aprons tied at their waists and colorful ribbons circling their necks. Their hair was combed and neatly braided. The men wore navy blue suits with brass buttons and trod in single file. The women marched in twos and threes, many with children at their skirts. No one spoke. It was a nightmare beyond belief.

She looked down at the sheet of paper in her hand and the first words she saw were "lively stock," before a tear hit the page. Her vision was blurred and she was filled with anguish, fear, and disgust. Again, she wanted to escape this place, but something kept her rooted to this spectacle of horror.

The parade ended and the marchers were commandeered into rows on the covered porches of the long, low buildings. The seller continued his spiel.

"Genuine Virginia and Maryland stock, folks! Compliant and gentle. Little to no marks on their backs. No whips necessary with this docile type!"

They were sorted by sex and size and made to stand in sequence. Men on one side, in order of height and weight, women on the other. A typical arrangement placed the youngest girl at one end of the line with a stair-step progression of women's ages along the line so that the girl's mother might actually be at the far end. This plan was obviously intentional, the first step toward selling children away from their parents.

Cory was expecting a kind of auction to begin, but there was no auction. A buyer chose a body, took the person inside for an examination and then haggled on the price.

Cory followed one of the buyers inside along with a few other prospectors who were interested. The man was made to undress until he stood naked. She kept her eyes on the ground and listened.

"What is your name, boy?" the buyer asked.

"William," the man answered.

"What kind of work you done, *William*?" the buyer asked, pronouncing his name like it was too fancy.

"Field hand. My master in Maryland done grow corn and wheat," he answered.

Next, the buyer told William to open his mouth so his teeth could be inspected.

"Now, do a little dance for me, boy," the buyer instructed afterward.

With her head down, Cory could only see William's bare feet moving up and down in a way that showed he was agile.

"Okay, turn around and let me see your back," the buyer demanded.

Cory was shocked by the order and briefly looked up. William had several long thin scars on his back. The buyer nodded his head.

"Not bad," he quipped.

Few scars meant a "slave" was obedient, never interpreted as a sign of a cruel master. A smooth back was rare and fetched a high price.

Satisfied, the buyer began to haggle in front of William's still naked body.

"One thousand," he offered.

"This is a prime buck, tame and strong. I ain't taking less than fifteen hundred," the seller answered.

"You've got a dozen others like him out there. Twelve fifty." the buyer countered.

"Thirteen hundred to get this done," the seller muttered.

"Done," the buyer answered.

William was handed rags to put on. The shiny blue suit was put aside for another sale and the new owner motioned for him to follow. William obeyed, keeping his head bent in servitude until they stepped outside.

"Suh, my wife and child is here, too. Can you please buy them, suh?" he asked.

"Which are they?" the owner asked.

William pointed to the porch next door. It was obvious who his wife was. The women were supposed to keep their eyes forward, but she was looking frantically toward William and his buyer.

"I been looking for another house servant. Don't need a child though," the buyer commented.

"My child done lots a prickly chores. She knows how to chop wood and pluck chickens. Be a good worker someday for whatever you want, suh."

The daughter was at the other end of the line from her mother and was also looking in her father's direction. She was small and beautiful with a defiant look in her eye. Cory worried for her. She reminded Cory of Dustu confronting the soldiers. She prayed that the girl would stay still and be quiet in the hope that the buyer would consider purchasing her with her mother. Cory hated thinking this way but at least they would be together.

Her hopes were dashed when William's buyer finished eyeing the mother and daughter.

"Not today," he said. "I may come back tomorrow after some thought about it."

"Please, suh," William pleaded.

"You want to get a whippin' in front of all of these folks?" the buyer threatened. He did in fact have a short whip tucked in his belt.

"No, suh," William answered, clearly desperate to calm things down in front of his family.

"Then get a move on. This way," he motioned.

William took a last look at his wife's face, slowly turned, and followed.

Cory was livid. She completely lost it and discarded the fact that she might possibly be throwing her life away.

"Stop!" she called out, not to anyone in particular, but as if to the universe in general.

Because the slave market, at least this one, was fairly subdued, everyone heard her and turned in her direction. She strode up to the porch.

"Who is in charge here?"

The seller stepped out of the building having heard the commotion.

"What's going on?" he demanded.

Cory threw back her shoulders and stood up as tall as her five foot seven-inch frame could manage.

"I'm here representing the United States government. I need to see your ledger book on these sales," she said loudly.

The farmers standing in the yard stared at her with blank faces. The seller gave her a mild quizzical look.

"You don't look old enough to be a government official, boy," said the man.

She took a breath and lowered her voice as deep as she could.

"I'm 21 years-old, sir, and I'm traveling incognito," she answered, indicating her shabby overalls. She went on. "I had to disguise myself because jurisdictions began forwarding information I was coming and they temporarily shut down their operations before I arrived. I am an inspector for the Washington Office of the Internal Revenue Service and I am checking to see if taxes are being collected at all markets in this region. This is a new law, gentlemen, and if you are not aware of it, Mayor Simmons is and so is the constable," she replied with authority. Luckily, she had seen the mayor's name on the Town Hall building and now crossed her fingers that the sign was current.

"We don't pay no taxes on slaves," the seller insisted.

"This is a business, correct?"

"It ain't your business," the seller snarled.

She put on the most lawyerly countenance she could muster.

"Do you own this land?" She challenged. "Is this your home or your farm? I'm guessing it is not. Either this "lively stock" is being sold at an illegal market or you need to prove that you are paying taxes on these transactions. She called out to the farmers. "You are tax-paying American citizens, am I right? The City of Natchez is owed taxes on every 'slave' you buy or you are operating unlawfully." She turned back to the seller. "For today, until I see a ledger that proves that you are collecting taxes, you are now closed for business. Anyone that doesn't leave these premises immediately, will answer to the law."

She stared down the crowd until she saw Lucas standing at the edge of it. His mouth was hanging open and he was wide-eyed with disbelief.

The seller stepped up to her and faced her down.

"Why don't we step into my office and discuss this," he proposed.

"Okay," she replied, "but unless you can produce what I'm asking for, there is no discussion. She pointed to William's new owner. "You, sir, need to come with us," she added. Apparently the owner didn't want to break the law by not paying taxes on his transaction because he shook his head in disgust, but followed. Not sure what to do, William came with him.

Inside the low building, the seller tried to be persuasive. He pulled out a bag of gold coins and set it on the table in front of Cory.

"Look, young fella, what would you need in order to turn around and go on down the road to the next town?"

"Are you trying to bribe me?"

"Either you accept this token of our appreciation or you may not make it to the next town, son. Who from the government knows exactly where you are anyway?"

"I do." said a voice at the door. Lucas stepped in the room.

"Who are you?"

"I was hired to protect this...person and was paid good money to do so," he said eyeing the bag of gold on the table while at the same time patting his rifle.

Cory made a sudden decision. She clearly couldn't end slavery here, but she might be able to do something that was not going to end in a violent altercation.

"On the other hand, Lucas, let's not get hasty," she said. She looked right into the eyes of the market seller and steeled herself to use the words he would understand.

"I can't take your money, but I could use some extra hands on this job. I would be willing to take slaves as payment to look the other way."

Lucas was caught off guard, but kept silent.

"Well, now we are talking," the seller said. "why don't you pick the one you want, and we have a deal."

"Not one. I want three," she said and pointed to William. "I'll take that man and his wife and child. I can use all three."

"Now looky here, young man...," William's new owner objected.

"I'd take her offer, mister," Lucas suggested to the seller and raised his rifle. The farmers outside were getting anxious and starting to call out their frustration at having to wait for the market to continue.

"Done," the seller announced. He switched the bill of sale for William and transferred the two others to Cory.

Cory crossed her fingers behind her back for her forthcoming lie.

"I will report back to Washington that your books here are in order and you will not be bothered in the future about taxes. I would; however; consider a payment to the Mayor that would satisfy the City needs, a bribe or compensation."

*

They were back on the flatboat quicker than Cory could believe. All of them. Lucas, Dustu, William, his wife, and daughter.

The adrenaline was still pumping through Cory's body as Lucas shouted to her to get up on top of the cabin and work the rudder. She followed his order without hesitation. She expected to see an angry mob follow them to the dock at any second. Lucas threw the lines, jumped on board and poled them away from the dock.

William and his family stood huddled together on deck and Dustu was crouched warily a few feet away from them.

Cory called down to William as she pushed the long pole as hard as she could.

"I'm sorry," she began. "I didn't know what to do and I know you don't know what's happening and I know you don't know us at all, but that sale was just to get you out of that place." She was panting and rambled on. "I'm not sure what to do, but when we get to New Orleans, I'll try and forge some papers to get you free or figure out something. You'll have to hide for now, but it'll be okay, I promise."

William and his wife stared up at her, looked at each other, and back up to her.

"What is your name, miss? You are a woman, not a man, right?" asked the woman.

"Yes, my name is Cory."

"Miss, Cory, I beg your pardon, but we don't believe in no promises except from the Lord. No matter what happens, we are free today and that's all that matters right now."

William climbed up on the cabin and took the pole from Cory's shaking hands.

"You go on now. I gots this," he said. He manned the paddle, rowing with all his strength to move the boat quickly out to the channel.

Cory climbed down and shock began to settle in.

"You is shakin' like a leaf, Miss Cory," Charlotte said. Dustu fetched a blanket and Charlotte wrapped it around Cory's shoulders and rubbed her arms.

"I..I'm f...fine. Thank you," Cory replied with chattering teeth. Everyone on the boat became quiet as the boat pulled away from the dock and sailed from Natchez free and clear. A few minutes later, Lucas left the gouger and reached his hand up toward William on the roof.

"I'm Lucas," he said.

William reached down and shook his hand.

"William. And this is my wife Charlotte and daughter Catherine."

"Nice to meet you, ma'am," Lucas said.

It was at that point that Cory looked around in a panic.

"Where's John?!" she cried.

Lucas was at her side in a shot and put his hand on her shoulder to calm her.

"John's all right. He's at Robinson's house. Robinson has a friend that was traveling up the Natchez Trace. I saw the look on John's face when he heard that news. He wanted to go, too, back to Ellie. I told him to go. I wasn't sure how we would manage the boat, but..."

"You got no worries 'bout dat," William assured Lucas, still manning the pole.

"We'll have to be careful," Cory said. "Word will travel about what I did."

"I was going to start selling produce when we got to the sugar coast plantations, but it's too risky. We'll wait to sell everything in New Orleans," Lucas said.

Chapter Eight

THE CRESCENT CITY

They decided to keep moving on the river that night and took turns watching for any debris missed by the Snag Boat. The full moon helped them, but also made them more visible. They drifted past other flatboats and Cory realized that there was more traffic now. With every river junction, the number of traders on the Mississippi grew.

During her watch, Dustu stayed close to Cory, curled up on the deck at her feet like a sleeping cat. Lucas didn't have a plan yet for Dustu's future, but Cory guessed that it would involve re-connecting him to his family either in Oklahoma or back in Georgia. He seemed tense with the strangers that were traveling with them. She was so glad that he had not been with her at the "slave market," but she sensed that he felt the danger they were in now.

William, Charlotte, and Catherine were asleep in the cabin and Cory hoped they were resting peacefully.

The next morning, Cory woke to the smell of food cooking. Charlotte was making a breakfast of fried pork and potatoes for everyone and Lucas was standing on the roof eating from his plate as he manned the steering pole.

Catherine was watching Dustu work on his carving. He was whittling the piece of wood into the shape of a bird and she was clearly interested. Catherine was not shy and as they sat cross-legged on the deck facing each other, Dustu seemed to enjoy her company. She and her mother still wore the nice dresses and aprons from the "slave market." The seller had forgotten to switch out their clothes during the quick sale and exit from the market.

"My Cat likes your 'lil boy," Charlotte remarked.

"Dustu is not mine or Lucas's. We took him from some soldiers in Missouri. They were transporting his people to Indian Territory," she explained. "His mother got sick and died on the way."

"Poor baby. Yessum, we heard about the people being moved. We are from Maryland. People moved Indians from there a long time ago. They movin' everybody now. Callin' this Indian travel a 'trail of tears.' Is fo' sure. We know about that. Our people are on a 'slave trail.' My momma and sister are back in Maryland. I might never see them again."

"Cotton fever is what I call it," William said. "The masters have done gone crazy with the gold they make sellin' cotton. Tooks the soul right outta them. Black folk had it bad before, but we done figured out how to survive. Now the masters are selling us a second time, splittin' up families and forcin' us to travel halfway across the country. These owners walk and breathe and acts like they human beings that loves they family, but they got no real feelin' 'cept greed and hate. Present company don't count," he added.

"How did you get to Natchez?" Cory asked.

"Our master walked us from Maryland," Charlotte explained. "We lived on a farm in what they call the 'eastern shore,' near the ocean. We could see the water from the corn fields. Then one day he and the missus told us they were sellin' us. "

"Our master was tryin' to make money off this cotton fever, too," William lamented. "The ones of us he could spare, he took west. Six of us. He be hopin' to sell us before he got too far from home, but we walked all the way to

Nashville before he found a buyer, a slave trader. The trader's men walked us down the Natchez Trace to the Five Forks where you done found us."

"They chained William," Charlotte said bitterly. "We saw other gangs of people in chains along the way. It was terrible."

"What you said about taking us to New Orleans? Is that true?" William asked.

"That's where we are headed," Cory answered.

"It's a bad place, miss, bad for us."

Lucas had been listening. "After we sell our produce, I'm headed home to Illinois, a free state." he said. "You could come, too."

"How you get there?" William asked.

"I walked last trip," Lucas said. "Was thinking of taking a steamship back this time. Work for passage, chopping wood for the boiler."

Cory heard this and was filled with apprehension. She and Lucas hadn't talked about what would happen after New Orleans. She guessed Lucas figured she might stay in the city, which was a natural assumption. She looked at him, but he lowered his eyes, avoiding her. Her heart sank.

"You can get off the boat anywhere you want. If you are careful, you can make your way north on your own," Lucas said to William.

"You said you could make us papers, Miss Cory. Papers that say were are free. Can you really do that?" Charlotte asked.

"I don't know. If I could see what they look like, yes," she said. "New Orleans would be a good place to find out."

"In the meantime, we is your slaves," William said.

"Yes," Charlotte said.

"I don't wanna be a slave again, Mama," Cat said.

"You aren't!" Cory said to Cat and to her parents.

"The best thing for you to do is stay out of sight as much as possible," Lucas warned them. "Especially when we get to Baton Rouge. With so many sugar plantations, boat traders will be everywhere. Slave traders, too,".

"I seen you got pork barrels to sell. You don't need to stop at these sugar farms to trade?" William argued.

Cory knew he was right. Waves of enslaved blacks were being moved from the east coast to be resold in the steamy hot southern Delta marshland that was perfect for growing sugar cane. Lucas had told her that many flatboat traders stopped along the sugar coast of the Mississippi River to sell produce and meat even before they reached New Orleans. He knew that plantation owners needed to buy the potatoes and pork that he had on board. The "barrel pork," the least desirable hog meat preserved with salt in oak barrels, was a low cost, high energy food for "slaves." Plantation mules needed corn and the owners always welcomed fresh produce from the north. Lucas told her that some flatboat traders sold their entire cargo along the coast and exchanged some of it for sugar they then traded in New Orleans. Cory was witnessing in person the genesis of the term "pork barrel" economics. She could literally see why this cheap food became the metaphor for the appropriation of government spending by local politicians. It seemed wrong to her that modern scholars still used the phrase considering its negative origin.

They passed by Baton Rouge and two days later, they began hearing the din of New Orleans. It made them so nervous that they decided to come into the docks late in the evening. As they poled into the port, Cory was shocked by the river traffic. The steamboats alone were berthed five or six deep and the line extended as far as she could see.

She could also see why it was nicknamed the "Crescent City." As their boat traveled along the riverfront, they experienced the curve of land that New Orleans was founded on.

They found a spot as secluded as one could be in the masses of flatboats docked along the shore. Lucas and Cory decided to explore the city in the cover of darkness. William, Charlotte, Cat, and Dustu stayed on board.

Cory sensed that Lucas was incredibly tense as they left the boat. They had to step along the roofs and decks of a line of boats to get to shore. When they stepped onto the dock, they entered a throng of people and cargo that covered every square inch of the quay and included bales of cotton, barrels of meat, and crates of produce. Even at night, they could barely move between the crowds of people. Lucas had warned Cory that New Orleans was dangerous. It had a reputation of being a city filled with thieves and assassins. He kept a grip on her arm as they squeezed their way through the multitudes of travelers. Cory was indeed wary, but she wished she could explain to Lucas that she was streetwise and the present threats were not unlike some of the busy avenues she roamed at night in her south Chicago neighborhood.

"I want to try and find the trader we dealt with last time," he said. "He bought everything we had," he explained. "I shouldn't have brought you along," he mumbled. "Stay close."

"I'm okay," she answered and tried to pull away from his tight grip.

They found a building along the wharf and Lucas was satisfied that the trader was still in business though closed for the night. Cory suggested they keep walking for a bit and Lucas reluctantly agreed. Though it was late, bars, brothels, and cafes were booming with business. The atmosphere was raucous, an entire riverfront in need of entertainment and relaxation. She and Lucas were gaping tourists gathering in the sights after spending months in the natural world. They were finally here, the place where she knew for sure that someone from her family lived! They were walking along Vue Chartres when she noticed something that made her pause. Up ahead was a sign hanging above a shop that read: "Madame DeCour, Fortune Teller." When they got to the door, it was open and candles were glowing inside.

"Can we stop here for a moment?" she murmured to Lucas, but didn't wait for his answer and stepped inside. He glanced up at the sign to see what type of store it was, raised his eyebrows, and followed her.

The shop did not fit the stereotype of a fortune teller. There were no astronomy images on the wall, no exotic posters of faraway places and no table with a crystal ball. The furniture and artwork were sparse and the style was distinctly Art Deco, which sent a chill down Cory's spine, considering it was decor from the next century not this one. There was a hall table with geometric wooden inlays and on it sat a lamp, lit by a gas flame, but with a leaded glass Tiffany shade. A sleek leather Bauhaus style couch rested on an area rug with a Mondrian-like design woven into it. No one was in the front room, but an open door led into the back of the shop.

"Good evening," said a woman's voice. "I'm Madame DeCour." She stepped out from the back room and stood in the soft light of the lamp. She was tall and thin with short, cropped hair and wore pleated slacks and a silk blouse, not the typical costume of a fortune teller.

"Curious what's in store for your future?" She asked.

"Yes, I've come a long way to find you," Cory answered.

Madame DeCour looked at her intensely.

Does the name "Amelia Earhart mean anything to you?" she asked

Cory's heart stopped. "Y...yes. Why?" She was excited. This woman really did know the future!

"I'm Amelia."

At first Cory thought it was a bad joke born from some kind of supernatural knowledge. It was not humorous; however, and she felt uneasy and unsafe.

"Are you feeling alright, dear? You look a little pale," the woman said. "Please sit down."

Cory sat on the sleek, leather couch and the woman sat next to her. She took her hand.

"I am who I say I am," she said.

Cory was speechless, but somehow she knew it was true. A million thoughts were racing through her head, but foremost was the fact that Amelia Earhart crashed her airplane in the Pacific Ocean in 1937. And yet, sitting next to her was a living, breathing woman that looked just like her.

"Don't be shy. You came for a reason, right? Let me help," Amelia said.

Cory looked up at Lucas instead. He seemed confused and uncomfortable amid the odd decor and Amelia's effect on Cory.

"Perhaps your gentleman friend would like to visit a tavern and come back for you after we are finished?" Amelia suggested.

"We should be getting back to the boat," he responded.

Cory wanted to go, but didn't move. She looked at Amelia again and was transfixed. Lucas sighed.

"I'll go for a pint of ale and be back."

The two women watched him leave and then Amelia turned to Cory.

"What time period are you from?" she asked abruptly.

"I...I..." Cory was stupefied.

Amelia got up and went to a side table. "There is always a look about someone from the future." She poured a small glass of whiskey from a lead glass decanter, handed it to Cory, and sat down again next to her. "To me you stick out like a sore thumb," she said emphatically.

"Two thousand seventeen," Cory answered. "You've met others?"

"2017. Amazing. You are the second most modern person I've met. There was a young man from two thousand thirty, but he couldn't tell me much. The people who found him thought he was insane. He kept rambling on about the 'explosion...everything gone...nu..nuclear,' yes, that was the word. Nuclear. The poor dear was in shock and I couldn't do much to help him. He disappeared and no one has seen him since." She paused for a moment, remembering. "But, please, tell me about you. Where did you come from?"

Cory was startled over the man's description of the future, but she forced herself to remain in the present...sort of...since she was sharing her story from another time.

"I'm from Chicago. I was visiting my sister...and...I'm sorry...this is blowing my mind."

Like Lincoln, Amelia Earhart had been an inspiration to her. The famous aviator, heroine, and champion for women's rights. She had aged a bit, but she still wore the iconic outfit captured in print and film—khaki trousers and a tailored blouse with a white silk aviator scarf circling her neck. She must have had them made special by a seamstress.

"How did you survive? Everyone thought you were dead!" Cory exclaimed.

Amelia laughed. "You are the first person to recognize me. The young man had no idea who I was, but you recognized my name instantly! I must have become somewhat famous. People remembered me for a time?"

"Yes, you were remembered. People wrote books and made movies about you," Cory told her. "They tried for years to find out what happened to you and there are dozens of theories."

This news made Amelia happy. Cory recalled that Amelia Earhart had a streak of narcissism along with incredible determination and courage.

"Our plane crashed on an island, but we both survived," Amelia explained. "Fred, Fred Noonan, my navigator, was certain we would never be rescued and then, after about six months, a boat came close enough for us to signal. Fishermen from a larger, nearby island took us to their home. We were skin and bones at that point, having survived on fruit and the few fish we were able to catch. We stayed with the islanders for several years until we decided to find our way back to civilization." She pronounced "civilization" like it was a dirty word. She continued, "The islanders helped us get back. They passed us along a network of islands to the west until we reached Indonesia." She looked off in the distance, remembering. "Fred developed a fever and died there. He was an incredible navigator, you know. And a good friend. I blame our crash on those damn, new-fangled instruments I insisted on buying for the plane. I didn't know how to use them properly and we flew into unbelievable weather. A massive storm. Fred got us to the island or we would have crashed in the ocean for sure. When we were able to understand their language, the islanders told us that the atoll we landed on was a mythical place for them. The story was that their ancestors also landed there after a terrible storm. They survived and created a new tribe of people."

"How did you get to New Orleans?"

"I relied on the kindness of strangers," she said, using the popular phrase way before Tennessee Williams made it famous.

"I traveled across the Indies through Europe with a constant goal of reaching America and returning home," she continued. "I didn't realize at first that I was in a different time. There was no indication of that when we were on the island or living with the Polynesian people. The first village I got to where there was significant trade, I noticed that there were only wooden sailing ships. That is when I realized something was strange. I began to understand the unbelievable fact that somehow when we crashed the plane, we traveled through time."

"Yes, it was so hard for me to believe, too," Cory agreed.

"In France, I arranged to board a sailing vessel bound for America. It was headed to New Orleans. When I arrived here, I still wanted to return home, but I became nervous about traveling north into the unknown where my ancestors were just arriving in Illinois and Kansas. People befriended me here and New Orleans was so lively with so much going on that I decided to stay awhile. A friend took me in and gave me a room. I often slipped up in conversations and accidentally made references to the future. People started thinking I was like a fortune teller or a seer. I needed a way to make money and so I decided to become what people already thought I was. Predicting people's lives is actually quite easy. They give you so many clues without saying a word, like your gentleman friend. He's obviously crazy about you."

"No, we're just friends," Cory insisted, feeling her face flush.

Amelia smiled at her. "I foresee that he will drink that pint of ale and be back in ten minutes."

Cory explained her mission. "I met a Mr. Johnson in Illinois who said he had a woman friend who could predict the future. You are part of the reason I came to New Orleans. To see if you could help me get back."

"You met Robert?! Why, he is the one who took me in when I arrived. He's a great friend," she exclaimed, and then her expression changed. "But I'm sorry. I haven't a clue how to get back. When the reality sank in that I might never be able to return to my time, I was depressed for months." She was quiet for a moment then her cheery demeanor returned. "I can't believe you met my Robert! The world seems so vast here with no telephone or radio, but I guess it is becoming smaller very quickly. I hear people are moving west in droves."

"Yes, people are moving and people are moving other people," Cory said. "We saw Native Americans being driven west on foot by soldiers and we saw a slave market in Natchez, Mississippi that was horrible. Enslaved people are being re-sold from the east coast to the southern Delta."

"It is horrible," Amelia said and looked down at her lap. "You know, Cory, I look back at my life in the 1930s and think how lucky I was, how privileged without knowing it. It has been my greatest awakening to realize that I did not understand the black experience at all—past, present, or future. I did not have the slightest notion of what they are subject to at any moment and for their entire life. The first time I saw a slave market here, I was horrified. It was beyond belief. I thought about the future and I was ashamed. We fought a huge bloody war to stop slavery, but it didn't really end. And why would it? It's too damn profitable to keep people oppressed."

"Amelia, we are helping three people escape. They are on the boat with us. I'm going to try and get papers to emancipate them."

"Well, now I have to reassess you. A young heroine from the 21st Century."

"I'm not a heroine and I'm terrified that we will get caught," Cory answered.

"Yes, what you are doing is very dangerous, especially here with so many people who might want to stop you. I will help you any way I can."

Cory was touched and a bit overwhelmed by Amelia's revelations. "Yes, we might need your help," Cory answered. Her thoughts were now running to tomorrow and everything that needed to be done. At that moment, Lucas walked into the shop and Cory stood up.

"Can I come back to see you tomorrow?" Cory asked.

"I'm counting on it," Amelia answered. She stood and walked Cory to the door to join Lucas."

"What is your name, young man?" She asked.

"Lucas."

Amelia looked at Cory and Lucas.

"Where are you staying?" Amelia asked.

"On the boat, ma'am," Lucas answered.

"Well, if you need accommodations for any reason, I have extra room here."

"Thank you," Cory answered and she and Lucas left the shop.

It was close to midnight, but the streets were still crowded with people. Gas lamps lighted the sidewalks. Laughter, singing, and the tinkling of piano music spilled from saloons. Some shops remained open, doing business the same as daytime. The whole atmosphere of the city felt festive, especially in the warmth of the southern, spring air. As they walked along, Cory heard as much French spoken as English and she marveled at the mix of people—French Creole, European French, Spanish and German sailors, British merchants, and flatboat farmers. There was some shouting and pushing by drunks or ruffians, and it was rowdy to be sure, but also exciting, urban, and familiar. She had wanted to keep talking to Amelia, but felt the pressure from Lucas to leave. He was pulling her along through the crowd at a fast pace and she finally jerked away from him and stopped. He grabbed her again and backed her against a storefront.

"It's dangerous here," he said.

"Let go of me. I can take care of myself," she answered stubbornly.

"Can you?" he challenged. He let go of her arms, but stayed in place, blocking her path.

"I feel comfortable here," she informed him.

"So did she tell you your fortune?" he asked, seemingly annoyed. "Did she tell you that you will meet some rich stranger and live happily ever after?"

"I'm not looking for that kind of guy," she answered. She could feel the tension between them and realized that it had been building up the whole journey downriver. From St. Louis and Givens, finding Dustu, and escaping Natchez, so many things had happened. He was right. It was a perilous world, but so was hers in the future. Nothing had changed much.

"I'm sorry if I've put you in danger," she said sarcastically. "But we made it safely and I have things to do! So get out of my way!"

He glared at her, his body taut with anger, and she glared back, obstinate and defensive.

"You are a selfish...," he bit his tongue, "woman!" he seethed, trying to keep his voice from rising.

"I think you meant 'bitch'! And you are an ignorant bastard!" she yelled in his face.

"Go. Go find your 'kind of guy'!" he roared, livid.

"And you go to hell!" she fired back.

They were nose to nose in a furious standoff, and then abruptly, Lucas stepped aside.

She bolted away down the sidewalk, walking briskly. She could barely breathe and her eyes were stinging with tears. She paused and whipped around. Lucas was standing watching her and she saw that his anger had dissolved. He quickly looked down at the ground to hide his pain, but then swallowed his pride and looked back up at her. She saw his heartache at the same moment that she felt hers. Their eyes stayed locked and they started walking towards each other. They both pushed past people on the sidewalk until they finally met. His head bent and she raised hers. Their lips joined and they kissed with the urgency of all they had kept pent up inside and not shared. The city melted away, the sounds, the lights, the voices. It was only the two of them standing on the sidewalk, unaware of the people having to step around them.

"Get a room," a sailor snickered. Cory heard him and pulled back from their kiss for a moment to smile in recognition of how old that expression was.

She took Lucas's hand and led him back down the block to Amelia's shop. Amelia was surprised when they walked in, but she saw the look on their faces and pointed upstairs.

"First room on the right."

They climbed the stairs, entered a bedroom, and Lucas shut the door.

There were no words now. They had lived and worked and looked out for each other for twelve hundred river miles. She knew him in so many ways except one.

They removed each other's clothes slowly as if savoring the moment, this last bridge to full connection. She had seen his bare torso many times, but when he stood naked before her, she saw that his whole body was muscular and tight. She was both shy and eager as she tried to be relaxed about her own body. He scanned her figure appreciatively then looked in her eyes and breathed a sigh of relief as if he had waited a long time for this. He ran his fingers along her neck and down her chest then cupped her breasts. She circled her arms around his neck and pulled him in for another kiss. Their naked bodies pressed against each other and they were unable to stay still. They clung together as they moved to the bed—a real bed with a silky coverlet. She reached back and pulled the cover aside and they fell onto the soft mattress and cotton sheets. There was a brief moment of laughter at the amazing ecstasy of this moment, and then she pulled him close and they began a night of bliss.

In the early hours before dawn, Cory woke from the deep, relaxed sleep only multiple orgasms can provide. She was on her side with Lucas spooned around her back. The fullness in her heart was something she had never felt and she was both unbelievably grateful, but also scared. Her old anxieties about the realities of life crept in. She also thought of Dustu, William, Charlotte, and Cat. They would be worried that she and Lucas hadn't returned.

She turned over to face Lucas. "We should get back to the boat."

He groaned in sleepy resistance.

"Come on, we should go," she repeated as she sat up and turned to swing out of bed. Lucas caught her wrist.

"Wait. What's that on your back?"

The dawn light was beginning to bathe the room and Cory's naked body was visible now. She unconsciously reached her hand back to cover her right shoulder blade and glanced shyly at Lucas.

"It's a tat. Tattoo."

"I know what it is," he said. "The Cherokee and other tribes have them. Why do you?"

Is this when I tell him the truth? she wondered. She sat on the edge of the bed and looked down at the floor. Amelia could back her up her time travel. Lucas would understand. She still felt the warmth from his body and their newly formed bond. Her mouth opened to speak and then doubt swept in and she paused. If she told him the truth, would he question their future together, a future she wasn't sure of either?

She began a pretend story instead, keeping her face hidden from Lucas while she spun her quick tale. "I did it on a whim when I was twelve. A peddler came to Chicago who had the idea of... tattooing horses, under the lip, since horse thieving was getting worse in our area.

"Good idea. Better than branding," he noted. "Go on."

"Well, I had the idea of tattooing myself just to try it. I didn't want my parents to know and it was summer, so I just pulled one side of my blouse off my shoulder and he put the tattoo on my shoulder blade."

"Why wings? and a cloud? It's a cloud, right?"

"I don't know why," she answered honestly. When the tattoo artist in her Chicago neighborhood had asked what she wanted, she had replied instantly as if the words were not hers. "I want a pair of wings with sun rays shooting through a cloud."

Lucas gently traced the design with his index finger. The image was the size of her fist and finely drawn. The artist had needled a perfect set of wings, copper feathers with cream tips so detailed they seemed real. They spread, hovered over a floating cloud emanating golden rays of light fanning across her tan skin. She had been stunned when the artist held up a hand mirror so she could see her back, bloody and breathtaking, mysterious and comforting at the same time.

"I like it," Lucas said. "It's one more thing about you that is strange but beautiful."

She turned, climbed back into bed and into his arms until the dawn fully unfolded.

*

When Cory and Lucas got dressed and slipped silently downstairs, she saw the package with her name on it that Amelia had set by the door. She grabbed it and left, hoping to return later that day. The streets were quiet now as they made their way back to the docks. Sleeping bodies filled the port. Men, women and children were curled up on bales of cotton, boxes of produce, and even atop wooden barrels. Rats scurried along the quay and more than one shifty human cracked a drunken eye as they passed by.

What Cory did not notice was the man in a black shirt and jeans standing behind a stack of crates. As Cory and Lucas searched for the line of flatboats that led to theirs, Givens watched them with a vengeful sneer. "I made it," he thought to himself. "I'm worse for wear, but I'm alive and I'm going to get myself out of this mess."

When Lucas and Cory got to the boat, no one was on deck, but as soon as they stepped aboard, William crept out of the cabin.

"You okay, Miss Cory?"

"Yes. I'm sorry we are so late getting back." Cory answered.

"We didn't sleep a wink, but maybe now," William said, yawning.

"Yes, go back to sleep. We'll watch out," Cory said.

William nodded and stepped back into the cabin.

Cory looked back toward the city and Lucas put his arms around her. She turned and kissed him. "You are awesome," she whispered.

"You are 'awesome,' too," he said using an expression that clearly felt new to him.

As the sun rose, she thought about the tasks ahead. "I'll figure out how to get papers for William, Charlotte, and Cat," she said. "I'll also look for my relative."

"And I'll try and get the cargo sold as fast as I can," Lucas said.

"And then what?" She thought, but swallowed the question, afraid to consider their future together.

Chapter Nine

FINDING NEVERLAND

Four hours later, Cory woke completely disoriented. She had no idea where she was and it took her a moment to recall the night before with Lucas. She was lying on the deck of the flatboat, having fallen asleep near him. He was sitting against the cabin, but had drifted off to sleep, too, despite their promise to William to stay watchful. Even before she touched him; however, his eyes snapped open, alert.

"Good morning," she said, resting her hand on his thigh.

He shielded his eyes from the hot sun as he looked up at the sky.

"More like afternoon, I wager."

"You've probably never slept this late in your life," she teased.

"I've never spent a night like that before," he grinned as he leaned down and kissed her temple.

"Any regrets?" she asked.

"No! I've been waiting to do that since the morning I met you at John at Ellie's."

She laughed. "With my puffed up black eye and swollen face? You didn't even stay for breakfast!"

"Then when you threw up in the street and I still yearned to kiss you, I figured that you were the one for me," he teased.

She tried to playfully push him away, but he pulled her close and gave her a proper kiss on the mouth. It lasted a while until they were interrupted by Dustu who crawled out from the cabin and squinted in the sun. Lucas beckoned him over with a whispered greeting in Cherokee. Cory sat up and they nestled him between them.

Dustu and Lucas proceeded to have a short conversation that Lucas translated afterward.

"He is nervous and wants to leave. I told him that we will leave as soon as possible and that he should stay on the boat."

He then looked at her gravely. "When I get the cargo sold, we'll need to book passage on a riverboat going north. After I break down the boat, we should go right to the ship or find a safe place to camp."

"Maybe Amelia can help or my cousin can take us in when I find her," she said.

"That's asking a lot with the six of us," he noted.

"I'll find us a safe place," she said with determination.

Luckily, no flatboat had pulled in behind them, but there was a risk that any moment, they would be blocked in. They had actually moved one space closer to the dock because one of the boats ahead of them had sold their cargo and been moved to a site where it could be broken down. The hardwood lumber was a valuable commodity for building homes, churches and sidewalks.

Cory opened the package Amelia had left for her and found a clean set of clothes. They were fine quality and comfortable fabrics. She shed her overalls in a shielded spot at the stern of the boat and donned a white blouse, long blue chambray skirt, and a tailored jacquard vest.

Lucas grinned at her fancy clothes and made a fake bow to tease her. She smiled and then ducked into the cabin to talk to William, Charlotte, and Cat. When her eyes adjusted to the darkness, she saw that they were waiting to hear her plan.

"Lucas will talk to the trader today and try and get his produce sold. I'm going to get your papers if I can. Please stay hidden. Thank you for watching Dustu. He's really scared. I have to tell you that I don't know what will happen, but I will do my best to make sure you are safe."

"Pardon me, miss, but you is not our savior," William said. "We is grateful for all you done and now God will make the way for us. We will stay here one more day and see what happens, but if you finds us gone, it's cuz we had to go."

Cory nodded. "Okay. One day. Give me a day. Just don't leave Dustu alone. Make sure he is okay. Please."

"I'll make sure of that," Charlotte said and stared her husband in the eye to secure his promise.

Cory gave a last look at the family and ducked out of the cabin.

She saw Lucas standing with his hand on Dustu's shoulder.

"I changed my mind," he said. "I'm taking him with me today to do my business."

Cory was starting to feel scared about the day ahead, but she pushed away her anxiety and smiled at Dustu.

"He will be a great help, I'm sure," she said. Dustu smiled back, took her hand and squeezed it.

She conveyed the new plan to William and Charlotte that Dustu was going with Lucas and then she left.

It was now early afternoon when she stepped onto the dock. She was in search of records—records of her great, great grandmother and records of free blacks. She asked at least a dozen people before she was directed to the New Orleans Courthouse. She arrived at the stone, Greek revival building and noticed crowds of people gathered across the street. Something about the atmosphere was familiar and then a sales sheet was shoved in her hand, confirming her suspicions. The sheet announced today's sales, describing the gender, age, and condition of each "slave" along with a price, of course.

It was the very last thing she wanted to do at the moment, but her anger compelled her to bear witness. She left the courthouse and walked across the street. A sign was stenciled in the stone facade over the building where the crowd gathered outside. It read: THE EXCHANGE. She stepped into the building and followed a line of mostly men heading down a hallway that ended in a beautiful, light-filled marble rotunda. Enslaved blacks were being presented to buyers under the rays of sun shining down from the round, glass ceiling. It was both a stunning and sickening sight that made Cory's stomach clench. An auctioneer was in the middle of a sale featuring a young woman, healthy and strong. She was half-naked with her breasts exposed. The bidding was animated and reached a crescendo.

"Five thousand!" yelled a buyer.

"Eight Thousand!"

"Twenty thousand!"

The auctioneer yelled, "Sold!"

Cory turned to see the buyer. An elderly white man was standing proud and leering at his new acquisition. Cory's judgment of him could not have been worse and the words "lecherous" and "debase" were top of mind. She wanted to kill him on the spot. She could not stop the sale here like she had in Natchez. She was powerless. Instead, she stumbled out of the building blinded by tears and stood outside taking deep breaths. She knew she had to keep herself together, but it was a struggle. A man walked up to her.

"Are you alright, miss?" he asked.

"I'm fine!" she answered angrily and strode away without looking at him.

Given's face darkened as she walked off. She hadn't even acknowledged him. He consoled himself with the fact that he had found her and that he was not going to let her get away this time. He watched her hurry across the street and enter the courthouse. He decided to wait for her outside before he took action.

Cory was more determined than ever to fulfill her mission. Inside the courthouse, she found the Office of Deeds and Property. With bitterness, she realized this would be the likely office to change human "property" to the status of a free human being. The clerk was young and courteous with a thin face and long, brown hair tied in a ponytail. He didn't raise an eyebrow when she asked him for samples of manumission papers.

It was actually a fairly simple procedure. The transfer in Natchez had taken only minutes, leaving her with papers that declared her the owner of William, Charlotte, and Cat. She was now relieved to learn that the process to free them would be just as quick.

The clerk provided her with paper, pen, and ink and she immediately sat at a nearby table to draft the documents.

"To all to whom these presents shall come," she wrote, copying the language of the sample papers. "I do further certify that the said William..." She didn't know William's last name. She debated whether to wait and ask William and Charlotte what they wanted, but fear for their safety made her take immediate action and she wrote: William Douglass is a free Citizen of the State of Louisiana entitled to all the privileges of a free White man of said State and the United States of America." She was forced to describe him according to the protocol that would ensure accuracy. William is of medium-dark skin color, approximately five feet nine inches tall, and bears a permanent scar over his left ear. He is accompanied by his wife and female child, Charlotte and Catherine. They, too, are free citizens of the State and the country. She paused for a moment and wondered how she would describe herself for this purpose. Coraline Dupont is of tan skin color, five feet seven inches tall, and bears...a large tattoo on her right shoulder.

She wrote two more documents describing Charlotte and Cat as free citizens and kin to William in order to remove any doubt that they were a family. She presented the documents to the clerk for his official, notarized signature. When he signed the last document, she held them in her hands and stared at them.

"Is there something wrong?" the clerk asked.

"Everything is good," she said as she tucked the documents inside her vest and walked out of the office.

She couldn't wait to get back to the boat, but then stopped and remembered her other mission. She walked back into the Deeds office.

"I have a relative living here, but I don't have an address. How would I find her?" she asked.

"Is she married? Does her husband own property?" the clerk asked.

"She isn't married yet," Cory replied, frustrated that there wasn't even a chance she could find her great, great grandmother through legal records unless she was married and her husband owned real estate.

"You could try the Postal Office on Canal Street. I hear they are making a directory of people's addresses," the clerk shared.

"Yes, I'll try that," she said.

He gave her directions, she thanked him and left the courthouse. She avoided looking toward the Exchange and instead touched the papers in her vest for reassurance as she headed for the Postal Office. Amelia's shop was on the way, and Cory decided to stop there and thank Amelia for the change of clothes...and use of the bedroom the night before.

As she walked from the Courthouse south through the busy French Quarter, she had the sense that someone was following her. She turned several times but didn't see a recognizable figure among the throngs of people. She reached Amelia's shop and stepped inside.

Amelia was just finishing with a client and said her good-byes as Cory waited.

"I'm so glad to see you, my dear," Amelia said.

"I stopped by to thank you for last night and for the clothes," Cory said.

"As I said before, I have lots of room," Amelia smiled. "And I sensed you might need a change from those raggedy men's clothes you were wearing."

"I did, especially today. I went to get legal papers for my friends and the outfit made me feel a lot more credible to say the least."

"How did it go?" she asked.

"I got the papers!" she said excitedly. "I can't wait to tell them."

"I'm so glad it worked out," Amelia replied. "I did not stand up for blacks in my time. Most especially, I did not stand up for black women. I thought I was such a defender of women's rights, but it was a sham. There were women of color trying to become aviators. I heard about them and didn't support them. I was too caught up in my own desire to become famous. I remember hearing about one young woman, Bessie Coleman. She was in the newspapers. Do you know how good a flyer she must have been to make it into white newspapers? She was a passionate, expert pilot and she was teaching other women to fly. I wish I could have met her. I wish that more than anything."

They were interrupted by a man's voice. "Good afternoon, ladies."

They turned and Cory froze.

"Get away!" she shouted, a directive meant for both Givens and Amelia.

"Hey, that's not very polite," Givens responded and walked toward Cory, pulling a gun from his belt. "I'm taking you with me, and if your friend here doesn't want any trouble, she will sit down and keep her mouth shut," he warned.

Amelia did what she was told and sat on the couch.

Givens grabbed Cory by the arm and put the gun to her back. He pushed her toward the door. "Let's go."

"Stop right there, mister!" Amelia shouted.

Givens turned and found a shotgun aimed at his heart.

"I keep a gun stored under here," she said as she stood up from the couch. "I'm never quite sure who is going to come through that door. In any case, I grew up on a farm hunting game and I know how to use this," she informed him, handling the firearm like a natural.

Givens glared at Amelia. "How about that? Another smart ass bitch. Guess we're at a standoff, lady," he said to Amelia. He pivoted Cory around so that she acted like a shield for him.

Cory appealed to Amelia. "Please, put your gun down, Amelia. I don't want you to get hurt."

"Haven't you heard? I'm like a cat. I have nine lives. This guy doesn't scare me. He wants you for a reason and he's not going to kill you, am I right, Mr. What's-your-name?"

"The name is Givens. Now that you mention it, she came here cause she thought you knew how to get us back. Maybe I don't need her. I need you, am I right?"

At that point, Amelia burst out laughing. She looked at Cory and at Givens.

"Damn, he's from the future, too!" Her expression hardened. "Maybe I didn't guess because you seem so backward, Mr. Givens. I hate to tell you, but I don't have a clue about how to get back to your time. I'm from the future, too, and stuck here like you. None of us are going anywhere."

"You are lying," he said.

"As I see it, you have two choices. Either you drop the gun and walk out of here, or we start shooting."

Since Givens still had his gun at her back, Cory took a quick inhale of breath in anticipation of being shot.

Givens thought for a moment, then lowered his gun.

"I'll leave...for now," he said, tucking the gun in his waistband and backing toward the door.

"Does that work for you, Cory?" Amelia asked, still aiming her shotgun at Givens.

Cory's gut reaction was to blow Givens away, but she exhaled and stepped next to Amelia.

"Let him go," she said. "Just stay away from me, Givens, or the next time it may not work for me.

"I'll do what I want and you both better watch out," he said as he scooted out the door, not taking any chances that Amelia would change her mind.

Once he had exited, Amelia lowered her gun and collapsed on the couch.

"Jeezus, who is that?"

"The day I came through time, he came with me. He had attacked me and tried to kill me."

"Ex-boyfriend? Husband?" Amelia asked.

"He tried to kidnap schoolchildren and hold them hostage in exchange for money and safe travel so he could escape from a crime he committed. I convinced him to take me instead. Once he found out that I wouldn't pay off as a kidnap victim, he tried to kill me. As he was attacking me, something happened...and we ended up here."

"I wish you had let me shoot him. What a bastar....," Amelia went quiet and her expression changed from anger to curiosity as something dawned on her. "The spot where you were attacked. Do you know if anything else happened there?" she asked.

Cory thought for a moment and then remembered Ellie's story about the woman being attacked in the exact same spot. "Yes, apparently another woman was mauled by a bear at the same location two years before me. Why?"

"It was the same with me. Remember I told you that the place I crashed the plane was a special place for the islanders because their ancestors had wrecked their ship there?"

Cory nodded, but still didn't see the connection to time travel.

"Don't you see? This is the answer! Somehow, we connected to the event from another time and it pulled us to it. Oh my god, that's it! I've been trying to puzzle this out for years!"

Cory was still confused as Amelia continued.

"I remember now having the oddest feeling right before we crashed. Like I had been at this spot before, which of course, was impossible."

Cory suddenly recalled the sensation she felt right before she went back through time.

"I had a similar sensation when Givens dragged me to the place in the woods where he attacked me. It felt familiar. Almost like a deja vu."

"A deja vu, yes!" Amelia said. "That sense that you have been there before," Amelia pondered. "What if deja vu could also be about experiencing what someone else felt before in the exact same place."

Cory picked up her thread. "Are you saying that if that feeling was strong enough, it could draw you to that time?"

"Maybe," Amelia answered with excitement.

"Holy shit," Cory said. She had to admit that this explanation of their time travel had merit considering they both experienced the same thing.

"Of course, it doesn't solve our dilemma of how to return to our time," Amelia said. "Still, it's amazing if it's true!"

"It is...amazing yet scary if there is no way back." She visibly shivered and Amelia took her hand.

"Don't give up. Whatever happened, be it miracle or science, it means that anything is possible and that includes returning to our time."

Cory nodded and let herself shift to her present reality.

"I should probably get going. I was on my way to the postal office. I haven't had the chance to tell you, but I have a relative here. She is my great, great grandmother and I'm trying to find her."

"What is her name?"

"Rebecca McNeely. I know that she came here and..." she stopped because Amelia's jaw dropped open in surprise.

"Why, I know her! She came to my shop not more than two months ago. She was a beautiful young woman, about twenty-years-old, and very unhappy."

Cory was at first astonished that Amelia actually knew her relative, but then she realized that every world can be a small world. Besides, Amelia probably interacted with a lot more people than most. Fortune tellers and bartenders were the only therapists during this time.

"Why was she unhappy?"

"She had come to New Orleans from Virginia. She ran away from home and thought she could get work here. As you know, life is not easy for unmarried women unless they want to sell themselves. She came to me asking what she should do. Her mother had written that relatives were traveling west to Illinois and suggested that she visit them."

"Do you know where she is staying here?"

"She's not here, Cory. She left on a steamboat traveling up the Mississippi and then hoped to find a stagecoach to Chicago."

"You're kidding," Cory said, but it was really a comment to herself. She wanted to kick herself for not knowing her family history better. She had known that Rebecca McNeely eventually moved to Chicago and married a mapmaker, but she had banked on the fact that Rebecca would still be in New Orleans at this point. She wasn't wrong, just "a day late and a dollar short" as her dad used to say. "Time sucks," she added.

"I'm not familiar with your term, but if I get the negative connotation, I might suggest that it is life that 'sucks.' At least at moments. Time is just a construct. Isn't that what Mr. Einstein was trying to tell us?"

"Yes. And he was right. Time feels like a totally made-up thing to me now," Cory said with exasperation. "Sometimes it goes fast. Sometimes it goes slow. Time is short. It's long. I used to wish I had more if it or less of it. I worried constantly about the future. I'm really sick of thinking about the past and the future. I just want to be here...now."

"Me, too," Amelia said.

Lucas and Dustu walked into the shop. Both of them were covered in sweat and looked exhausted. Cory looked up at them calmly for once, not anxious about whether their news was good or bad. She was just glad to see them.

"Hello, ma'am," Lucas greeted Amelia.

"Hello, and who is this handsome young man?" Amelia asked, smiling at Dustu.

"Dustu," Lucas told her.

"Dustu is traveling with us until we find his family," Cory explained.

"I see," Amelia said with a wry smile. "Still another part of your journey I haven't heard about. You mustn't leave until I've heard it all. Would anyone like some lemonade?"

"Not sure what that is, ma'am, but if it's something to drink, we would be mighty grateful," Lucas said wiping moisture from his brow.

Amelia disappeared into the back of her house and Cory told Lucas about Givens.

"He came here," Cory said.

"What?!" Lucas swung around toward the door, now wary and alert. "Did he hurt you?"

"Amelia chased him away with a shotgun, but knowing Givens, it's not over. We need to watch out," she warned.

"Okay, but if I see him again, the man is done for," he said.

"I got the papers for William and his family. They can travel freely. They are free," she told him.

"Awesome," he said, making Cory smile. "What about your relative?" he asked.

She's gone. She left New Orleans," Cory said.

"Oh. Sorry to hear that. You came a long way to find her."

"What about you? Did you have any luck with the cargo?"

"We came here to tell you. We sold everything!" He said with a smile. "The one trader bought it all just like I hoped. He wants the lumber from the boat, too. We'll pole over to a spot tomorrow and unload the cargo and then I'll help break down the boat. My labor made the price better."

"That is great news," she said.

Amelia walked in with a pitcher of lemonade and some crystal goblets.

"Here you are," she said as she set down the tray and filled two glasses.

"Thank you, ma'am," Lucas said as he took a glass and gave one to Dustu.

Lucas downed the lemonade in one long gulp. Dustu took a small sip, smiled at the taste, and then guzzled it as well.

"It's mighty tasty, " Lucas remarked.

"I have a lemon tree growing in my courtyard," Amelia said as she refilled their glasses. "I cut the lemons and squeeze the juice into water and then add honey or sugar and 'voila,' lemonade."

She picked up a lemon fruit from the tray and handed it to Dustu. He rolled it around in his palm, smelled it, and then started to hand it back to Amelia, but she waved it back to him.

"Keep it," she said smiling.

Dustu slipped the lemon in his pocket and Lucas took another long drink. "It sure takes the thirst away."

Amelia eyed the three of them. "Would you like to come to dinner tonight? Your friends on the boat, too?" Amelia asked.

Cory looked at Lucas and he nodded.

"Thanks. I'll ask them," Cory said. "I'm anxious to get back so I can give them the papers."

"Go on then and come back at sundown for supper. And be careful," Amelia added. "I know the constable for our ward. I'll ask him to look out for this...Mr. Givens," she said.

"He's a vengeful son-of-a-bitch, excuse my language, ma'am, so you be careful, too," Lucas warned her.

She nodded, Cory gave her a quick hug, and they left.

When Cory put the papers of manumission in William's hands, Charlotte burst into tears. Cat took them from her father, sat on the deck, and started sounding out the words. Dustu sat next to her and listened.

"To all to who...whom these pres...presents shall come, I do further ker..cer...ti..fy that the said William...Dug...Douglass?" she asked and looked up at Cory.

"I'm sorry. I forgot to ask what your surname is and I didn't want to wait so I picked Douglass," Cory explained.

"We were named after our masters," Charlotte said, frowning at the memory. "Douglass is a fine name."

"I'm not done," Cat piped up. Everyone focused their attention back on her and quietly listened in solemn gratitude as she continued.

*

Dinner at Amelia's was gay and delicious. They dined in her courtyard, a beautiful garden filled with the scent of gardenias and roses. Metal lanterns hung in a magnolia tree and candles lit a handsome iron dining table with a black locust wood top. Amelia had hired a cook for the evening and they feasted on local creole favorites including crawfish étouffée, smothered greens, red beans and rice. She poured glasses of red wine for the adults and lemonade for Dustu and Cat. They ate and talked only of the happy times in their lives, funny stories about misadventures and family gossip. Charlotte had a wonderful, raucous laugh that was contagious. Cory couldn't remember ever feeling this happy.

Amelia had asked her friend Caleb to play music for them. He was a classical violinist, but also a fiddler. After dinner, everyone danced in the open patio to popular regional tunes. Amelia and William were best at leading dance reels as the fiddler called out the steps. Lucas pulled Cory from her chair and she tentatively joined in. She had always loved to dance, and though her modern moves were entirely different, she began to experience the same uninhibited joy as Lucas swung her around and guided her through the fast-paced steps. Dustu and Cat danced their own steps, whirling and scooting between the adults like mischievous elves. The merriment had its greatest effect on Charlotte. She mostly sat on her chair, but clapped fervently to the music and filled the courtyard with huge whoops of delight.

Lucas kept to Cory's side the whole night. They were constantly touching hands, shoulders, thighs, and finally, during a slower tune, he took her in his arms and they pressed their bodies together in a lazy waltz under the magnolia tree. They both stopped, drawn by need, and kissed. The others noticed and felt their love infuse the warm spring air like a sweet perfume. William pulled Charlotte off her chair and they tenderly rocked each other to the music.

They were all drunk on happiness and wine when they stumbled back to the docks. Lanterns lighted the way, but it was dark farther out on their line of flatboats and they stepped carefully from bobbing vessel to vessel. As they approached their boat, Lucas noticed a figure on deck and he quietly signaled for everyone to stop. He crept forward across the next two boats and William followed him.

As they got closer, they saw a man pouring liquid along the starboard side of the deck. Lucas caught the scent of kerosene and tensed with fear and anger. He guessed that it was Givens and pulled a knife from his boot as he stealthily approached. William signaled to him and moved off to board the boat on the leeward side. When they were both at the rails, Lucas hopped over, landed with a thud, and faced Givens who swung around in surprise. He dug in his pocket and pulled out a lighter.

"I'd stay there if I were you," he warned and held up the lighter. He flicked the ignition and the flame appeared. "Ever seen one of these?"

"Looks like some kind of special flint," Lucas remarked calmly. He caught William out of the corner of his eye moving along the other side of the boat in order to come around from the stern behind Givens.

"Much better than flint. It's instant," Givens informed him and let the flame go out. "You need to step back off the boat. Now." He drew his gun from his belt and now held the lighter in one hand and the gun in the other. "Back away and I will follow."

Lucas took two steps backward and Givens moved toward him. Lucas's back touched the railing.

"Climb over real slow and easy."

Lucas did as he was told and now stood on the deck of the boat behind him.

"Now, take that knife of yours and cut your boat from the others. No use getting a whole bunch of rivermen upset." He was now at the railing, too, and beginning to carefully climb over as he kept the gun on Lucas. "We'll just watch a nice little fire on your boat."

"I'm not going to let you burn the boat," Lucas warned.

"We'll see about that." Givens reached the top of the railing when William grabbed him from behind. Givens was completely caught off guard but grasped at William and they fell over the railing into the water.

William was not a swimmer and neither was Givens. They desperately pulled at each other to stay afloat, shouting with fear, but both sank into the Mississippi.

Cory and Charlotte rushed toward the spot and stepped onto their flatboat as Lucas dove into the water. After a moment, he came back up, looked around, and dove down again.

Cory climbed onto the boat and grabbed a rope. Charlotte and Cat scanned the dark surface of the water, terrified. Suddenly, Lucas and William popped up through the surface, gasping for breath. Cory threw the rope and William seized it. She pulled him to the boat and she and Charlotte heaved him on board. Lucas hauled himself up and then he and William laid on their backs breathing and coughing. Charlotte helped William turn to his side and vomit water from his lungs.

Cory bent next to Lucas. "Are you okay?"

"Yup," he said, still catching his breath.

"Where is Givens?" She asked.

"Gone," William answered in a raspy voice. He cleared his throat. "We wuz holding onto each other sinkin' down and then he just went away."

"What do you mean? Did he let go and swim away?" Charlotte asked.

"No, one minute he there then he gone," William answered.

Lucas nodded. "I only found William and was lucky at that. It's dark and he was down deep."

Cory stared at the river. It made the most sense that Givens had drowned and been pulled away by the current, but she had an eerie feeling about what William described. Another dramatic incident, another instant disappearance. Another deja vu? If so, where had Givens gone?

"If God saw fit to take that man's life, I say, good riddance," Charlotte said.

They sat and talked for a while, going over what had happened and trying to soothe each other from the trauma. Finally, when everyone had calmed down, they stood up, bid each other goodnight, and went to bed. The deck smelled of kerosene so Cory and Lucas took blankets up to the roof of the cabin. Dustu followed them and they tucked him in between them as they lay under the waning moon. Dustu had restless dreams and thrashed in his sleep. Cory felt sad about all that he had witnessed. The joy and peacefulness of Amelia's party had vanished when Givens tried to destroy the boat. She placed her hand on Dustu's back to try and comfort him. She realized that she could never make him safe, but she vowed again to try and protect him. She looked over and saw that Lucas was awake, too, staring up at the night sky. He turned on his side to face her.

"The boy has seen a lot of trouble in his life," he said quietly.

"I know. I want to make sure he is okay," she answered.

"I don't know how we can do that. I'm thinking we should try and find his family."

"Back in Georgia?"

"No, out west. His aunt and his baby sister. First, I have to get the money back to John and Ellie and then I could take him."

"We could take him," she corrected. "I want to go with you."

"Are you sure? It's a long way and could be dangerous."

"Is your question really about danger or about us?" she asked.

He smiled. "Both I reckon."

"Do you want me to go with you?"

"I want you to go. I want to be together," he said.

She smiled at him and reached out to touch his arm. He took her hand, kissed it, and held it to his chest. Cory watched him close his eyes and drift off to sleep. Dustu was resting peacefully now between them. Cory was still wide awake.

Givens had said to her in St. Louis that he needed her, that she might be the key for traveling through time. What if he was right? Now that he was gone, was she stuck in this time forever? She hadn't thought about Jill and Sam and Michael in a while. All the years since their parent's death, Jill had tried to help Cory be okay. She thought back to when they were growing up and how her sister had always looked out for her. She remembered a time in second grade when a classmate taunted her, calling her a "boy" because she liked to play kickball on the playground. Jill had left her circle of fourth grade friends, walked over, grabbed the girl, and taken her to a spot away from the others. Cory had watched her sister face the girl eye to eye, not losing her temper, but calmly saying words that made the girl break out in tears and never bother Cory again. Would she never be able to tell Jill she was sorry for the last fews years of pushing her away? Would she never get to tell Jill how much she loved her? She looked at Lucas's silhouette in the dark and wished she could talk to him about her life before. She ached to tell him the truth and have him somehow understand. How would she explain it? Givens' words about their connection scared her. If he was gone, how did that affect her? She finally fell asleep and had a disturbing dream about walking endless beaches full of dolphins, beached and gasping for breath.

Lucas was up early, excited to trade their cargo. The rest of them moved a little sleepily through the morning tasks after the events of the night before. They pushed the boat out of its berth, poled it down the river, and guided it to the new dock where the cargo could be unloaded. Charlotte cooked them their last breakfast on the little iron brazier in the sandbox stove.

William and Lucas did most of the unloading and when they were finished, they moved the boat to a riverbank, pulled it ashore, and then immediately began the job of dismantling the vessel. Lucas had warned Cory that this was always a bittersweet task and she understood what he meant as she watched their home of the last two months being ripped apart. Several other men helped, and within a few hours, the boat looked like a skeleton of its former self. The light was fading so the trader paid Lucas and told him that his men would finish the rest of the breakdown in the morning.

It was done. They were all free to leave New Orleans. Cory had purchased tickets that day for a steamboat. Because Lucas and William would work for their passage by loading wood into the steamboat boiler, the tickets were discounted for Cory, Charlotte, Cat, and Dustu.

Amelia had insisted that they all come back and spend their last night with her, but William and Charlotte respectfully declined. Charlotte had met a coffee vendor named Rose Nicaud, a former enslaved woman who had bought her freedom. Rose invited Charlotte, William and Cat to visit with a group of free blacks and other people of color who had formed a council to support artisans and small business owners. William and Charlotte were interested to hear more.

Lucas, Dustu and Cory arrived at Amelia's shop exhausted. She had prepared a delicious dinner of barbecued chicken, roasted potatoes, and a fruit pie. Cory helped Amelia wash dishes while Lucas and Dustu perused the books in Amelia's library. An avid reader, Amelia had started collecting books the moment she arrived in New Orleans. Cory could tell that neither Dustu nor Lucas had ever seen so many books before as they scanned the shelves wide-eyed.

They settled on a botanical journal with colorful ink sketches of flowers and trees, and sat on the couch together gazing at the illustrations. Amelia glanced at them from the sink in the kitchen.

"The boy is very fond of Lucas," she remarked.

"Yes. They bonded instantly. Lucas thinks we should try and reconnect Dustu with his family out west."

"I see. And will you go with him?"

"Yes."

"I've been waiting for the chance to talk to you," Amelia said as she set her washcloth down for a moment and continued in a whisper. "I've been thinking a lot about how we came through time, or how we think we came through. If being at a spot where something traumatic happened is the reason we were pulled back in time, could it work the other way? In other words, if we went to a location where we knew something powerful occurred in the future, could it take us there?"

Cory thought for a moment. "If what happened to us was like a deja vu, I don't know if it would work for something that hasn't happened yet. Even if it did, wouldn't we have to put ourselves in some sort of dangerous situation that matches the event?"

"I've been thinking about that, too," Amelia said. "Maybe it doesn't have to be perilous, but merely intense. Maybe it's about making a conscious connection. If we go to the spot and connect ourselves physically and emotionally to the feeling of that future event, maybe it will take us there! I've been pondering specific places where something momentous happened in my time."

"There are a lot of places like that in my time," Cory said.

"So much the better! If it doesn't work in one location, you'll have other opportunities!" Amelia noted. "I've been trying to remember the powerful events happening in

America in 1937," she said. "Or elsewhere. I can always travel to America once I get back to my time."

Cory was aware of momentous events in 1937, including those in Nazi Germany, but obviously that was not a place where she would want Amelia to go.

"Robert will be so amazed at this discovery! He knows all about me. I can't wait until he returns to discuss it with him." She paused. "I would miss him so much if I left. And my other friends. It would be difficult to say goodbye."

Cory was thinking the same thing. Deliberately leaving the few people she knew here was unimaginable; however, the idea of never seeing Jill, Michael, and Sam was unthinkable, too.

"I just realized," Amelia continued. "I've lived here longer than any other place in my life.

Cory looked at her. "Maybe we should just..."

"Think about it," Amelia chimed in. They laughed and it caused Lucas and Dustu to glance at them from the library. Amelia grabbed the dishcloth and continued washing.

"I've been considering something else about my life," Amelia said in a whisper. "I may give up this whole fortune telling business. I remember the work of the psychologist Carl Jung. I had just begun reading his books when I came through time and I found his theories fascinating. I believe I could assist people a lot more if I helped them understand their lives in the present instead of trying to predict their future."

Cory smiled. "Not easy for most people, but you are on the right track. Despite the technology that is supposed to connect people in my time, people suffer from anxiety and trauma more than ever. Psychotherapists, life coaches, Yoga instructors, naturopaths, holistic health care providers, breathworkers are all working to help people find peace in the 21st Century."

"That's astounding, but encouraging. So I might be able to do something that will help the future?" Amelia asked.

"I don't know. To be honest, what is happening now will be hard to stop. This country was built on slavery and oppression. If you cannot do something to turn that tide, America will never really be a democracy and anyone who has benefited will end up suffering no matter how much money they make though they are not my concern. It's the people they are harming overtime that is my focus now."

Cory wondered about her own ability to make a difference. It made her think about her encounter before she left New Salem

"Did I tell you that I met Abraham Lincoln?"

Amelia stopped washing again and looked at Cory with her jaw dropped open. "No! Oh my goodness," she thought for a moment. "He would be a young man now, right?"

"He lives in the village where I came back through time in Illinois."

"So what is he like?"

"Exactly like everyone wrote about. Tall and lanky, black wavy hair and brown eyes, more handsome than I thought. Smart and humble and funny."

"Who are you talking about?" Lucas said, appearing at the door. "First you are giggling and then you are talking about a tall, dark and handsome man. Should I be jealous?"

"I'm talking about Abe Lincoln," Cory said.

"Oh, Abe. Yup. I would be jealous if I didn't know that he already has a sweetheart."

"Ann. Ann Rutledge," Cory said.

"Do you know her? She likes him back real fine. If he would just get up the gumption to ask for her hand, they'd be married in two shakes of a pig's tail."

Cory smiled, but knew that would never happen. Ann got sick and died in August of 1835. They would hear the news when they got back to Illinois.

"I admire Abe and am glad he will go to the legislature," Lucas said. "He will make us proud," he added.

Cory and Amelia looked at each, knowing Lucas was right, but also knowing the cost of his future greatness.

Dustu had fallen asleep on the couch so Lucas carried him upstairs and laid him on the soft pallet Amelia had made for him on the floor next to the bed. Cory figured he wouldn't stay there, but she and Lucas climbed in bed under the sheets and made quiet love to the sounds of Dustu's gentle snoring. Some time in the night, Dustu climbed onto the bed nestled under Cory's arm and instantly fell back to sleep.

*

Cory woke to heavy knocking on Amelia's front door. Lucas jumped up, quickly donned his trousers, and trotted downstairs with his rifle. Amelia followed him in her robe and nightgown and grabbed the shotgun from under the couch. Cory and Dustu stayed upstairs and listened from the landing.

Amelia called out, "Who is it?"

"It's us, Miss Amelia. William and Charlotte. We come with good news."

Amelia immediately opened the door and Cory and Dustu came down the stairs. William, Charlotte, and Cat stepped in the front room, their faces full of excitement.

"Last night, we met with folks from round here. Black folks that is free, always been free and they want to help us. The long and short of it is, we decided to stay in New Orleans," Charlotte informed them.

"I is goin' to school!" Cat piped up.

"Where will you live?" Amelia asked, surprised. "If you need a place..."

Charlotte waved a hand to stop her. "There's a little place over in the ninth ward. A Negro businessman is goin' to set up a blacksmith shop for William. I can cook and sew clothes for all the fancy houses in the Garden District for now. But I've got plans beyond that!"

"and I is goin' to school!" Cat announced again.

"There is a Negro school in the ward, too," Charlotte explained, smiling.

"That's wonderful!" Cory said.

"We just wanted to come and tell you since we knew you were leavin' today. Thank you, Miss Cory and Mr. Lucas, for all you done for us. It's truly a miracle what happened!" Charlotte said and then she turned to Amelia. "Miss Amelia, we are going to be neighbors!" she laughed. "We going to pay you back for your kindness."

"Not necessary, but I am glad that you are staying. Cat, please come over anytime and borrow books, okay?"

"We're going now. Lots to do," Charlotte said. She stepped up to Cory and gave her a hug. "You keep fightin' for people to be free," she whispered to Cory.

"I will," Cory promised.

Lucas and William shook hands.

"Good luck to you, sir," Lucas said.

"You be safe goin' upriver," William answered.

Dustu bolted upstairs and at first Cory thought he was upset, but he ran back down and put the little carved bird figure in Cat's hand. She smiled and hugged him and then she looked him in the face, her brown eyes staring into his.

"You iz goin to be alright, you hear?" she said to him. He nodded as if he understood. "Alright then," she said and joined her parents at the door.

They turned, hurried out, and were gone.

Chapter Ten

UP A CREEK
WITHOUT A PADDLE

The steamboat was fully booked with passengers. Cory and Dustu stood at the crowded rail of the upper deck waving at Amelia who was standing on the dock trying not to cry. Lucas was already down in the boiler room loading wood since the engine was running and they were steaming away from the shore. The ship was named "Lookout" and she was a cookie cutter version of the many riverboat packets pulling in and out of New Orleans. She was not fancy, but her large paddlewheel, tall smokestacks, and pilot cabin made her look charming and exotic to Cory. She watched as Amelia's figure grew small on the dock and disappeared as they rounded the crescent shoreline of New Orleans.

On most packet steamboats there was a single first-class deck with the rest of the space cramped and uncomfortable. Cory and Dustu shared a corn husk mattress in a small space of the open air main deck on the same side as the waterwheel. Dustu liked watching the wheel's wide, wooden paddles churning the water and pushing them upriver. Later that day, Cory entered the boiler room to visit Lucas, but she quickly sensed that women were not welcome there. The men were of various backgrounds, including enslaved blacks.

They sorted wood from huge piles and loaded it into a pair of iron boilers. Cory noticed the twin pistons pumping up and down nearby, driven by steam from the boilers. The pistons cranked metal arms that ran outside to the paddlewheel. Cory was covered in sweat within seconds and felt bad that Lucas was working in these sweltering conditions. He glanced over and nodded at her, but she could tell he preferred that she leave. She exited the boiler room hoping to see him on deck later.

Lucas collapsed near Cory and Dustu sometime after dark. She sat up and leaned over him.

"Are you okay?" She asked.

He rolled over and put his head in her lap. She stroked his hair and kissed his temple.

"Are you hungry? I saved you some food," she told him.

He just groaned and shook his head. They had shared a small meal together earlier that day. Their ticket included two meals a day of beans and rice, and every other day, some pickled cabbage. Within minutes, Lucas fell asleep and Cory lifted his head, laid it on the mattress and then slid down next to him. She rested her arm across his chest as she watched the night sky and the ever turning paddlewheel pushing the water.

Toward the end of the following day, they reached Natchez. The steamboat stopped in the port, but Cory, Lucas and Dustu stayed on board.

"No use risking it," Lucas said. Cory agreed. The Five Corners slavery market was forever embedded in her memory and she sent silent thoughts to Charlotte, William and Cat in hopes they were safe. It was unlikely that anyone in Natchez would recognize her. She was dressed completely differently from their previous stop, wearing the outfit Amelia had given her. Though the skirt was less practical than trousers, it was much cooler. Amelia had also given Cory undergarments, which allowed her to wear the thin blouse without it being too revealing. When she rolled up her sleeves and felt the air moving beneath her skirt, the southern heat was almost bearable. She slept in her clothes and hoped there would be a chance to jump in the river during a stop and thus rinse herself and her clothes. Dustu still wore his deerskin trousers and calico shirt, but Lucas bought him a straw hat to shade his face and he wore it out of practicality. Lucas had traded his own old clothes for a short-sleeved linen shirt and khaki trousers that he rolled up to his knees. He wore his boots to protect his feet from burning coals that often fell from the boiler and were swiftly stamped out.

Over the next few days, Cory and Dustu tried to occupy themselves by reading the several books that Amelia had given them. They also walked a circuit around the boat though they avoided the stern where the enslaved men were chained at dusk. She had already asked the steamboat captain why he was using enslaved labor when passengers paid him for accommodations and merchants paid to transport freight.

"I work hard to make ends meet, but paying crews and having to compete for freight charges mean that my profits are slim." He explained. In other words, free labor helped him make more profit.

"Why do you have to chain the men? We're out in the middle of the river," she said.

"The first-class passengers get nervous seeing them. Besides, half of them would jump ship and escape if I didn't chain 'em," he responded.

"I didn't see any water for them to drink."

"I let you and the boy ride for almost nothing so I wouldn't complain about things that ain't your business, little lady, or you'll be put to shore at the next port," he warned.

For Lucas's sake, she didn't argue whether the captain could fulfill his threat to kick them off the boat. She pivoted and walked away, feeling the Captain's disapproving eyes on her back. She continued to check on the water supply for the enslaved men and brought cups or buckets of water to them whenever she could.

Between Natchez and Memphis, the boat pulled into several spots along the shore. At each stop, the hired crews jumped off the boat with axes and disappeared into the forests. They cut trees and gathered deadwood and then hauled it in carts back to the boat to feed the boiler.

In Memphis, the enslaved men were removed from the boat and presumably sold to a cotton plantation owner in the area. Cory was anxious to leave the south.

When they arrived in St. Louis, all passengers and most of the crew disembarked for a one-day layover before heading farther north. Cory, Dustu and Lucas; however, remained on the boat. Lucas had discovered that one of the passengers was getting off in St. Louis and he knew which first-class cabin was now open. Dustu asked Lucas if he could wander about the boat and after a promise that he would stay out of the boiler room and behind the railings of the second deck, Lucas let him have his wish. Cory and Lucas entered the first-class cabin, shed their clothes and laid on the down-filled mattress of the large bunk.

"I want to be with you in a bed like this forever," Lucas said.

"I'm just glad to be here now," Cory answered as she rolled on her side and rested her head on his shoulder. She ran her hand across the straight soft hair on his chest down to his muscular abdomen and flat stomach. He turned to face her. His hand started at the hollow of her neck and followed the curves of her body like a ship on the ocean, moving along her breasts to her belly to her hips and around to her bottom. He pulled her on top of him and she laid full length, letting gravity work as her whole body relaxed into his. She felt every part of his flesh from his lips to his pelvis, thighs, and toes. She sighed and he responded with a satisfied rumble in his throat. She rose up to a sitting position, straddled his hips, and let him enter her. He brought her almost to climax and then deliberately stopped, waited a moment, and then started again. She discovered the agony and ecstasy of this maneuver and when she finally came, the waves of sensation rocked her body like never before. She settled beside him afterward and he fell into a much needed nap after his weeks of hard labor. Cory slipped out of the cabin and found Dustu. She played hide-and-seek with him and then they made up a new game where they each dropped a stick off the ship's stern and bet which one would win a race on the river. They woke Lucas at dusk to warn him that the crew was returning, and the three of them left the luxury of the cabin and returned to their corn husk bed on the lower deck.

They disembarked at Alton, Illinois with a plan to walk the rest of the ninety miles home to New Salem. Despite all that she had been through during their river journey south and north, Cory was a bit nervous about a four-and-a-half day trek through the forest along a path not much wider than a deer trail; however, Lucas talked about it in such a nonchalant way that she let go of her fear. They bought supplies in town and configured them into bundles they could carry on their backs. Before setting out, they decided to eat supper at a tavern.

An elderly woman in drab clothes and black shawl stood outside the tavern handing out leaflets. Cory took one and when they were seated at a table inside, began reading it.

The notice described a gathering in a nearby church where Minister Elijah Lovejoy was speaking. The minister's name rang a bell in Cory's mind, but she could not remember the details.

Dustu loved eating at the tavern and gobbled down his beef stew topped off with a slice of apple pie. The rustic tavern had a warm ambience and Cory relaxed into her chair, savoring the food and her mug of ale. She smiled at Lucas across the table and her foot found his calf beneath it. He felt her toes sliding up his leg. He grinned back at her and then reached across the table, took her hand, and stroked her wrist.

"Where we sleep?" Dustu asked.

"That is a good question, which Lucas will now answer," she laughed.

"I reckon we'll camp outside of town," he said as if it was obvious.

When they left the tavern, they walked by the church referenced in the leaflet. Through the open door, Cory heard a man's voice preaching loudly.

"Can we stop and listen for a moment?"

Lucas knew better than to do anything but nod especially since she was already stepping up to the door of the chapel.

The seats were filled and a man stood at a podium. He wasn't much older than Cory and his round face and stern expression reminded her of a young John McCain. He was fervently delivering a speech to the congregation.

"When I was in St. Louis I felt myself called upon to treat at large upon the subject of slavery as I was in a state where the evil existed. Now having come to a free state where that evil does not exist, I feel myself less called upon to discuss the subject, but ladies and gentlemen, as long as I am an American Citizen, and as long as American blood runs in these veins, I have the obligation to preach against slavery everywhere for we must all fight it whatever the risk!

His words triggered Cory's memory of who Lovejoy was. Elijah Lovejoy had been killed by a mob, not for his abolitionist preaching, but for his writing. She pulled the leaflet from her pocket and realized that he had printed it. He continued his speech.

"If I could hold my peace on this subject with a clear conscience, I would most assuredly do it. My views against slavery have cost me many a valued friend. But I cannot, and I am sure you do not ask or wish a Christian to connive at what he believes to be sin for the sake of popularity. Those who don't fight slavery are fighting against God. All attempts to justify slavery from the Word of God are gross perversions of its precepts and principle. My printing press was destroyed in St. Louis, but I've come here tonight, my friends, to share with you that my new press arrived today! I will begin again to editorialize on the evils of slavery. I shall hold myself at liberty to speak, to write, and to publish whatever I please on any subject. Anyone who tries to stop me is a threat against freedom of the press!"

Cory heard some cries of "here, here!" in support of Lovejoy's declaration, but most of the audience seemed a bit overwhelmed. She admired Lovejoy's courage and lamented his fate. She remembered that Abe Lincoln often quoted Lovejoy after he solidified his own views and began speaking against enslavement.

They stepped out of the church and Lucas led them to the road they would follow to New Salem. He took them off the path to a quiet spot in the woods and they laid out blankets on the soft bed of needles under a White Pine tree. The night was warm and they needed no covering. They nested into their pod of three and fell asleep under the branches and open sky above.

*

It was a sunny, late June morning as they followed the narrow road into the woods. Dustu hopped, ran, and explored the path, sometimes falling behind, but often trotting ahead.

Cory and Lucas began talking about a plan. It was really the first time they had discussed their future together.

"I will be glad to get back to New Salem and give John the money from the sale. I'll see what help he needs and then we can figure out how to get to the Indian Territory and find Dustu's family."

"Would we go by boat again?"

"Yup. Probably head down the Mississippi to the Arkansas River and find a steamboat going west. Or join a wagon train that follows the Arkansas to the territory."

He stopped for a moment and turned to her. "Are you sure you want to go? You could stay at John and Ellie's. It might be a help to Ellie to have you there with the baby and all."

"Are you trying to get rid of me?" she teased.

"Yup," he said as he put both hands on her waist. "You've gotten kinda scrawny lately and maybe aren't much use for anything," he noted. He lifted her up in the air to demonstrate how light she was.

She circled her legs around his waist and he settled her on his hips as he kissed her. "A better idea would be to take you over to that patch of meadow yonder and show you that I mean to keep you after all."

Dustu came running up to them.

"Cory hurt?"

"Cory not hurt," Cory answered. "Lucas offered to carry me the rest of the way."

"You need walk," Dustu answered.

Lucas set Cory back standing on the path.

"I walk," she said, smiling at Dustu. "No free ride."

Dustu seemed satisfied and padded away to explore some new spot ahead.

"Have you asked Dustu if he wants to find his family?"

"No."

"I think you should ask him."

"Okay, but I just figured he would want to be with his kin."

"If he said he doesn't want to find them, what would you do?"

"I don't know. He might say 'no' to somethin' he would regret when he is older. This way of life of white men is not his way."

"I guess I'm trying to answer the same question about myself. I want to be with my family, but I want to be with you and Dustu."

"You said they were in Chicago. We can go visit them."

It was time. This was the moment.

"They aren't there," she told him.

"Where are they?"

"They are there, but not yet."

"I don't get your meaning."

"They won't be there for a very long time."

"You are not making any sense."

"I'm not making sense because what happened to me doesn't make sense. That day when you first saw me, when Givens attacked me and you shot him, what exactly did you see?"

"I was hunting. I heard you cry out and I came and found you."

"Nothing seemed odd about it?"

"I heard you and I ran...back." He paused. "I suppose I did think somethin' was amiss. I had just been past that spot and I did ponder why I hadn't heard anything before, some sound of trouble." He stopped walking and looked at her. "It was peculiar. It was like you appeared out of nowhere."

"Exactly," Cory said.

"Cory, what in tarnation are you trying to tell me?"

"Ellie said a woman had been attacked by a bear at that same spot. I think when Givens attacked me, I felt the same terror that the woman felt and it brought me here."

"Brought you from where?"

"I'm trying to tell you!"

"Then just say it!"

"From the future. I'm from a future time!" she shouted and then said more calmly, "I'm from the year two thousand and seventeen."

He looked angry and annoyed for a moment and then his expression changed to one of recognition and then to a look of fear.

"But you are real," he said.

"I am," she said. "I was totally confused and scared when it happened. I wanted to go back to my time. I went with you to New Orleans to find my relative, but also to find someone like Amelia. I thought maybe a fortune teller could help me."

"Go back to your time?"

"Yes. She has an idea, but I don't know if it would work. I don't know what to do."

He stood quietly for a long moment thinking.

"This is a lot to take in. Why didn't you tell me this before?"

"I tried to tell you. When you and John rescued me from Givens in St. Louis, I wanted to tell you then, but I couldn't find a way that didn't sound crazy. I thought you would think I was insane."

"I do admit that I always wondered why you are so different than other women, other people."

"A stranger in a strange land," she said.

"More than a stranger. Like you didn't belong at all. Except..."

"Except what?"

"I had such strong feelings for you right from the start. I figured you couldn't be that different if I liked you so much.

Or maybe I liked you because you were different. When did you say? Two thousand and seventeen?" She nodded and he whistled in astonishment.

They heard a huffing noise and looked down to see Dustu with his arms crossed and looking frustrated at Cory and Lucas standing immobile on the path.

"We best keep walking," Lucas said.

They continued on, but Lucas made Cory tell him everything that happened that day when she came through time. After he let it all sink in, he began to ask her questions about the future. Her relief that he believed her was unmeasurable. Another layer of anxiety peeled away.

"Those exhibits we saw about locomotives in New Orleans. Does that become real?" he asked.

"Yes, there are lots of trains all over America and they go really fast. Cars and jet airplanes, too. Uh, cars are machines that replace horses. You steer them with a wheel. Airplanes fly in the sky and can carry hundreds of people from place to place." She stopped when she saw the look of "too much information" on Lucas's face. She decided to hold off telling him about space travel, cell phones, and the digital world until later.

Talking about the future felt odd to her. Until now she hadn't missed technology much at all. Hot running water for a shower maybe, but not all of the gadgets and machines she had depended on in modern time. On the contrary, her life felt very full now—full of feeling, purpose, and love. She had cluttered her life before with way too many objects and too many anxious thoughts. There hadn't been room for a real existence.

She let the feeling of the forest surround her. She took Lucas's hand and he stopped asking questions. They let silence fall between them and kept walking.

Chapter Eleven

DOCTOR ANNA

An hour later, Dustu came running down the path, anxious and upset. A family was ahead. A sick family. Cory and Lucas followed him to the spot where a family of five had settled in a small clearing. A man was on his knees tending to a woman and three children lying on blankets. Their faces were pale and feverish and their clothes were damp with sweat. As they approached, one of the children abruptly sat up and vomited into the dirt. They also noticed a cow standing nearby nudging her calf lying on the ground, mewing and shaking.

When the man saw Cory and Lucas, he got up and came over to them. His face was full of anguish and helplessness.

"You best stay away," he said.

"Milk sickness?" Lucas asked.

"Most likely," the man said.

"We can try and find a doctor," Cory offered.

"A hunter told me the only doctor is a woman who lives east of here."

"Did he say her name?"

"He called her Dr. Anna."

"I'll go find her," Lucas said.

"I would be forever in your debt, mister."

"My name is Lucas McCain," he shook hands with the man.

"Daniel," the man answered. "And that's my wife Mary and my youngins'—Jacob, Sally and Thomas."

"I'm Cory and this is Dustu." Cory said with her hands on Dustu's shoulders, wanting to keep him close.

"I best get going," Lucas said to Cory.

"We'll go with you," she said.

He pulled her aside.

"I can move faster on my own." He looked over at the family. "Stay away from this sickness. Camp nearby, but don't nurse them. And don't go near the cow."

"Be careful," she said.

He nodded and started to leave and then turned back to Cory. She tried to hide her fear as she kissed him. He hugged her tightly and whispered in her ear. "I'll be back," and then he released her and took off through the woods.

*

Cory had tried to keep distance between the family and a small camping spot she and Dustu set up, but cries from the children tugged at her heart. In the end, Dustu had suggested making soup for them so they did. He fetched water from a nearby creek while she gathered wood for a cooking fire. Dustu killed a chicken by wringing its neck and then he deftly plucked its feathers. He borrowed the man's knife and Cory cut the bird into pieces and dropped them in the boiling pot on the fire. As the soup simmered, Cory watched Daniel move between Mary and the children who were trembling and taking turns vomiting, clearly experiencing severe intestinal pain. Mary was petite with blond curls that stuck to her feverish temples. The children were all close in age and favored their father's looks—brown hair with sharp noses and prominent cheekbones. The youngest, Jacob, seemed the sickest. He was listless, clinging to his mother and whimpering. His sister and brother, Sally and Thomas, were quaking and holding their stomachs in pain.

When the broth was ready, Cory poured it steaming into a bowl, added a wooden spoon, and carried it to the family. She meant to hand the bowl to Daniel so he could feed them, but she discarded Lucas's warning and knelt by Mary.

"I made some broth. Could you try some?" she asked.

"I can't eat," the woman answered, gripping her stomach.

"They can't seem to keep anything down," Daniel said, kneeling beside Cory.

"Maybe if you just try a spoonful at a time," Cory suggested. "It'll help keep your strength up," she said to Mary.

Mary shook her head, but nodded toward the children. Cory tried to get each child to sip some of the broth, but without much success.

"They need to drink or they will get dehydrated," she said, repeating the words her mother used to say during Cory and Jill's childhood flu episodes.

"Let me try," Daniel said and took the bowl from her. He sat down next to Thomas who was able to tolerate a few spoonfuls of broth. Cory had noticed that Thomas seemed to be doing slightly better than the others.

Cory offered a plate of chicken meat with boiled potatoes to Daniel. He sat with them for a few minutes, but always had an eye out for his family.

"When did they get sick?" Cory asked.

"Yesterday. I don't drink milk is why I'm okay. The sickness is in the milk. I know it on account of the calf is sick, too. I'll have to kill the cow," he told her.

She had never heard of "milk sickness" and wondered what kind of illness it was. Whether a virus or bacteria, she couldn't do much to help other than provide comfort and liquids. She took their soiled clothes to the creek, washed them, and hung them to dry. When she came back to the clearing, Daniel was digging a hole. The calf had died and was lying still next to the hole.

Dustu squatted on the ground nearby watching the whole scene with a blank expression. His mother had died of fever on the forced march with the soldiers and Cory imagined the distress he might be feeling even if he didn't show it. She found some pieces of soft pine and handed them to him with a knife. He took them and immediately began whittling the wood.

That night Cory had a restless sleep. It was a very warm night and she woke thinking Dustu's body felt feverish next to her, but after checking his forehead and cheeks, she realized that he was actually cool to her touch. The family was quiet and she fell back to sleep. She dreamed that she was a bareback rider in a circus with the crowd watching as she stood balanced on the rump of a white horse that cantered around a center ring that kept getting bigger. Her legs ached and her stomach roiled, but she was afraid to jump down from the moving animal.

The next morning she and Dustu were awakened by an anguished cry. Mary had discovered the dead body of little Jacob lying next to her. Tears streamed down Daniel's face as he picked up the child in his arms and held him close. After a while, he tried to carry Jacob away, but Mary cried out at him to leave the child so he set Jacob's body back down next to her. She was very weak, but cradled Jacob as she wept uncontrollably. Daniel left Mary and went to Sally's side. She was slipping into unconsciousness and her body was shivering. He tucked the blanket around her and sat holding her hand.

Cory checked on Thomas and discovered that his condition had improved. He was able to sit up clear-eyed and had no fever. He looked around at his family and saw that his mother was weeping.

"Your brother passed away in the night," Cory said.

Thomas's lip quivered and he looked toward his father who nodded to confirm the sad news.

The family was like a grove of trees connected by the roots and Cory saw their common pain over Jacob's death. She tiptoed around them, bringing water and food, gently bathing them, and helping them into clean clothes.

Dustu sat and whittled away and sometimes walked to the stream to just sit and stare at the water. When Cory saw him do this, she understood more than ever the power of nature to heal. No matter what was happening in the human world, she watched him draw comfort from a larger world that continued on. The birds flew, the water flowed and the clouds still moved across the sky.

That evening, Mary passed away still clinging to her youngest child. Daniel had already been digging graves in a nearby meadow. He wrapped them in blankets and carried them to the site. Cory and Dustu bore witness as he slid them into their resting places, forever connected to the earth now. Under a crescent moon, he spoke a few heartbreaking words.

"God, I don't know why you took them from me, but please take care of my darlin' wife and beloved son. I will never forget them and the pleasure they brought to my life every day."

Cory thought back to her parents' funeral and how numb she had felt. All she remembered was the claustrophobic feeling of the funeral home and the heavy drapes in the small room where the two caskets lay side by side. It was a freezing cold day and the burial at the cemetery had been unceremonious and quick. This burial in the woods made death so real and yet somehow so connected. She felt Daniel's pain, her own loss, and the death of all beings, human or animal, whether quickly or through suffering.

Lucas was still not back and Cory was beginning to worry. Dustu posted himself near the trail, looking for any sign of Lucas's return.

The next morning, Cory and the family kneeled around Sally who seemed already to be a ghost. Her breathing was slow and shallow.

"I don't know what to do," Daniel said.

"There is nothing you can do," a woman's voice answered.

Cory turned and Lucas stood nearby with a woman clad in plain, grey clothing and wearing a bonnet. She walked over and knelt at Sally's head.

"She is in God's hands."

Sally took a last, deep breath and passed. Thomas called out to his sister. "Sally?"

Daniel pulled him close. "She's gone, son."

He pulled the blanket over his daughter's face and Thomas broke out sobbing. He clung to his father, his only remaining family member.

The woman sat quietly and silently prayed.

Cory got up and walked to the stream and then collapsed on the bank and broke down crying. Lucas came to her side and sat, holding her tightly. Dustu crouched behind her, stroking her hair as if she was a hurt animal.

Cory had never been able to grieve over her parents. For so many years, she had kept her anguish buried inside. She had been lost for so long. Now she wept for Jacob, Mary and Sally, for her parents, and for her younger self.

"I wish I could tell my parents how much I love them," she said.

"Me, too," Lucas said.

Cory pivoted around and looked at Dustu and realized that the three of them had all lost their parents. She pulled Dustu into her lap and hugged him. "We need to find Dustu's family."

When they returned to the clearing, the woman was folding bedding and tidying up the family's belongings.

Daniel finally rose from Sally's side and greeted her.

"Doctor Anna?"

"Yes, Anna Bixby," she said.

"I thank you for coming. I hope you will stay a bit. I need to bury my child."

"I will stay," she said.

Daniel and Lucas dug another grave next to Mary and Jacob. Daniel climbed into the opening and Lucas handed down Sally's body shrouded in a blanket. Daniel gently laid her in the earthen bed and uncovered her face to give her a last kiss on the forehead.

"Sweet girl," he softly murmured then covered her face for the last time.

He pulled himself out of the grave and though Lucas offered to finish the burial, Daniel helped shovel every last bit of loose earth onto his daughter's resting place.

Cory, Lucas, and Dustu surrounded the earthen mound. Anna held Thomas by the elbow as he stood near his father. She had confirmed that Thomas was recovering and rejoiced that he would survive.

Daniel looked down at the grave. "There wasn't a soul sweeter or braver than Sally," he shared.

"We used to fight a lot, but she was my best friend," Thomas added with a quiver in his voice.

"Whoever enters heaven showered with love, will be forever bathed in peace," Anna said.

That evening Cory prepared a stew using dried beef and fresh potatoes and they all ate together.

"I lost my mother and sister to the milk fever three years ago," Anna explained while they ate. "I searched for two years to find out the cause of it. I discovered that it wasn't a sickness in cows, but a powerful poison from some herbaceous plant they were eating. I couldn't determine which one, but finally, one day in the woods, I met an elderly Shawnee woman gathering plants and she told me. The Native people call it White Snakeroot. Now that I know it, I see it everywhere. It's that pretty plant in the woods with the white flower umbels. So innocent looking, but so deadly. The puzzle was solved, but the tragedy continues because people don't know. As they leave the pastures in the east to pioneer in the west, they graze their milk cows along the woodland routes. The cows eat the snakeroot and it taints the milk. I have been traveling around talking to people who settled near the travel routes, asking them to help eradicate it. I hope that it works." She looked at Daniel. "You need to put down your cow, sir, for the toxin will stay in her body for a long time. You cannot eat her meat either."

At dusk, Daniel led the cow into the woods and Cory heard the gunshot. He returned after a few minutes carrying the empty halter and rope

The next morning, Cory woke and immediately vomited. Lucas turned to her startled with a stricken look on his face. Anna came to her immediately and knelt at her side.

"Did you drink any milk or touch the cow?" she asked.

"No," Cory answered and abruptly wretched again. Anna checked Cory's eyes for dilated pupils and then palpated her stomach. She sat back on her heels and scanned Cory's face and body.

"How long has it been since you bled?"

Cory tried to clear her head and think. She had menstruated right after she came through time, but she hadn't since New Orleans.

"Two months maybe," she said. "Why?"

"My dear, I believe you are with child."

"No," Cory answered. "I have very irregular periods." She sat up, but became short of breath and threatened to vomit again.

"Are your breasts tender? Have they changed lately?"

"Yes," Lucas answered before she could.

"This can't be," Cory answered. It was beyond belief. Lucas smiled at her and she looked away feeling embarrassed.

"You are blessed, Cory," Anna said.

Lucas hopped up and began to gather their belongings.

Anna grinned as she watched him. "Fathers never know quite what to do so they try and act useful," she said.

"I can't have a baby now," Cory said.

"Well, you will have lots of time to prepare," Anna noted. "Will you be settling nearby?"

"I..I don't know," Cory replied. Her world was suddenly turned upside down.

"I must get back, but send for me when your time is near," Anna told her.

"Please don't leave," Cory said in a sudden panic.

"I must. I will share something with you, Cory. I'm afraid for my future. My husband is in trouble. He has fallen into bad company, consorting with men who are evil. I worry that I cannot pull him away from a dark path. I must return and keep trying."

Cory saw the fear in Anna's eyes. "Will you be okay?"

"I will put my life in God's hands and trust him to help me," she said. She hugged Cory. "Eat lots of greens and berries," she commanded and then stood up, gathered a small bag, and walked away. Cory watched her say good-bye to Daniel and then she was gone.

Lucas came back to crouch down next to Cory.

"Are you feeling better?"

"I don't know what I'm feeling."

"I'm happy about the baby."

"You are?"

"Of course," he said and took her hand in his.

"But everything is so uncertain."

"It's more certain now."

Cory wanted to believe that.

"I care about you, Cory. I will do anything to make sure you are okay."

Dustu arrived with a tin cup of water.

"Thank you," she said and drank a few sips of the cool water that soothed her throat from vomiting. The nausea was starting to fade away, but her pregnancy was looming very real.

Daniel was relieved to learn that she was not sick and he congratulated them about the baby.

"You'll be needing Dr. Anna in a few months," he smiled.

Cory remembered what Anna had shared with her and turned to Lucas.

"Was Anna okay when you found her?"

"She was delivering a baby at a neighbor's cabin."

"She told me she was afraid and that she needed to go back to help her husband who was in some kind of trouble."

"Folks said as much when I was looking for her. They said she had married a no account thief."

"She seemed like she really cared for him but was also afraid," Cory said. "If that's true, we should help her."

"What is the distance?" Daniel asked.

"It took me a good day's fast walk," Lucas replied.

"When Thomas gets his strength back, we could go and see that she is well."

"We could all go," Cory said. "Lucas knows the way."

"We maybe should get to John and Ellie first," Lucas said to her.

"It would only be a few days' difference," Cory answered.

"S'cuse us, Daniel. I need to speak to Cory in private."

"Sure thing," Daniel said and walked away.

Lucas sat on the ground facing Cory.

"We don't really know the woman and if her situation is dangerous, it's not the kind of place I want to be taking you."

"Taking me somewhere dangerous never stopped you before," she said a bit snidely.

"I had some knowledge about where we were going. And you weren't with child then."

"Actually, considering it's been close to eight weeks, I was with child then. So, now I'm a burden to you?"

His face was turning red. "That's not my meaning at all. What has gotten you so fired up?"

"I saw the look of fear on Anna's face. You are right. I don't know her well, but she came to help us and I think we should help her. John and Ellie would understand that, wouldn't they?"

Lucas sighed. "I reckon they would. Maybe she would come to Ellie when she gives birth."

"Another reason to help her. Let's just make sure she is okay and that she has people around that can look out for her."

He smiled at her. "You are a stubborn woman. You know, you can't take care of every person we meet."

She grinned back at him. "I didn't help Dustu. You did. You also saved a woman you didn't know much at all...three times."

"Three times?"

"You saved me from Givens twice. And I don't think I would have made it out of Natchez in one piece if you hadn't shown up and pretended to be my bodyguard."

"I don't know what a 'bodyguard' is but I mean to protect your body as long as we live," he said and gently pulled her to him as he laid back on the ground. "You are wrong. I knew you well enough," he said and kissed her.

She looked in his eyes and felt amazed at her life. She was stretched along a 19th Century man's body in the middle of the woods with no belongings, no home, and pregnant, and yet she was happier than she had ever been in her life.

"Okay. So we are agreed. We'll go find Anna, right?"

"Christ almighty, woman. Yes, we will go. And if anything bad happens, I will strangle you." They kissed again for a very long time.

They left mid-afternoon the next day. Thomas seemed fully recovered from the milk fever and Dustu's company provided him with constant distraction from his grief. Already that morning, the boys had fished in the stream, built a fort of branches, turned a log into a flatboat, and put a fallen baby bird back in its nest.

In the end, it took them three days to get to Dr. Anna's home and Lucas was not happy about it. When he had sought her out before, he had found her at a cabin about 15 miles away. She was delivering a baby and he assumed she lived nearby. Her home; however, was much farther south and east, close to the Ohio River in a small village called Elizabethtown.

No one complained about the lengthy detour except Lucas. Daniel was completely adrift and finding Dr. Anna gave him purpose. Dustu and Thomas saw it as another interesting exploit. Cory was completely preoccupied with what was happening to her body. She vomited every morning, but recovered quickly and became energized and filled with wonder about the baby growing inside her. She walked along the trail in high spirits.

"Do you think it's a boy or a girl?" she asked Lucas.

"I think the baby will be born before we find Dr. Anna," he answered grumpily.

"You'll help me take care of it, right?"

"What do you mean?" he asked.

She saw the blank look on his face and burst out laughing before she realized he was serious.

"Am I really going to have to train the first modern man in the world?"

"I do not have the slightest notion what you are talking about."

"Changing diapers, getting up in the night, washing clothes."

He looked at her, incredulous, and then started to talk as if she was a child.

"Don't worry," he said. "Babies aren't much trouble. Cherokee women just put them on their backs and go about their chores. Besides, my job is to hunt, grow crops, and tend livestock."

"Spoken like a true nineteenth-century man."

They were interrupted by the bleating of a herd of goats shepherded by an elderly man. He wore a tattered straw hat, brown trousers, and a white untucked shirt with various stains vouchering the front. He stopped to say hello and his goats crowded around them to taste their clothes as possible sources of food. Dustu giggled as one of them nibbled his shirt.

"Do you know a Doctor Anna, sir?" Lucas asked.

"What's that you say?"

"Dr. Anna," Lucas repeated in a louder voice.

"Ah, yes, I do," replied the man. "Keep following this road another two miles and when you see the rooftops of Elizabethtown, take the road on your left. There is a mighty Sycamore at the junction. The road leads to her farm. Watch out for that Bixby fella. He's a pirate you know."

"No, we don't know," Cory remarked.

"Dumb as a door. He tried to pay for dry goods with counterfeit money in his own town!"

Thomas and Dustu were busy petting the goats who loved the attention.

"Nice goats," Thomas remarked as he ran his hand along the head of a pretty, black and white spotted kid goat.

"Yes. Oats are good. Wish I had some."

"Goats," Thomas said louder.

"Of course they're goats. Are you daft, boy? Come along, girls," he said and used a wooden rod to steer the animals gently along.

They all watched the old man totter away with his herd.

"At least we know it's only another few miles to Dr. Anna," Lucas remarked.

"You say you want a banana?" Cory asked, mimicking the old man.

"You are the one that is daft," Lucas grinned. "Let's go. I want to get there before dark. If Bixby is like the old man described, I'd rather confront him in daylight."

When they arrived at the farm, they discovered a neat and trim little cabin on a knoll with a beautiful view of the surrounding meadows and woods. The door was wide open. They knocked at the door frame, but no one answered.

"Hello? Anna?" Cory called out, but was met with silence. She stepped into the room and walked around the cabin. The cabin was a tidy arrangement of the kitchen and dining area with a separate bedroom. When she walked into the bedroom, the covers were pulled back as if someone had just gotten up.

Lucas walked in and met Cory coming out of the bedroom. "The paddock gate is open. Someone saddled up and rode off. I can track them."

"I'll go with you," Daniel said.

"I think it's best if you stay here with Thomas and Dustu. You, too, Cory. I won't travel far," Lucas said. I'll only go a mile or two then loop back."

"I need to go with you. I can keep up for a mile or two," Cory insisted.

Lucas tried to argue, but in the end, he and Cory set off on foot into the woods where the horse tracks led. They climbed a hill and ended up at a sharp cliff.

"Something happened here," Lucas said with certainty. The ground was disturbed and a length of chain was left in the dirt. Cory looked down from the steep bluff. "We need to go down there."

They carefully descended using a deer trail of switchbacks. They found nothing at the bottom and yet the hair on the back of Cory's neck stood on end.

"Listen," she said.

They heard a faint whimpering in the distance, but could not tell where it was coming from. They began to circle the area and call out.

"Anna! Anna, is that you?!" Cory shouted.

A sharp cry rang out. They honed in on the direction and hurried toward it. Within a minute, they heard something in the brush and spotted a body scooting on the ground towards them in obvious distress.

"Anna!" Cory shouted and ran to her.

Once Anna saw them, she stopped moving and lay quietly gasping for breath. Her clothes were covered in dirt and her right leg was battered and bloodstained.

"Oh my god, what happened to you?" Cory asked.

"Fell. Fell off the cliff," she whispered, her words restricted by pain. "Leg is broken. Some ribs, too, I think."

"Don't worry," Cory told her. "We'll take care of you."

"Thank you," she whispered. "My husband tried to kill me," she added and then fainted.

Cory splinted her leg with sticks held together with vines. Lucas fashioned a stretcher with branches tied into an "H" frame that he could drag behind him. He carefully laid Anna on it and they headed back to her farm. Daniel, Thomas, and Dustu were glad to see them, but upset about Anna's attack. Daniel volunteered to go into the village and notify a constable. Thomas asked to go with him.

"I go, too?" Dustu asked.

"Okay. Stay with Daniel," Lucas said and then the three of them left. When Lucas started to pick Anna up from the stretcher to carry her to the cabin, she woke, jerked away in fear, and then moaned in pain.

"Anna, it's Cory and Lucas. You are safe."

"Oh," Anna replied weakly and relaxed. Lucas brought her inside and over to the bed in the corner of the cabin. Cory pushed back the jumbled spread. "Let me sit up," Anna said, but winced in pain as Lucas set her down so that she could sit against the headboard. "There is a box of willow bark on the shelf. Would you kindly steep some twigs to make a tea?"

Cory scanned a shelf filled with herbs in glass jars and boxes and found the container labeled "willow." Lucas started a small fire in the hearth and poured water from a pitcher into a kettle that he hung over the flames.

"I think my ribs are only cracked, but if you would help me, I want to make sure one of them doesn't break and puncture a lung. There are bandages in the drawer of that sideboard," Anna told Cory as she pointed to the drawer. Cory nodded and found the rolls of cloth. Anna unbuttoned her blouse and Cory eased it off her shoulders and down her arms and then wrapped a wide bandage around her chest beneath her bare breasts. Lucas occupied himself at the fire, dropping the willow twigs into the kettle. When Cory finished bandaging Anna, she slipped her arms into a nightgown and helped her rest back against the headboard.

"Thank you," Anna said, breathing through the pain. "Now, would you set the bone in my leg?"

"I can't do...," Cory began, but Anna interrupted her.

"You can do it. Lucas can help and I will talk you through it," Anna assured her.

Cory cut the vines and carefully pulled the splints away. The bottom half of Anna's shin bone dropped to one side and left it looking curved and distorted. Cory felt immediately sick to her stomach but vowed not to throw up. Anna reached down and gently palpitated her leg.

"I think it's a clean break, not shattered. I remember hitting it on a rock when I fell."

Cory and Lucas looked at each other, but didn't ask any questions.

"Help me lie down again. Now, Cory, hold the upper part of the leg just below my knee and, Lucas, take hold of my ankle, straighten that part of the leg and pull it toward you. When it's all lined up, gently push until you feel the bone touch bone." She sucked in her breath as the bones made contact. "Hold it there. Cory, place the splints back on the sides. They are nice straight pieces and will do just fine for now. Wrap a bandage as tightly as you can around my leg to hold everything together." They followed her directions as best they could and when they finished, she let out another long breath. "Good. Very good. Now, I could use a cup of that tea, please."

Lucas ladled out the willow tea into a china cup and brought it to Anna.

"Are you hungry?" Cory asked.

"Just sit with me a moment if you would."

"Of course."

Cory placed a chair next to the bed and sat quietly while Anna slowing sipped the hot tea.

"Any sign of Eason?" she asked.

"No, ma'am," Lucas answered, but walked to the window and looked out.

"He's likely gone...for good." She smiled sadly. "I was here alone, sound asleep. Someone knocked on the door and a man's voice called out that his wife needed help. It happens often. I didn't even light a lantern, but just grabbed my bag and went outside. It was rainy and windy and very dark. The man had his hat pulled down and the collar of his coat pulled up to his chin. He stood waiting with two horses and helped me climb onto one of them and then I followed him as he rode off. It was stormy and I got disoriented, not knowing where we were going. We hadn't gone too far when a huge bolt of lightning flashed nearby, and in the light, I saw that the man was Eason! When he knew that I recognized him, he grabbed the reins of my horse and shouted at me to get off. I slid off the horse and we stood on the ground as another flash of lightning shone on his angry face. I was so shocked that I hadn't recognized his voice before. I asked him what was going on and he said I had to tell him where the treasure was buried."

"Treasure?" Cory asked.

"Not a treasure really, but that is what Eason called it. My first husband had saved some money over time and when he died, I hid it. I don't know how Eason found out about the money, but he continually asked me where it was hidden and said that since we were married, that it was his money, too. I refused to tell him, but last night I guess he decided he would find it without me. He was so angry. He bound my hands and gagged me and then he reached in his saddlebag and I heard the rattle of chains. I knew right then that he meant to kill me. I took off running. I crashed through the woods and it was storming and I didn't know where I was. He was after me, shouting my name in a rage. Then it happened. I took a step and there was nothing there. I had run off a cliff. I fell and hit the branches of a tree. It slowed my fall, but I still hit the ground hard. I lay still for a while, but then I saw a lantern moving down a path from above and I knew he was coming for me. I crawled the best I could to find a place to hide. I found a large hollow log and scooted into it. He came nearby, but didn't see me. Through a crack in the log, I finally saw him turn and walk away. I crawled out in the morning and began to drag myself back toward home. That's when I heard you calling my name. I still can't believe you found me. Why are you here?"

"Cory was worried about you...with good reason," Lucas said.

"We all came," Cory told her. "Daniel is here, too. You helped him and we wanted to make sure you were okay."

"Bless you. Bless you all. I thought I could help Eason. He was so good to me after my first husband died. If you saw him, you would see that he has such a sweet face. I fell in love with him and refused to see the part of him that was not good. I pleaded with him to stay away from his thieving friends, but he wouldn't listen. Maybe he never cared for me at all. Maybe he was always after the money."

"I'm sorry," Cory said.

"I hope the law catches him," Lucas said.

"He'll go west. He always talked about it."

Daniel, Thomas, and Dustu arrived. They had relayed what happened to people in town and one of them rode off to the closest village with a sheriff to report the news.

"No one seemed very hopeful that your husband would be apprehended, Miss Anna," Thomas explained. "Somebody ran into him yesterday and his horse was packed with provisions. He said he was leaving town. He said you were off delivering a baby and that you would follow him by stagecoach when he sent word."

Thomas interrupted. "Papa, I'm hungry."

"Poor dear. How are you?" Anna asked him.

"Much better, ma'am. But now my stomach is growling something terrible," he answered.

"We'll find a place to camp and cook some supper, son," Daniel said.

"You will not!" Anna announced. "I have chickens and cornmeal. There is a garden out back. You cook up a nice meal for this boy. For everyone. You stay here as long as you like."

"Thank you, ma'am," Daniel said. "So long as you insist."

"I insist."

Lucas made a fire on a brazier outside to prevent the cabin from becoming stifling in the summer heat.

Cory made a pot of chicken stew, adding carrots and turnips from the garden. Dustu and Thomas picked blackberries and then they brought the food into the cabin and all shared a meal around Anna's table while she watched from the bed.

"Lucas, would you fill a pipe with some of the herb in that small brown pot on the shelf? The willow took away the pain some, but I could use something a bit stronger."

Lucas lit the pipe for her and then he and Cory stepped outside to sit on the porch steps. There was a spectacular sunset that filled the sky with red and orange. The smell from Anna's pipe wafted out from the cabin and Cory recognized the unmistakable scent of cannabis. She turned and looked through the door as Anna puffed on the pipe and held each puff a few seconds before blowing it out. Cory smiled.

Daniel had moved to the chair at Anna's bedside and opened a small book of poetry he carried with him.

Cory and Lucas listened to his voice as he read a poem about a young man's search for love.

"It's beautiful," Anna said when he finished.

"It was one of my wife's favorites," Daniel told her, looking down at the page.

"Mary is with God, but she will always be with you, too. Please tell me more about her if you'd like."

Daniel began telling Anna how he and Mary met, the good times they had raising the children, and their plans for a new life in Missouri.

Cory listened from the porch as she rested her head against Lucas's shoulder. When she stepped inside later, Anna was asleep with a peaceful smile on her face. Daniel had fallen asleep in the chair, but woke when he heard Cory's footsteps. Cory leaned down to whisper in his ear.

"I'll sleep on the floor next to her in case she needs anything in the night," Cory said.

Daniel nodded and got up to join Thomas, Lucas, and Dustu outside. They camped under a large Hickory tree in the front yard. Lucas kept his rifle at his side, not taking any chances that Eason Bixby might still be in the area.

Cory curled up on the floor next to Anna's bed, but sometime in the night she woke to the touch of a hand on her shoulder. She looked up and Anna motioned for her to come onto the bed. Cory crawled into the bed, gently lay next to Anna, and fell into a deep sleep.

The next morning, Cory looked over at Anna who was silently praying with her eyes closed. Her lips formed an "Amen" and then she turned and smiled at Cory.

"This will be a new day for us all."

"I'm worried about how you will manage," Cory said.

"I have many good neighbors to call upon," Anna reassured her.

Daniel walked in and heard Anna's words. "You need someone here with you, not just neighbors stopping by and bringing you supper. Thomas and I are unsure about our future. If you would have us, we could stay and look out for you until you can walk."

Tears formed in Anna's eyes. "I prayed that you would stay," she said. "I am a stubborn, independent woman, but I see that I am a bit helpless at the moment."

"Then it's settled," Daniel pronounced.

"I will be forever grateful," Anna said.

*

Cory, Lucas, and Dustu were outside the cabin with their bags packed and ready to leave when Anna called Cory to her bedside.

"I want you and Lucas to do one more thing for me. There is a small cave exactly a five-minute walk due east of here. It's tucked away behind a large boulder, but you'll know the place because there is a stand of Sassafras there. Inside the cave, on the right-hand side you'll find a rock set into the wall. Behind the rock, is a canvas bag. Would you bring it to me?"

Ten minutes later, Cory and Lucas walked out of the cave with a bag of what they were sure was filled with coins. The place was exactly where Anna had described, a small cave opening well hidden behind boulders and the mitten-shaped leaves of Sassafras trees.

Anna took the weathered canvas bag in her lap and carefully opened it. It was filled with gold coins, and Anna sat for a moment touching them, deep in thought.

"I haven't seen these in a while. My dear first husband worked so hard to earn these. He was not a handsome man, but such a good man," she said. Cory guessed she was comparing him to the supposedly dashing Bixby.

Anna removed a handful of gold coins and held them out to Cory.

"We can't, we..." Cory protested.

Anna cut her off. "I insist. For all that you've done for me."

"But you'll be helping me someday soon I hope," Cory said, placing a hand on her belly.

"Yes, I will come, and this money will hopefully give you a start on your new life with your new family," she said, smiling at them both.

"Thank you, ma'am," Lucas said and Cory took the coins in her hand.

"You are welcome. There, now go. Be safe and send word when it's time.

"We will," Cory said and gave Anna a final hug good-bye.

Chapter Twelve

HOMECOMING

L ucas had gone ahead to hunt and Cory and Dustu were following a small road heading north to New Salem. The road cut through the woods and Cory was thankful for the cool shade in the August heat.

"Tell me again where we go?" Dustu asked.

Cory could see that spending time with Thomas had improved Dustu's English.

"To where John and his wife Ellie live."

"And Lucas," Dustu corrected.

"Yes," she smiled.

"And us," Dustu added.

"Well, we will see. Maybe we will live somewhere else."

"Where?" he asked.

"I don't know," She told him. "Hold on a second," Cory said as she quickly stepped to the side of the road and vomited onto a patch of moss.

Dustu unhooked the canteen from her backpack and handed it to her.

"Thanks," she said as she wiped her mouth on her sleeve and took a sip. Dustu had stopped asking questions and she was relieved not to talk about the future. Lucas hadn't told Dustu yet about going to find his aunt and sister. Cory was not sure how Dustu would take this news.

They heard a cry in a nearby treetop and watched a large red-tailed hawk lift out of its hidden spot in the leaves, swoop across the path above them and disappear into the canopy again.

"Good sign," Dustu noted.

"Why?" she asked.

"Seeing with no fear."

"That does sound good," she said.

He nodded and held up the canteen. "I go fill. Wait."

She watched Dustu dive through the brush toward the stream that paralleled their path. She wanted to see with no fear. It was so opposite to her normal way of viewing the world. She looked toward the direction the large raptor flew. She touched her belly. Her baby would be strong and fearless. She resolved to use the hawk as a symbol to guide her and she nodded a thank you to the treetops.

Dustu darted back out of the brush with a full canteen and tied it back on her pack. His leather trousers were wet and she guessed he had splashed in the stream to cool off. She was still wearing her skirt and blouse, which kept her cool and allowed her to pee more easily, a frequent occurrence these days. There was only a small bulge in her belly and she hadn't felt the baby move yet, but there were lots of other changes in her body. She was less nauseated and more hungry and her breasts kept growing in size. She thought back to that night in New Orleans when she and Lucas first made love. That was the beginning of May and it was now the middle of August. She was close to four months pregnant.

Lucas was trying to treat her the same as before, but she could see all of the ways he was being more attentive. He was also more tender and she woke up often in the night with his arm around her. Her pregnancy made her extra warm in the summer heat and she would gently lift his arm and lay it aside so she could breathe and cool off. Then she would lie there watching his sleeping face in the dark as the crickets and cicadas filled the night air with their percussive music. "I love you," she often whispered. Dustu was usually curled up on her other side. He was really trying to stay on his own separate blanket at night, but he almost always ended up cuddled by her in the morning. She knew he missed Thomas. They had bonded during the three weeks they spent together. There were children in New Salem and she hoped he would find new playmates. If Lucas decided to take Dustu to his family in the Indian Territory, she figured she would have to argue with Lucas about going with him. He would want her to stay back because of the baby. But she did not want to be separated from him and she wanted to see where Dustu was going to live and grow up. Thanks to Anna, they had the money to pay for steamboat tickets down the Mississippi River and west along the Missouri River to the new settlement of Kansas City and then walk or ride south to the army fort near Tulsa. She would convince him to take her with him.

*

Two days later, they arrived at John and Ellie's farm. Ellie was in her eighth month of pregnancy, but her round belly did not slow her down. After all of the greetings, unpacking, and settling in, she cooked a dinner of chicken, potatoes, and fresh green beans from her garden. As Cory helped her wash up, they chatted about the trip and goings-on in New Salem. Lucas had shared the news about the baby the moment they arrived. Ellie and John congratulated them though Ellie hadn't seemed surprised.

"He was smitten the moment he saw you," Ellie told her as she washed and Cory dried dishes. "We'll raise our babies together!"

Cory nodded and smiled, but her future still seemed uncertain despite how much Lucas reassured her that everything would be okay. She had not fully accepted that she would be in this time forever. She was happy about the baby, but also terrified. She felt physically comfortable living in this simpler and rustic era, but it made her nervous thinking about raising a child in a world without modern medicine and technology.

"Should we have a wedding?" Ellie asked her.

"We...we haven't talked about it," Cory said, embarrassed.

Lucas had stepped into the cabin and heard Ellie's question about marriage.

"Yes, if she'll have me," he said as he stood behind Cory and wrapped his arms around her. He cupped her belly in his palms.

Cory turned beet red and was speechless. A wedding hadn't occurred to her.

"Do we need to get married?" she blurted out.

She felt Lucas stiffen behind her and she saw Ellie glance at his face. Cory turned around and saw the disappointment in his eyes.

"We don't have to have a wedding," Lucas said. "We could just have a justice of the peace marry us," he said hopefully.

"I guess that would work," she answered mechanically, averting her eyes. She spotted her bag sitting on the floor and pulled away from Lucas.

"Where did Dustu go? He was supposed to clean out my backpack and air it out," she said as she walked over, picked the bag up, and headed outside, leaving Lucas and Ellie standing awkwardly in silence.

Cory strode out in the yard.

"Dustu!" she called and then spotted him with John cutting wheat in a field far from earshot.

She turned her bag upside down and shook out any loose dirt and food particles. She then batted it with her hand to clear any dust and walked over and hung it on Ellie's clothesline. She turned around and saw Lucas standing there, quietly watching her.

"We don't have to get married," he said.

"Everything is happening so fast," Cory said.

"You don't want to be here," he said.

"I do! I'm just scared."

"Ellie said women have a lot of different emotions when they are with child."

"Hormones. It's caused by hormones. But that's not what's going on. You don't really know me, Lucas. In my time, I was scared all the time."

"But you are one of the bravest people I know," he argued.

"Stubborn, combative, not brave," she countered.

"I won't argue the stubborn part," he said. "But I saw what you did in Natchez and New Orleans to stand up for William and his family."

"It's easy for me to stand up for other people. It's much harder for me to stand up for myself." She struggled for words to explain. "Making a home, having a baby, being married. These are things I thought would never happen to me. In my time, my generation is super informed, but super anxious. The world is so fucking fragile. You can't imagine how screwed up the planet is. There are a billion people trying to survive and after two world wars and dozens of smaller ones, we still haven't figured out how to take care of each other or the planet."

She stopped for a moment and took a breath.

"The thing is," she said. "People here can't afford to worry. They survive. They keep going, and as we saw, people are taking what they want with no regard for other humans. That will continue. Even after slavery is abolished. Even after women get the vote. Even after the Civil Rights movement, a gay rights movement, and an environmental movement, we still keep making the same fucking mistakes, but with bigger consequences because weapons and technology are so powerful. My time is supposed to be the Age of Aquarius, but it feels like we're heading toward an Apocalypse."

Lucas stared at her.

"I don't understand even half of what you are saying," he said. "But if the world is so bad there, why would you want to go back?"

"Because, despite everything, there are hospitals and technology and people *are* still trying to change things," she said.

"I don't have any more words to convince you," he responded. "I only know what is happening with us, now. I plan on leaving in two days to take Dustu out west. You should stay here and decide what you want."

He turned and headed down the road toward town.

"Lucas!" she called, but he didn't turn around and she didn't go after him.

*

Later, Cory and Dustu were asleep on a pallet in Ellie and John's main room of the cabin when Lucas slipped inside in the darkness. Cory woke instantly, but didn't move and stayed silent. Lucas stretched out on his back beside her, but didn't touch her. She wanted to turn over and hug him, to lay her head on his chest and say she was sorry for doubting their future together. Instead, she closed her eyes and touched her belly. She lay thinking about hospitals and cell phones and ambulances. She also thought about Amelia's idea for traveling forward in time. "Find a place where something momentous will happen. Go to that spot and concentrate on the feeling of what transpired." She went over the events right before she stepped back in time, trying to recall one with a large positive impact. 2017. A new president inaugurated. Then it dawned on her. The Women's March in

January 2017. Downtown Chicago, tens of thousands of people, but mostly women in "pussy hats" standing for equality and justice. Other than Obama's inaugural speech, the Women's March had been the most positive and exhilarating political experience of her life. She felt a sudden burst of homesickness for Chicago. She could go there now and see what 1835 Chicago was like. She could find the spot where she stood at Jackson and Columbus on January 21, 2017 when the crowds grew so large that there was no room to march so it became a gigantic rally. If she concentrated on the positive feeling she experienced there, maybe, like a deja vu, she would be drawn to the future already lived. She looked over at Lucas now sound asleep. She felt Dustu's small frame pressed up against her shoulder. She felt like a traitor for thinking of leaving them. She was carrying Lucas's baby. And where was her promise to see Dustu safe?

At that moment, she felt a flutter in her womb. It felt like a butterfly taking flight. She froze and waited. It happened again. It was the baby, her baby. In that moment everything changed. She saw her daughter standing with all women of her time trying to make a better world. She knew now what she had to do.

Chapter Thirteen

THE FUTURE

She didn't tell Lucas about her plan and carried the guilt from it. She convinced herself that it was better that he not know and decided to leave a letter for him with a postman in Chicago to be mailed if she didn't return in two days to retrieve it. She would leave for Chicago while Lucas was away and after Ellie's baby was born. In the meantime, she helped Lucas and Dustu get ready for their trip, packing their bags with smoked pork, dried beans, and corn cakes. She and Lucas acted as if nothing was wrong, talking about the journey and the routes he would take by boat and by horseback using some of Anna's coins to avoid hardship. Beneath the polite harmonious preparations, there was an unspoken question about their future together. She knew he was pretending everything was okay. He kissed her in the morning when they woke and they smiled at each other when they interacted throughout the day, but there was clearly a tension between them. Ellie noticed it right away, but misconstrued the cause.

"Don't worry about Lucas and Dustu. They will be fine," Ellie said as she carefully lowered herself into a chair after making breakfast. Her baby was due any day now and she often took the weight off her feet, closed her eyes, and tried to breathe.

"You must have been so happy when John got back from the river trip," Cory replied.

"I was! The first day, I just wanted to be near him, but then I started asking him questions about the trip and chattering about all the news from town and he probably wished he was back on that flatboat! I was so lonely when he was gone."

Cory didn't comment. It was as if she had switched off her emotions, closing her heart as the only way to keep focused on her mission—to get back to the future, to her time.

The morning Lucas and Dustu left, John, Ellie, and Cory stood out in the yard and said their good-byes in the hot August sun. Dustu was quiet and looked at the ground as John and Ellie wished him well.

"You will grow up to be a fine young man, son," John told him.

"Your family will be so glad to see you," Ellie added.

Dustu walked over to Cory, wrapped his arms around her thighs, and buried his head in her skirt. She put her hand on his head and stood quietly as Lucas watched. Dustu looked up at her.

"You go with us?" he pleaded.

Cory had never seen him cry, but tears were forming in his dark brown eyes, so like her own.

"She needs to stay here safe," Lucas said. "For the baby."

Dustu touched Cory's belly.

"I will come to see you and him," he said, already deciding the gender of the baby.

Cory knelt down and hugged him. Tears were streaming down her cheeks and she quickly wiped them away and looked Dustu in the eye.

"Remember what Cat told you?" She asked.

"I iz going to be alright," he said repeating Cat's exact cadence and tone.

"Yes, you are," Cory said. "Take care of Lucas, okay?"

"I will," he said.

"Let's go, Dustu," Lucas said. He stepped up to Cory and gave her a brief hug.

"A month most likely," he said.

"Okay. Take care," she answered.

He and Dustu grabbed their bags and walked off. Cory froze in panic.

They got about twenty steps away and then Lucas turned and walked back. He took Cory in his arms and kissed her fully on the mouth. She was stiff at first, but her feelings took over and she relaxed in his arms and kissed him back with complete abandon.

He broke away and walked off again. He and Dustu disappeared down the road and around a bend as Cory watched. She felt sick and scared and hated herself. Ellie came up and put an arm around her shoulders.

"We could pray together for them if that would bring you some comfort," she said.

Cory gave Ellie a half-smile of thanks and shook her head slowly.

"I just need to be alone for a bit," she said and walked off. She crossed the road and headed into the cornfield, losing herself in the tall stalks. She crouched down among the rows and a sob escaped her lips. Her body started quaking and she began to weep. Her emotions fought with her mind and she knew that whatever was driving her was in opposition to her heart. She missed Lucas and Dustu already and wanted to jump up and race after them. But another instinct had kicked in. Something was demanding attention, asking her to be very sure about her actions. She stopped crying and took long slow breaths, listening and alert. The fluttering in her womb began immediately and she regained her focus. She needed to know if she could return to her time. She wasn't sure how it would happen, but she needed to try. She stood up, walked back to Ellie and John's, and helped Ellie with chores. That night, she stopped short of telling them about her plan to go to Chicago.

"What was the news from town, John?" Ellie asked at supper. They sat at the simple wooden table eating fresh corn and beans from the garden.

"The mill broke, but Elton fixed it fine. Folks are still coming down with the typhoid fever. Best to stay away from town. I saw Abe and he seemed pretty downhearted about Ann's death. He wasn't himself at all.

"He is getting ready to go off to Vandalia for the legislative session, right? Maybe it will help take his mind off his loss," Ellie said.

"I've never seen him so low," John commented.

They were finished eating and Ellie rose to clear their plates when she stopped and winced in pain. She held her large belly. John jumped up from his chair and went to her side.

"What is it?" he asked

"It might be the baby is coming, John," she said.

"Shall I go fetch Granny Stevens?" he asked as he helped her back down in the chair.

"Not quite yet. I've had these pains before and they went away again," she said.

But the contractions continued and Cory watched the unfolding of the labor process. She cleared the table and washed the dishes as Ellie relaxed and then ten minutes later felt her womb cramp again. This went on for about an hour and then the squeezing pains came every five minutes.

"Maybe you should get Granny Stevens now," Ellie said after a particularly heavy contraction.

John was out the door in an instant and Cory stood at the washing tub looking at Ellie.

"Can I make you some tea?" she asked.

Ellie was covered in sweat from heat and exertion and shook her head.

"Some water with mint leaves would be nice," she whispered, but another clenching overtook her and she let out a loud moan. Cory fetched her a glass of water and added some sprigs of mint they had picked together that morning. Ellie took some deep breaths and used her hands to massage her lower back.

"I'm starting to get terrible pains in my back. I'd like to lie down for a spell."

Cory helped her to the bedroom and then brought her the water. Ellie sat on the edge of the bed and drank it in one gulp. She laid back and placed her hands on her belly, but the pressure on her back made her roll to her side. Another contraction came and she groaned in pain.

"Would you rub my back a bit, Cory? The pain is awful," she whimpered.

Cory climbed on the bed, knelt behind Ellie, and began to knead her lower back.

"It feels like the baby is pressed against my backbone," Ellie said.

Cory had noted that the contractions were getting very close together, which was confirmed when barely two minutes later, Ellie cried out in pain. Cory's eyes darted to the door as she prayed for John and the midwife to walk through it.

Ellie sat up and changed her position so that she was on her hands and knees on the bed, hoping to relieve the back pain, but when that didn't work, she changed to a sitting position and Cory pressed her knuckles into the muscles at the top of her buttocks.

"Keep breathing," Cory said, the only thing she knew to offer, having seen movie versions of childbirth.

"I want to walk some," Ellie announced and climbed off the bed. Cory took her arm and they paced the floor next to the bed. Another contraction caused Ellie to yell with pain and shout at Cory. "Don't have a baby, Cory! Oh, yes, I forgot. You ARE having a baby! Damn horrible men!"

Cory had no response other than to continue supporting Ellie as they walked out into the main room of the cabin and made endless circles, stopping every two minutes for Ellie to absorb the pain of her clenching womb.

Finally, John and Granny Stevens walked through the door. Granny was small and hunched-back with a top knot of silver hair and crevices of wrinkles in her weathered-face, but as she went into action, it was clear that she was more than capable of handling the heavy work of delivering a baby. Cory breathed with relief as Granny led Ellie back into the bedroom, examined her, and then called out to John to boil water and get the blanket that Ellie had put aside for the birth. Cory peeked into the room and Granny motioned to her.

"Come on girl," she said. "Hold her hand and mop her brow. She needs your strength." Rusty scooted into the room and sat on the floor in the corner like a sentry watching over the proceedings.

Ellie was sitting propped against the headboard and sweating profusely. Cory took a damp cloth and wiped her brow.

"You are close, dearie," Granny told her. "You are doing a fine job. Your body is just about ready to push this baby out."

"I want to push now," Ellie told her.

"Not quite yet, just a little longer. Breathe like your old dog there does when he's hot. Fast little breaths like this," Granny said as she opened her mouth and panted like a dog.

At that moment, a rush of water flooded the bed beneath Ellie. It soaked the old blanket Granny had put under her.

"There, you see! Your baby is coming soon."

It didn't seem that soon to Cory. Ellie panted and cried, screamed, and huffed through another hour of contractions and finally Granny called to her.

"Now, when the next squeeze happens, you push, dearie. Bear down and push."

Ellie was exhausted as she squatted on the mattress with Cory bracing her arm.

Granny called out to John. "John, get in here!"

John walked in and his face went pale when he saw his wife panting and red-faced. Granny had pulled off her dress and put a nightgown on her, but the gown was lifted to her thighs as she squatted on the bed.

"Stand on her other side and hold her up, just like Cory is doing," Granny said.

John grabbed Ellie's arm and put his other arm around her back.

"I hate you, John," Ellie growled.

"I love you, Ellie," he replied.

"Push," Granny commanded as another contraction overwhelmed Ellie's body.

She closed her eyes and braced herself against John and Cory.

"It's coming!" Granny called. Her hands were below Ellie's body as if she was holding something. Cory caught a glimpse of a round, wet, and hairy bulge emerging from Ellie's vagina.

Ellie gave another massive push and a little body shot out onto the bed.

"Whooee! And there is our baby!" Granny called out.

Ellie cried out with relief and John and Cory gently lowered her down. She scooted up to lie propped against the pillows.

Granny pushed open Ellie's nightgown, lifted the baby, and laid him against Ellie's bare chest.

"He's a healthy boy, Ellie. He's already turning a nice color," Granny said.

Cory and John remained a bit stunned by the arrival, but were smiling quietly at each side of the bed.

John kissed Ellie on the forehead.

"Do you still hate me?"

"What are you talking about? I could never hate you! Look at him, John. He's so perfect!"

"Congratulations," Cory said to them both. The baby had lots of fuzzy reddish-brown hair and did indeed seem perfect though his tiny features also made him look like a little alien creature. She watched him in awe, wondering what her baby would look like.

Granny was gently kneading Ellie's belly and after about five minutes, Ellie bore down and expelled the placenta. Cory watched Granny examine it and smile.

"Everything's there. All good."

*

An hour later, the umbilical cord had been cut, the baby swaddled and nursed, and everyone was sitting on the bed with Ellie.

"You got a name for this child?" Granny asked.

"Oh...yes, we do!" Ellie said realizing she hadn't even thought about the name, that it was enough that the baby was born safely.

"Abraham. We like Abe's name," John said.

"He'll be tickled about that. I best be getting back," Granny said.

"You are welcome to stay the night, Granny," John said.

"I like to sleep in my own bed when I can. I never know when I'll be needed somewhere else soon."

"I'll walk you home," John told her.

"No, you will not. I'm perfectly fine getting home. It's a full moon and the road is like daylight. You stay and enjoy that baby. Keep sipping the tea, Ellie. I'll come check on you in a day or two. Good night."

When Granny departed, Cory immediately felt like a third wheel with this new little family. Both John and Ellie were exhausted and Abe was fast asleep, but not for long she guessed.

"You should get some sleep before he wakes to feed again. I remember that my sister was up every two hours when my nephew was born," Cory said. "He's very beautiful and I'm happy for you," she added awkwardly.

They turned to look at her a moment.

"Thank you, Cory," they answered in unison and then continued staring at the baby lying between them as they snuggled in the bed together.

Cory quietly slipped out of the room.

Over the next three days, she took care of everyone, cooking, and washing diapers. Ellie was up and moving easily the day after the birth so Cory's help was not so much a necessity as a much appreciated effort. She was impressed that Ellie was able to function so well after giving birth. Her delivery had been a normal one by pioneer standards or any standards for that matter, and there really was no reason that she couldn't carry on her normal routine except for the need to stop and feed Abe or change his diapers. Still, it was impressive to see her take on all of her duties and she was an inspiration to Cory.

Most of the day, Abe slept in the cradle John had made for him. It sat in the middle of the cabin and Cory viewed his tiny body often. And then there were times when Ellie finished nursing and thrust him into Cory's arms as she closed up her bodice. Every time this happened, it felt to Cory like she was receiving a surprise package, and she stood there staring at the precious contents. Ellie would always laugh at her.

"He's just a baby, Cory. You act like he is a basket of eggs you might drop."

He was not "just a baby" to her. Cory looked at his tiny fingers waving in the air and when he looked up at her, she melted, completely in love. Though she was terrified to become a mother, she was beginning to feel the anticipation of wanting to see her baby. Would it look like her? Like Lucas? Any thought of Lucas or Dustu made her immediately sad. She rocked little Abe and watched his face scrunch up, which usually meant he was pooping in his diaper. Ellie stood up and reached for him.

"I'll take him now if you want," she said.

"I'd like to hold him for a while if you don't mind," Cory replied. She carried him outside and sat on the porch, placing him lengthwise on her knees so she could keep looking at his face. Ellie followed her and stood at the door a moment observing.

"I've never seen anybody so interested in a baby before. After all, they don't do much! Well, I need to start washing diapers. Just put him in the cradle when you are done."

"Okay," Cory murmured as she continued to stare at Abe. Ellie shook her head and headed for the washtub.

"I will miss you, little guy," Cory said to Abe. She had decided to leave New Salem in two days. There was a stagecoach heading north and the driver thought he might be going all the way to Chicago.

"If I don't come back, grow up big and strong."

Abe looked at her with a serious expression that made her smile. He smiled back, which newborns are not supposed to do, she noted.

"That is definitely a smile and you are obviously brilliant," she said. She took his little hand and held it in hers then leaned down and kissed the tips of his fingers.

Chapter Fourteen

THE WINDY CITY

As Cory waited in New Salem for the stagecoach driver to announce their departure, she noticed Abe Lincoln walking into town. He caught sight of her as well and came over to greet her.

"The young lady from the road. I apologize that I've forgotten your name. Wait, Cory is it?"

"Yes," she replied, shyly.

"I do try to remember folks' names. If I'm going to represent my district in the legislature, I darn well better act like a politician. I suppose I will be kissing babies, too," he said smiling. "Speaking of babies, Ellie and John have a new arrival, am I correct?"

"Yes," she answered. "And they named him Abraham!"

"Well, I'll be a monkey's uncle!" he exclaimed. "I hope he doesn't favor me in any other way! Landsakes, it is good to hear about new life coming into the world. It lessens the pain a bit over those we lose for seemingly no cause."

"I heard about Ann Rutledge's death. I'm sorry for your loss," Cory replied.

Abe stared at the ground. "Yes, it hit me very hard. To be truthful, I did not see much use in living after she passed," Abe said. "How in tarnation would it serve any purpose to take a life like hers?!"

"I don't know."

"She had the kindest heart and wrote the most beautiful poems," he said as he looked off in the distance. There was a long pause, and then he turned back to Cory. He noticed the bag at her feet.

"Are you traveling again?" he asked. "I haven't gotten to hear the stories about your journey on the Mississippi."

"I am going to Chicago...perhaps to seek out a relative and for other reasons," she said.

"I hear that Chicago is a swampland. You be careful. This fever seems to favor a humid climate," he warned.

"I saw amazing things on our trip to New Orleans," Cory shared with him. "We ended up harboring an enslaved slave family. The slave markets are the worst thing I have ever seen in my life."

"I am impressed by your bravery. I have seen those markets on my two trips south. As we discussed before, I do not know the solution, but I will seek a legal course to stop it. Your words have stuck in my mind. I will not be the person who stands by and does nothing," he said with determination.

"I believe you." She looked him in the eye. "If it's a choice between keeping the country whole and ending slavery, choose to end slavery."

He looked at her curiously. "That's a hard choice. I would not want our country to be split apart."

The stagecoach driver walked over and interrupted them.

"Time to go," he said, glancing at his pocket watch. He flipped the case shut and slipped it into the small enclosure of his vest and then tossed Cory's bag on top of the coach.

"Perhaps we can talk again when you return. Have a safe and productive journey, Miss Cory," Abe said.

"Thank you," she replied. "I hope you enjoy the legislature. I know you will do great things."

"I will strive to live up to your expectations," he said with a grin.

She stepped into the coach, sat down on the hard bench seat and looked out the window at Lincoln standing in the New Salem dusty road—young, tall, and with an air of both sadness and hope. She would remember this image of him forever.

*

She had started the trip with only one other passenger, but Cory was now surrounded by travelers as the coach bumped along the road, previously used only by wagons and horseback riders. They had already stopped twice to help push the coach out of a muddy rut since it had rained heavily the day before. Today was dry and sunny, and after moving past her morning queasiness, Cory was staring out the coach window trying to keep her thoughts positive.

"Are you traveling alone?" the woman next to her asked in a German accent. She and her husband had gotten on the coach in Bloomington. The woman had grey streaked blonde hair pulled back in a severe bun. Her face was round and her smile friendly, but Cory felt the slight ridicule behind her question. The woman's husband sat on her other side staring out the window. He was older with a hooked nose and long, expressionless face.

"I'm traveling to Chicago to see relatives," Cory answered. The story was not entirely false. She still hoped to find her great, great grandmother Rebecca McNeely who was now supposedly in Chicago. She was growing tired of half-truths and wished she could just answer: "I'm traveling back to the future."

"This is my first time traveling by coach and I daresay, I am glad it is only for a short distance," the woman told her.

At that moment the stagecoach hit a rut in the road and the passengers were tossed in the air. They landed and pitched to and fro until the wheels found purchase again.

The violent interruption caused everyone to become quiet and the silence continued as they settled back in their seats. Cory was grateful. The break was welcome even though the jolting had made her feel nauseated. Her morning sickness had almost disappeared...but not quite. There were still moments like this when she felt like sticking her head out the stagecoach window and leaving a trail of puke on the path behind them.

She sat and breathed instead. Dustu would have pulled the canteen from the ties on her backpack and offered her a drink to settle her stomach. Lucas would not have noticed that she retched, but would have turned to her a minute later and kissed her on the lips. She could feel that kiss now. She missed Lucas and Dustu. Her longing grew each day instead of fading. She touched her belly and felt the bump that could not be hidden. In fact the woman next to her began staring at her womb and Cory gave her a steely eye as if she dared the woman to ask where the father was.

The stagecoach stopped for the night at a horrible inn. Cory paid for a room by herself and after declining supper that looked more like slop Ellie fed the pigs, she went upstairs to her room and sat on the bed. She didn't risk looking at the sheets or bother to undress, but simply placed one of her blouses over the pillow, lay down on top of the covers, and was asleep within seconds. She woke hours later to loud laughter in the room next door. Her back ached from the lumpy mattress and she sipped water from her canteen to slake her thirst. The room was stuffy and hot so she opened the window and pulled over a chair. She breathed fresh air and looked up at the stars, thinking about her conversation with Amelia about time and space. As she rested her arms on the window sill, she had the sensation of time disappearing, of losing her sense of self, and of mingling with the dark expanse of the universe.

When the driver called out their arrival in Chicago, Cory was excited, but when she stepped down from the stagecoach she was shocked. Chicago was no more than a cluster of cabins sitting at the junction of the Wabash and Chicago rivers. The people moving about were from various backgrounds including the first Native Americans she had seen since Dustu's tribe. They were living in mud-walled, thatched-roof huts along the river. There seemed to be an air of tolerance here, but in truth, Chicago was so small that there didn't appear to be any reason to fight over resources...yet. There were no identifiable landmarks she could relate to at all. It took her only five minutes to walk from one end of the settlement to the other and it dawned on her that there was no location here that had any recognizable tie to an event in her future whatsoever. Only the strong, fecund wind blowing off the lake reminded her of the city she knew. It was merely a dusty village where people were just beginning to take advantage of the potential Joliet saw when he explored it a hundred years before. It might be years before she would find the spot to connect with her future.

Cory's hopes were dashed. She had come all this way to try and protect her baby's future and failed. In that moment, she knew she had been right all her life. She could never assure her baby's safety and that was why she had never wanted children. And yet she was already in love with the tiny human growing inside her. She was also in love with a man and a boy she had been willing to abandon.

She found the stagecoach at the town stable and spotted the driver heading toward the tavern.

"Hey!" Cory cried.

The driver heard her and stopped. She ran to catch up to him.

"When are you heading south again?" she asked frantically.

"After exchanging the horses and eating a proper meal," he answered.

"I want to go with you," she said.

"You only just got here," he noted.

"I know, but I want to go back!"

"Lady, you pay the fare, and you can go up and down this route all you want," he joked and then he noticed how distraught she was. "I'll be back to pick passengers up at that storefront across the street in one hour."

"Thank you," she said. "I'll be there."

She walked over to the general store and was ready to sit patiently outside for the next hour, but her stomach was growling and she decided to buy some food. There were others in the shop and she waited in line to be served. Her excitement was growing about finding Lucas and Dustu. She could barely wait to reverse her course and head west even though she knew it was dangerous. Plans were swirling in her head.

"May I help you, miss?"

Cory looked up and her heart stopped as she stared across the store counter into the eyes of her sister. The young woman cocked her head in such a familiar way that Cory's eyes immediately filled with tears. It was not Jill, of course, but the woman had Jill's blond hair and same high cheekbones, full lips, and slanted blue eyes. She was wearing a store apron over her green gingham dress and rested her hands in the apron pockets.

"Are you Rebecca McNeely by chance?" Cory asked.

The woman was startled at first and slightly wary, but just like Jill, had a trusting quality backed by strength.

"I am," she answered. "And who might be asking?" She spoke with the slightest remnant of an Irish accent that made Cory grin.

"I...I traveled here from New Orleans and my friend asked that if I met a Rebecca McNeely, to say 'hello' for her. My friend is Amelia...Amelia DeCour."

Rebecca broke into a huge smile. "Yes, yes, I know her! I have been meaning to write and tell her that I arrived here safely. My uncle runs this store and took me in. I am so lucky."

She was young and full of hope. Cory wanted, on the one hand, to stay and talk to her, but on the other hand, realized that Rebecca's life was just beginning and there was not much to learn from her besides the fact that she was alive and apparently happy.

The customer behind Cory grumbled about "female chatter holding up business" and Rebecca gave him a stern look, then smiled at Cory.

"Would you like to come to supper with me and my uncle?"

Cory was torn, but her decision was quick. "Thanks, but I'm catching the stagecoach to continue my journey. I hope to come back someday and we can visit then."

Rebecca seemed disappointed, but she easily shifted her manner. "You'll need some provisions." She grabbed a loaf of fresh bread and sliced off a chunk of cheese and piece of sausage from the items beneath cloth-covered dishes on the counter. She wrapped them in paper and handed them to Cory.

"Have a safe journey."

"Thank you," Cory answered, receiving the gift. She hesitated a moment as she stared into the face of her great, great grandmother and then she and Rebecca exchanged smiles, she turned and left.

Chapter Fifteen

MISTAKEN

Cory had made a choice and now sat in the coach as it bumped its way back south. She would find Lucas and if he hadn't found Dustu's family yet, she would help him. She ached to see Lucas now and silently told her baby that they were on their way to find her father. Lucas wouldn't have known about her notion to go back to the future, but she knew that he would have understood. He had told her many times that if she found a way, that she should go.

"I swear on my life, that I will take care of you and the baby," he had said. "But if you could return to your time where life is safer, I would want you to go no matter how much it would pain me."

Now she knew for certain that it would pain her, too. Unbearably so. She would ten times rather risk any hardship in this time than to leave Lucas. She wondered now how she could have ever considered leaving, but then the baby tumbled in her womb and she remembered what had driven her. Love is as important as being safe she transmitted to the baby. Lucas and I will do our best to love and protect you. She stared out the window and willed the stagecoach to go faster. She hadn't slept well at the inn and after a while, her head dropped, bobbing to the beat of the horses' trotting hooves.

Cory woke up when the stagecoach slowed to a stop. She looked out the window and saw two men at the side of the road, one lying on the ground and the other leaning over him. The driver called out to them.

"You need help?"

The kneeling man looked up surprised as if he hadn't heard the stagecoach approaching at all. He had blonde hair and a short beard and his face was stricken with sadness.

"My friend is sick," he said.

Cory immediately thought about Daniel's family. She opened the door and stepped out of the coach and then knelt down next to the man on the ground. His hair was jet black, long and braided and he wore a buckskin shirt and trousers. He looked up at her with feverish brown eyes and when she touched his brow it was hot and moist.

"We've been out for a month leading a wagon party to Iowa when he took sick. I've been trying to get him to a town with a doctor. My name's Efraim. This is George."

Cory looked up at the driver. "We can take them to the next town, right?"

The driver shook his head and started to respond, but George interrupted.

"Don't move me...," he said in a breathy voice. His hand slowly moved to his waist pocket and he pulled out a ring. It was a silver band beautifully encircled with engraved leaves.

"Give it to Rebecca," he continued then paused to catch his breath. "Tell her I'm sorry."

Efraim refused to take the ring. "You'll give it to her yourself when you get better." He turned to Cory. "They met four months ago. George aimed to propose to her when we got back to Chicago," he explained.

George pushed the ring into Efraim's hand. "Find her and give it to her. Tell her I loved her mighty."

A memory filled Cory's head, the story her mother told about the marriage of her two times great grandmother.

"What is Rebecca's last name?"

"McNeely," George told her.

Cory looked over at Efraim and realized she was staring at her great, great grandfather. The family tale was of two men, both hunters and scouts. As one lay dying, he asked his friend to deliver a ring to his sweetheart. Efraim would take the ring to Rebecca and fall in love with her himself. She would marry Efraim, not George. Cory continued to gaze at Efraim, but her words were for George.

"She will get the ring."

"Take care of her, my brother. Rebecca is with child," George said to his friend in a whisper.

A moment of surprise swept across Efraim and Cory's faces. Rebecca was pregnant with George's child. George was Cory's biological forefather.

Efraim did not hesitate as he held George with a steady eye.

"I promise."

George nodded then stared up at the sky and it was as if he was seeing a vision. His face became completely serene.

"George?" Efraim called, but George was already in another place. His body took a sudden last breath and then became still.

Efraim was stunned. Cory reached down and closed George's eyes.

"We need to move on, miss," the driver announced with little sympathy in his voice. He had a job to do, and after all, the man was dead.

Cory stood up, but the blood rushed to her head and she swayed on her feet. Efraim noticed and jumped up to steady her and they stood awkwardly over the body. She wanted to stay and talk to him, but she was driven by her need to continue her journey. She did the only thing that felt right. She hugged him and looked in his eyes.

"Find Rebecca and make sure she is okay," she said to seal his promise.

"I will," Efraim replied firmly yet obviously still reeling from his friend's death.

The driver took time to help Efraim lay George across the back of his horse. Cory hated leaving him alone to travel back to Chicago, but Efraim assured her it was a journey he wanted to make solo, his time to grieve. Cory started toward the coach and then turned back.

"What people was George from?" she asked Efraim.

"Ojibway. His real name meant Arrow Maker," he told her with a sad smile.

She nodded and continued to the coach, stepped inside and it took off down the road. She could have chosen to get acquainted with her ancestors. She could have stayed with Ellie and John and been safe until the baby arrived. This time she silenced her head and listened to her heart telling her to go west.

*

The stagecoach delivered Cory to the Illinois River at Beardstown where she bought a ticket on a small riverboat that took her to St. Louis. Cory had money to pay for a cabin on the boat and she stayed there most of the time. She tried not to feel guilty as she watched immigrant families with young children camping on the deck similar to what she and Dustu had done before. Many of them were German and spoke no English. Cory's relatives on her father's side were German, from Bavaria, and she had always thought they were the source of her brown eyes and dark complexion. Now she saw the possibility of a different line in her genes. Cory knew nothing about the Ojibway or any of the Mid-west Nations, but she vowed to learn more.

She sat for long hours on her bunk with her feet tucked under her, looking out the small cabin window at the Mississippi waters. She tried to draw from it the force that Abe Lincoln had described and that she, too, had felt on her previous journey south. From Minneapolis/St. Paul to New Orleans, joined by rivers east and west, the Mississippi flowed with energy. She used its power to push away her fear that she wouldn't find Dustu and Lucas. If she allowed herself to give in to her nervous thoughts, she would panic. Instead, she set her sights on getting to Fort Gibson in the Indian Territory, an area designated for Native Americans pushed off their tribal lands. She told herself that the path to Lucas and Dustu's whereabouts would reveal itself once she made it there. Whenever she felt the baby move, she reminded herself how happy they would all be together.

The moment she disembarked in St. Louis, she asked around until a constable directed her to a company that guided travelers westward. She hadn't realized before how big St. Louis was. As she walked the streets, she realized that during this time, it was even larger and busier than New Orleans. She also noticed the shabbily clothed "slaves" following their "masters" toting various items purchased for home or business.

It was now the first of September, but still hot and humid and Cory was grateful for the shade of hickory trees lining the streets. When she stepped into the small office of the Mt. Ozarks Wagon Train Company, she was greeted by a large woman sitting behind the front desk.

"Bonjour, Mademoiselle. How can I help you?" the woman asked with a heavy French accent. She wore a low cut peasant blouse over her plus size frame, and sweat beaded on her face and bosom. A child sat on a stool behind her waving a fan made of woven palm leaves. The girl yawned, but did not dare stop her arm from its up and down sweeping motion to cool her mistress.

"I need to get to Fort Gibson. Is there a stagecoach that goes there?" Cory asked curtly.

The woman frowned at Cory's manners, but quickly switched to her best customer-pleasing smile.

"I do not know this place you call Fort Gibson, mademoiselle, but we go to many places in Missouri.

"It is in the Indian Territory," Cory said.

"Oh, I see," the woman answered, hiding another frown along with curiosity. "We have a stagecoach that goes to Joplin. From there, you could perhaps join a wagon train heading to that area. Our coaches are beautiful with upholstered seats," she said, noticing the bump at Cory's waist. "You will be very comfortable," she added.

"When is the next coach?" Cory asked.

"You are fortunate! A coach is arriving tomorrow and will leave the morning after that," she announced proudly.

Two days seemed like forever to Cory, but she took out a coin.

"I'd like a ticket, please."

"Of course. What is your name, mademoiselle?"

"Coraline Dupont," Cory said, giving her full name, which she almost never did. She paid the woman and received her voucher.

"The coach will depart from the stable just around the corner," the woman noted as she pointed in the direction. The little girl behind her looked so tired.

"May I take the child to get some supper?" Cory asked abruptly.

The woman looked at her with both surprise and suspicion.

"You may not," she answered emphatically. She turned to the girl. "Louisa gets fed well and is valuable to me. I do not let her out of my sight. Au revoir, Mademoiselle Dupont. Have a pleasant trip," she said in a displeased tone, not hiding her expression since the ticket was now paid for.

Cory left the office and searched for lodging away from the docks, but not too near Main Street. She found a Spanish style hotel with an inner courtyard that was lush and inviting. Her room overlooked the courtyard and she opened the french doors and stepped onto a small balcony. A dogwood tree grew in the center of the garden and beds of azaleas lined the stucco walls. Nothing was blooming now, but the leafy vegetation seemed to cool the air. She came back into the room, unbuttoned her blouse, and lay on the feather bed, intending to take a short nap. She woke hours later in darkness to the sound of music in the streets. She was famished.

The hotel offered food, but she found a nearby cafe and sat outside at a small sidewalk table eating a plate of red beans and rice. St. Louis was open for business at night in much the same way as New Orleans, and the streets were full of shoppers and merrymakers. Cory finished her meal and then walked along in the warm, humid air seeking to satisfy her craving for a pastry. She found a French Creole bakery and her mouth watered as she scanned the rows of beignets, profiteroles, and eclairs. Chocolate eclairs had always been her favorite and she bought two. She found the Mt. Ozarks travel agency and saw Louisa still perched on the stool with the woman nowhere in sight. The girl couldn't have been more than eight years old. The fan was propped next to the stool and Louisa was slumped over asleep. Cory slipped silently into the office, but the girl woke instantly and sat up straight trying to appear wide-eyed and alert, her eyes blinking like a little screech owl.

Cory put her fingers to her lips to show that they needed to be quiet.

"Where is she?" Cory whispered.

"The Missus done gone to the tavern like always. She won't be back fo' hours. I'z sposed to watch the office while she gone and go get her if anyone comes in."

Cory sat on the floor and motioned for Louisa to join her. Louisa cautiously slipped off the stool and sat on the floor next to Cory. Cory opened the bag of pastries and offered one to Louisa who stared at it longingly.

"Missus wouldn't like it," she said.

"She'll never know if you eat it all up," Cory smiled.

Louisa giggled and took the eclair.

They sat quietly eating, both delighting in the sweetness and gooey cream center. After a moment, Louisa stopped.

"I should save some for my mama," she said.

Cory broke off half of her own eclair. "You eat all of yours and take this to your mama. Where is she?"

"She out back in the crib. She be asleep. My mama works all day washin' and mendin' clothes for the missus. Mama says one day my daddy gonna come back and make us free," she announced proudly.

Cory closed her eyes and hoped Louisa's wish would come true.

Louisa leaned her head against Cory's shoulder and sighed. "That was the best supper I ever had."

They fell silent and within minutes, Luisa's body became heavy with sleep. Cory guided her down to rest her head on Cory's thigh. Cory stayed awake as the girl dozed, but after an hour, she gently woke her.

"Oh!" Louisa said smiling and then she climbed back up on the stool to keep watch. She put the wrapped pastry for her mother under her loose shift.

Cory was stiff from sitting on the floor. She slowly got up and then reached in her pocket. She took out a gold coin and put it in Louisa's hand.

"Give this to your mama, too," Cory told her. She touched Louisa's cheek softly and quietly left.

The next morning, she slept in and allowed herself to luxuriate in the soft bed, knowing such accommodations would end soon. She finally rose, gave herself a sponge bath, dressed, and went to find a produce market. It was another hot day, and after buying some fresh peaches, she found a grove of hickory trees, sat in the grass, and filled up on the sweet fruit, licking the sticky juice from her fingers.

On her way back to the hotel, she stopped by the stables to see if the stagecoach had indeed arrived and was reassured to see a coach unloading. She continued on to the hotel and her route took her past the brand new courthouse. She stepped inside and felt the immediate coolness from marble walls that supported a beautifully painted dome. Others had wandered in from the street to sit on benches lining the lobby, finding respite from the summer heat.

That night she was almost too excited to sleep. The baby seemed excited too, fluttering in her womb like a nocturnal bat. Cory dreamed about making love to Lucas on the riverboat and woke up bathed in sweat and desire. She missed him more every day.

*

The trip would take twelve days if all went well the stagecoach driver had told her. It seemed an eternity to Cory. They would be traveling southwest across Missouri from St. Louis to Joplin, a passageway established by the Osage and Paiute. A hundred years later, this road would become part of the famous and scenic Route 66 that took travelers all the way from Chicago to Los Angeles.

The first leg of the journey was uneventful as they left St. Louis and crossed prairie land. The four other passengers seemed friendly enough though thankfully for Cory, not too friendly. James Cochran and Frank McMasters were businessmen traveling together to San Antonio to sell supplies to the new army forts being built there. Wiley Thompson was a recent graduate of St. Louis University and was called to be a missionary. His Bible was constantly at hand. His destination was similar to Cory's since he was headed to Indian Territory to become a teacher. Cory found out very little about the other passenger, only that his name was Johan Schindler. He was dressed in a fine, black suit and said only "big canyon," in a heavy German accent when asked where he was headed. He, too, carried a Bible, a small version that he kept in his pocket and read constantly. Cory had picked up a novel in one of several bookshops in St. Louis. As the stagecoach joggled along the trail, she pulled out her book and did her best to overcome the motion sickness that had plagued her since childhood. The bookseller had recommended a young author rising in fame for her science fiction tale *Frankenstein*. Cory had never read Mary Shelley's gothic classic, but had always wanted to, having been intrigued by the plot—a young scientist so devastated by the death of his mother that he became obsessed with bringing the dead back to life. Cory became engrossed in the narrative and related to both Victor Frankenstein and the creature he gruesomely assembled from body parts. She knew firsthand how loss can cause unbearable heartache, but without love and direction, that longing can become destructive. It reminded her of the trouble she got into after her parents were killed in the car accident.

She had just turned eighteen and missed her high school graduation because of the funeral. That summer, she began hanging out with a crowd her sister labeled "white trash." They certainly fit the stereotype; poor, uneducated, and uninformed. Cory had a different perspective. Every one of them was struggling to feel okay just like her. Like Lester. He was the self-appointed leader of their group. He could usually score drugs when others couldn't. He was a white, twenty-five years old male, but looked thirty-five. His part-time handyman job gave him a ruddy, weathered appearance and he spent his wages on beer, cigarettes, fried chicken, and drugs. He crashed at his girlfriend's apartment, the girlfriend he frequently beat up. He was constantly spouting hate toward minorities and ethnic groups, and yet, he looked out for his friends and they knew he would stick up for them.

One night, they were hanging out in an alley shooting meth. It was the same night Jill had called Cory a "slut" and kicked her out of their parent's house. The meth hyped her up and the anger she felt began to change to euphoria. Then Lester's girlfriend said something he didn't like and he hit her. He also used every word in his limited vocabulary to degrade her. Cory watched him hit her again, hating his actions, but not doing anything to stop him. Someone else did though. A cop stepped into the alley with his gun pulled, but not raised.

"Freeze!" he shouted to Lester.

Lester turned and looked at the cop. "Great. Now I have to deal with a nigger telling me what I can and can't do," he muttered under his breath to Cory and the others.

"Step away from the woman and lie face down on the pavement." the cop commanded.

"It's okay, officer. I ain't hurt," the girlfriend said, blood trickling from her nose.

Lester snickered at the cop and stayed standing.

"Sir, I told you to lie face down on the pavement," the cop repeated and raised his gun as he moved toward them.

Lester raised his hands and turned his back to the officer.

"I wasn't doin' nuthin'," he said, keeping his hands up while he began walking away.

"Stop, or I'll shoot," the cop threatened. Cory heard a siren and a moment later a police car pulled up behind the cop. Lester took off running and the cop shot him.

Lester fell to the ground screaming and grabbed his calf where the bullet hit him. Two more cops burst onto the scene. One of them directed everyone to stand back and the other one joined the cop who had shot Lester. They handcuffed him, read him his rights, and waited for the ambulance to arrive.

The girlfriend was crying and shouting as she tried to reach Lester, but two of her friends held her back.

"You motherfuckers!" she screeched at the cops.

Lester was spouting his own insolent diatribe.

"You cops think you are somethin'. Specially this nigger cop. Rule the world! You happy now? Are you happy now?!"

The black cop was kneeling at his side. He was Lester's age. Cory would never forget what he said next.

"Let me tell you somethin'," he responded. "Whatever your daddy or momma did to you or told you about niggers, I am not the cause of your pain and fear. My people trying to elevate themselves is not why you don't have a good life. Stop being a fool and victim and find out how to like yourself. No matter how much radio and TV glamorize it, it ain't dope to be trashy, mean, and fucked up."

"Fuck you, man," Lester responded though his anger had dwindled as the shock from his gunshot was numbing his spirit.

The EMT responders loaded Lester into the ambulance and took off.

"Fuck," his girlfriend said as she watched it drive away. Black streaks of mascara and tears ran down her cheeks.

The group dispersed from the alley, but Cory stood in the darkness alone and heard the cop's words playing in her head. "Stop being a fool and a victim and find out how to like yourself." That was her. Her parent's death had turned her into a victim of self-hate.

From that moment on, she was bent on changing her life. She went to college, got a job, and took care of herself. Cory had not; however, learned how to like herself. Lucas had made her feel lovable, but her baby would need a model for self-worth, a mother who experienced life fully. She remembered an inspirational workshop she took where the leader encouraged the roomful of participants to chant loudly together "It's okay to be fully alive!"

She looked out the stagecoach window at the passing wild landscape. This time period and its people did, in fact, make her feel alive. The moments she felt anxious now were usually related to actual physical danger. She realized that there was a difference between her nail-biting and constant worry in the 21st century and her new concerns for people here. She began to wonder if it was possible to leave all worry behind no matter how justified. What would that feel like? If she could find that sort of peace here, why would she ever leave?

Chapter Sixteen

HOME

In Joplin, Missouri, Cory and Wiley found another company that ran westbound stagecoaches. They left the city in the morning on a hot, muggy day. The heat was unbearable inside the coach and the odor of sweating passengers was beyond belief. She envied the travelers that covered their noses with scented handkerchiefs. They entered a wide meadow valley where the horses could make good time; however, the stagecoach began to slow down instead. Cory leaned out the window to get a breath of fresh air and her heart sank as she looked ahead. A procession of Native Americans was being escorted by Army soldiers carrying rifles fixed with bayonets. The soldiers yelled at people to move off the road, and as the stagecoach rolled past them, Cory counted over two hundred people as bedraggled and downtrodden as the group Dustu had been with. When they reached the front of the line, she looked back and the soldiers herded people onto the road again to continue walking. The stagecoach approached a bend in the trail and the group disappeared from her view. Her head was still out the window and she shouted up to the driver.

"Stop!"

The driver slowed the team of horses to a walk and scooted to the side of his seat to look down at Cory.

"What is the problem, miss?" he asked, clearly vexed by her demand.

"I'm getting out," she told him.

He pulled the horses up and stopped completely.

"Miss, we're in the middle of nowhere," he informed her as if it wasn't obvious. He twitched his bushy mustache, lifted his straw hat, and wiped his brow with a bandana. It was already a hot day, promising to become sweltering.

She stepped out the coach door. "Please hand me my pack."

He shook his head in disapproval, but grabbed her pack and handed it down to her.

"I ain't responsible for your safety, miss," he warned her.

"I know. Thanks. You can go."

"Wait! I'm going, too."

Cory turned to see Wiley disembark from the stagecoach. "Please throw down my bag as well."

The driver muttered something Cory couldn't hear, tossed Wiley's carpetbag down and then he slapped the reigns and the team of horses trotted off.

By the time the stagecoach disappeared from sight, the throng of people and soldiers had caught up to Cory and Wiley as they stood in the middle of the road. One of the soldiers shouted back down the line for the group to halt.

"Howdy, miss," he said and tipped his hat. Mister," he added, greeting Wiley. "Is someone comin' along to collect you?"

"No," Cory answered. "Where are you headed?"

"I'm Captain Rivers and we are escorting these savages to Indian country four days from here. Why did you get off the stagecoach?"

"I'm on my way to the Indian Territory, too, to join my...uh...husband and friend. My name is Cory Dupont and I am..a...historian. I'm writing about the Indian removal. I'd like to travel with you for this last few miles."

"We don't have accommodations for a woman…"

Cory cut him off. "I am used to roughing it. I have my own provisions. I will take care of myself. I simply want to come along and observe."

"Not much to observe unless you like watchin' 'em drop like flies in this heat. We got assigned to this duty, but it's the worst dang job I ever had. We got to get 'em to Fort Gibson and we can't get there soon enough for me."

"I won't be a bother and anyway, you are stuck with me now," she said since the stagecoach was long gone.

"What about you?" Captain Rivers asked Wiley.

"I'm a priest. I am going to the Indian Territory to set up a school."

Rivers rolled his eyes and let out a huff of resignation.

"Suit yourself. We need to get movin'." He turned, shouted to his sergeant to start the line walking again.

"Captain, what tribe are these people and how far have they traveled?" she asked.

"Cherokee, from Georgia," he responded and then continued on his way.

Georgia. It was the Cherokee removal Lucas had described. Cory calculated that the walk was at least a thousand miles. The journey had taken its toll. As she made her way to the back of the line, she saw people completely despondent as the blistering sun beat down on their heads. When the army stopped to camp for the night, she found a spot under a pine tree near the Cherokee women who gathered together. She spread out her bedroll blanket and sat down. Soldiers dolled out canned rations and Cory noticed the small amount the women received and the few canteens of water spread among them. Between starvation and dehydration, people were forcibly subdued. If someone did meet her eye, it was with an empty stare. Except for one man. His elderly body was emaciated and yet he stayed focused and alert. He had grey hair and wore a traditional cloth wrapped around his head like a turban, but his clothes were western style, not the calico shirts and homespun wool trousers of the other Cherokee men. His white shirt was frayed and yellowed and his black vest and trousers were covered in dust. Wiley had learned some Cherokee in preparation for his missionary work and was now talking to the man, but the man kept glancing over at Cory.

She was hungry and tired, but when she pulled out some beef jerky from her pack, she immediately felt guilty. Some of the women eyed her food and then looked away. There were three more days of travel and she had plenty of food so she took the rest of the jerky from her pack, stood up, and walked over to the women closest to her. She handed it to an ancient-looking woman who already had her hands reaching out. The woman quickly divided the food among the group. Everyone looked withered and starving.

Cory returned to her blanket, lay down and curled up in a ball. The evening air was still hot and suffocating. She heard a baby crying nearby and her hands slid to her belly to feel the life inside her. *What am I doing here?* she thought. She cursed herself for leaving the stagecoach. She had believed that somehow her presence might be helpful, that being a witness might protect the Cherokee from further harm, but the reality of the situation overwhelmed her. These soldiers were following orders from the top. As Lucas said, President Jackson mandated the removal and she was seeing a process that was bent on success. Like the new locomotives that were just beginning to roll, the momentum of empire building was on a track running full steam ahead. It made her sick, and tears of frustration streamed down her cheeks. She ached to be with Lucas and Dustu. *Why did I leave the stagecoach? Why did I put myself and my baby in danger?* She sensed that if she stayed, she would drown in sorrow.

Cory did not realize that she was making whimpering sounds until she heard someone shushing her. She opened her eyes and found women kneeling around her. They began to touch her and though she was resistant at first, the voice of the elder woman kept repeating a soothing mantra that made her relax. The others gently pulled her arms and legs from their tucked position. They turned her so she lay flat and set her arms at her sides with her palms up. They did the same with her legs, placing her feet slightly apart. Her body was now completely open and vulnerable, but she was not afraid. She looked up at each woman, each face that held both suffering and compassion. The old woman continued her incantation and placed a hand over Cory's eyes, urging her to close them. A collective worry about the future drifted away as she felt her baby fluttering to the rhythmic chant and she fell into a deep sleep.

When the soldiers marched the group onward the next morning, Cory spotted the old man in European-style clothes ahead. He gradually dropped back through the line until he was beside her.

"I am called Grey Feather. And you?" he asked in perfect English.

"Cory."

"Why are you here?"

"I somehow thought that if I was here, the soldiers wouldn't treat you badly."

"Maybe we deserve to be treated badly," he said.

"Why would you say that?" she asked, astonished.

"For abandoning our culture. For trying to adopt the white man's ways. Those ways served us for a while, but now...look at us," he said as he stared at the long line of Cherokee ahead. Then he smiled.

"No, we do not deserve to be treated like this, but the whites do not think of us as humans. They treat us like animals, enslave us, move us, and kill us. Our people have done these things, too, between tribes, but not in this way, not to annihilate." He reached into his vest pocket and took out a dog-eared page torn from a newspaper. "These are your President's words," he informed Cory as he handed her the paper.

Cory read it out loud. "What good man would prefer a country covered with forests and ranged by a few thousand savages to our extensive Republic, studded with cities, towns, and prosperous farms embellished with all the improvements which art can devise or industry execute, occupied by more than 12,000,000 happy people, and filled with all the blessings of liberty, civilization and religion?"

"He wrote it to convince Congress to sign his Indian Removal bill," Grey Feather explained.

"The benevolent dictator. How patriarchal of him," she said bitterly. "The attitude of our president is the same where I come from."

"Where do you come from?" he asked.

The way he looked into her eyes and grinned, she realized that he already knew.

"I'm from the future," she answered simply.

"Then you know that none of this matters," he said, receiving her announcement matter-of-factly. "And you also know that you cannot stop what is happening. And yet you are here."

"It is very painful to see history unfolding when you know the outcome," she said.

"What do you know?"

"I know that between this time and mine, tens of millions of people will die suffering."

"And yet you are here."

"You don't understand. In my time, humans are capable of destroying all life.

"Do you really think the Great Mother will let that happen?"

"I think humans cannot help themselves. They will use technology to play out every possible scenario of control they can imagine,"she answered soberly.

"And they may destroy themselves. They may destroy all living things. But they will not destroy everything. They will not destroy the Great Spirit."

They began to climb a long forested hill. The rise was gradual and the path winded so it wasn't difficult. The elevation actually provided some relief from the heat. The woods were dense with an understory of laurel, spicebush and viburnums. The soldiers were on alert for people deciding to leave the transport by disappearing into the foliage.

Grey Feather noticed the increased vigilance. "The soldiers do not understand that we have no knowledge of this land at all. We cannot go back to our ancestral home. We do not know the area we are going to, this land promised to us by the government. These are places where other people hunted and lived, not our people. It is this uncertainty that is more harmful than having bad food and hard travel. One cannot survive a broken spirit. These soldiers should not fear that we will escape into the woods. The white man moves anywhere and everywhere, even across oceans. That is not us."

His words "anywhere and everywhere" echoed through her mind. The phrase reminded her of the internet and global connection.

"In the future, people invent a way for everyone on earth to be connected," Cory said.

"My people are already connected. We are connected to all life, not just humans. That is the big difference between your people and my people. It is why whites that become captives, do not want to leave us. When you feel the vibration of all life, it is a song that fills your heart."

Lucas knew that song. That was why she loved him. He saw her, the part of her that she had shut off. He had helped her open her heart and be present to life whatever it brought. She looked at the women ahead on the trail, the women who had cared for her the night before. They were able to hold both anguish and compassion. How did they do that?

"How do you be kind in the face of brutality?" she asked him.

"It is not about being kind," he said. "My people are not more kind or generous than others. I have watched the whites for many years now. What I see are people that are desperate to own land and yet they are not really there with the land when they occupy it. They fight and kill to own land, but why?"

"I don't know. People will say they love their country and want to protect it. There will be great wars over land and ways of life."

"We have done this, too." he asked. "We have fought other tribes to protect our territory, but we have no experience fighting people who want us to completely disappear, people who have no respect for us, who see no value in us at all." He paused and looked up at the tree canopy and then into her eyes. "I see the worry on your face. You need to feel the coolness of the forest and breathe the clean air it gives us." He smiled. "Be grateful and you will find what you are looking for."

Over the next two days, Cory tried to practice what Grey Feather said. She stayed quiet as the group crossed a wide, forested plateau. It was marked by outcroppings of chert and below their feet were underground caverns and streams. Cory ventured into one of the caves during a short stop. She saw thin, colorless crayfish crawling in the water and a vivid orange and black salamander that skittered under a limestone rock. That evening an enormous flock of Gray Bats flew from a cavern and darkened the evening sky. The next day, the soldiers moved the group from the hills into a lower terrain of woods and meadows, but the air remained cool and a slight wind blew at their backs. They followed Shoal Creek to the Neosho River and were now deep into the northeast area of Indian Territory, later to become the northeast counties of the state of Oklahoma. She spotted her first wild elk. It was large as a horse, a regal looking buck with a magnificent crown of antlers. It stared back at her for a moment and then leaped into tall grass before any of the soldiers could take a shot. They came upon pristine, spring-fed creeks meandering through pine forests. They climbed a steep hill and descended into a narrow valley where Cory saw a small herd of buffalo. She had practiced gratitude and remained quiet, letting the beauty of the land wash over her.

A woman had begun walking alongside her. She seemed roughly Cory's age and carried a baby in a sling against her chest. The baby had thankfully survived the journey and appeared healthy. They finally spoke, but only to exchange names. The woman pronounced hers "aht-SEE-lah." Later Cory learned that it meant "fire." Atsila was shorter than Cory with copper brown eyes, heavy eyebrows and broad cheekbones that made her appear both fierce and beautiful. She wore her hair in braids and was dressed in a tattered calico dress mended with patches of cloth. Like many of the women who had repaired tears in their clothes, Atsila had used colorful diamond shapes and continued the pattern into a horizontal border around her skirt. The effect was festive and she guessed that the diamond shape had some meaning. Atsila touched the linen fabric of Cory's skirt and nodded in approval. She also touched Cory's belly and smiled. Cory grinned with pride and they continued on in silence. She was beginning to feel the comfort of being among the clan, but she woke the next morning and learned that two elders, a man and woman had died of starvation. Her silence ended. Cory went to Captain Rivers and demanded that he give out more rations. They would arrive at Fort Gibson within a day and she argued for doubling the portions of food. She was successful and the Captain gave the order.

They arrived at Fort Gibson in the early evening. The structure looked exactly like army forts in movies—walls made of pine poles with a large gated entrance. She glanced anxiously around at the people camped outside the fort in makeshift tents and deer-skin huts, but saw no sign of Lucas and Dustu. She entered the fort where an equal number of people camped in open areas away from the wooden barracks where the soldiers stayed. The Cherokee were herded to a corner of the fort to bed down for the night. Cory left the group to make a detailed search among the settlers, trappers and Native Americans inside and outside the fort, but to no avail. She rejoined the Cherokee and lay down exhausted without dinner.

The next morning, soldiers counted and organized the new arrivals. Of the two hundred that started from Georgia, sixty had died, a death rate that would be repeated over and over especially during the infamous "Trail of Tears" three years later when thousands perished. A soldier sat at a wooden desk planted outdoors in the dusty ground as the Cherokee stood in line before him. He questioned each person, identified the female head of the family and wrote her name on a piece of paper along with the number of people in her family. When presented to the supply sergeant, the information would indicate how much food should be rationed to her family. The Cherokee had managed their own farms and hunted game in the forests of Tennessee and Georgia for hundreds of years. Now they were relegated to eating canned food in order to survive. This indignity had the same effect on Cory as the slave sheets she'd seen in Natchez and New Orleans.

Angry and defeated, Cory lined up behind the group. Her practice of silence and gratitude had stopped. When it was her turn, the soldier looked up and was met by her defiant expression.

"Miss, this is for Indians."

"I know. I don't mean to take their rations, but I have no food myself," she told him. "If you could spare a can of beans, that would be great," she said curtly.

"Miss, I'm sure the Major would invite you to dine with him in his quarters," he said. "Let me send word...,"

"I would rather eat with civilized people," she said.

He scowled at her and motioned to a soldier standing nearby. "Private O'Donnell, bring this lady two cans of beans."

Basically, once catalogued, the Cherokee were allowed to leave the Fort and find land within their designated area of the Indian Territory. It was the first of September and the Cherokee had three months to prepare for winter. Their federal, designated land was in the northeast part of the territory, at the edge of the Ozarks and consisted of forests, prairie and rivers. They could farm crops and hunt for game though it was more likely that they would need to rely on domesticated livestock for meat. Soldiers and fur trappers had already decimated populations of deer, elk and buffalo in the region.

That afternoon, Cory was escorted to the commanding officer of Fort Gibson, a Major Townsend. He was sitting at his desk writing. He had a homely yet friendly face, greying temples and wavy dark hair. His uniform was clean and dust-free and his office was sparsely furnished and tidy.

"Come in, Miss...," he said as he stood respectfully.

"Dupont," she answered.

"I'm Major Townsend. Please sit down." She sat in a simple, wooden ladder back chair facing the desk and he settled back in his wooden armchair. "Thank you for giving me an excuse to stop working on these reports. I heard from Captain Rivers that you accompanied the Indian transport along with a...," he leaned forward to read the name off a ledger. "A Mr. Wiley Thompson."

"Yes, Wiley is a minister. I'm here looking for someone. His name is Lucas McCain. He was bringing a young boy here to reunite him with his Cherokee family."

"Haven't seen him. The Sergeant said you preferred to camp with the Indians. Why is that, Miss Dupont?"

"With all due respect, Major, if you don't see how the abuse of these people makes me want to avoid your soldiers, then I'd be wasting my breath trying to explain."

"Abuse? What were my soldiers doing to the Indians?" he asked.

"See?" she said as she stood up. "You don't get it."

She walked out the door and met Wiley on his way in to see the Major.

"Good morning, Cory!" he said with a big smile. "I haven't seen you in days."

"You look very happy," she remarked.

"I am!" he exclaimed. "I am going to a town called Tulsa where I will open a school for the Cherokee. The Major is providing an escort."

"I would like to wish you luck with that, but I can't. I do hope you will be okay though," she told him.

"Did you find your friends?"

"No, not yet."

"The Cherokee are headed for a place called Tahlequah. Maybe your friends are there. It is becoming a kind of central location for their people. I wanted to go there, but was told that I was not welcome. I must find the people who I can serve. There is a mission in Tulsa where I will be able to teach."

"Wiley, don't let the soldiers take children from their families in order to raise them Christian."

"What? That is not happening!" he protested.

"It will," she said.

"But...perhaps it will help them assimilate," he rationalized.

"Fuck you, Wiley," she answered. She lowered her voice so that no one could hear but him. "Forget my wish that you will be okay. I hope an 'Indian' war party attacks you and your escort of soldiers."

"But,...what a horrible thing to say. You don't mean it!" Wiley cried.

"Maybe not, but they are only bad words. You will be committing bad actions. Big difference. And if you take these children away from their families, you will face bad news when you show up at the pearly gates someday," she informed him.

Her words took him aback. He stood there speechless as Cory walked past him toward the Cherokee encampment.

She searched for Grey Feather. She was going to tell him that he was wrong. He should not let things be. He should fight for his people or they would be wiped out. She found him outside the fort lying on a blanket under an oak tree. Three women were seated around him. At first she thought he was dead. His eyes were closed and he didn't appear to be breathing. All of her sanctimonious anger instantly disappeared. She knelt beside him and he opened his eyes. He said something in Cherokee to the women and they giggled.

"Funny white girl. Causing trouble again," he translated for her. Flies were landing on the deeply furrowed lines of his face, but he didn't seem to mind.

"Are you okay?" she asked.

"I have one foot in the Spirit World and am full of joy," he told her. "I will miss my wives," he said and winked at them. Cory looked at the three women in surprise. They were all ages and all sizes and they watched him dispassionately. The wailing and grief would come later.

"You have not found what you are searching for," he said.

"No, Lucas is not here," she answered.

"That's not what I mean," he said, then he stopped to cough and clear his throat. "Go with my people to Tahlequah. Now I rest." He closed his eyes.

The women motioned Cory away. She stood awkwardly and watched the rise and fall of Grey Feather's sunken chest as he struggled to breathe. She finally turned, walked to her blanket in the fort and sat staring at her lap, numb and drained. She did not know what to do other than follow the old man's advice. Her stomach growled from lack of dinner or breakfast and she sat in a stupor, only vaguely aware of the bustling activity around her.

Images ran through her head, but they were fleeting and stirred no emotion inside her. They were glimpses of her past, of her mother and father, her childhood, college, work, her sister Jill, Michael and Sam. She saw the faces of people she had met in the present time—John and Ellie, Lucas, Dustu, William, Louisa, Cat, Amelia, Wiley, Grey Feather and Atsila. She saw the future—the birth of her baby girl, her tiny legs kicking in a bassinet, walking bravely into kindergarten, strolling down a wedding aisle. She saw generations ahead, advances in neuroscience, alternative energy, Artificial Intelligence, quantum computers. Also dark images of gang violence, police brutality, right-wing terrorists, sex trafficking, genocide, corporate fraud, dictatorships, refugees, cities flooding, nuclear explosions. The words of Martin Luther King, Jr. came to mind, his assertion that the arc of history bends toward justice, but she had experienced two time periods and his vision was paralyzed in her mind. The arc of time was frozen and threatening to fracture into a thousand pieces.

She was unaware that nearby, the chief and elders gathered in a council circle, a risky action since they were forbidden to do so during the journey. The women were busy packing their few provisions and preparing the children for travel. It was a beautiful day with blue skies and cooler temperature.

The Cherokee clan formed a line of their own volition as soldiers watched. The fort was open and when everyone was ready, they passed through the gates and out into the countryside. Atsila came over and pulled Cory up from the ground, keeping an arm around her waist and drawing her into the line. Cory felt like she was in a dense fog, moving her feet, but completely numb.

They walked into the forest and followed woodland streams eastward. A wooden sled had been fashioned to carry Grey Feather and when they stopped for the night, his wives discovered that he had died. The sled was remade with cedar to honor him and he was wrapped tightly in a blanket with cedar boughs laid around his body. The wives were with him and the sound of their grief filled the air. Cory remained in a daze, suspended in time and unfeeling.

The next morning, she was at the end of the line of travelers, following Grey Feather's travois as they broke out of the woods into a meadow clearing. The azure sky was filled with white billowing clouds that caught her attention for a moment. She remembered as a child lying in the grass watching clouds and finding familiar shapes among them. As she gazed up now, she noticed a human form, only the person had wings like an angel. Cory paused in the path and watched as the group of travelers continued ahead. As the old man's sled moved along, it came to a spot in her visual perspective that put him directly under the angel cloud. The image shifted in such a way that it appeared as if the figure was extending an arm with its palm open, beckoning Grey Feather from his sled. She froze and watched as a sort of vapor rose from his prone body and sailed up into the sky. It was a formless shape and Cory knew it was Grey Feather's spirit that had ascended. At that moment she felt a warmth at the crown of her head as if someone was touching her. She closed her eyes and sensed a diamond white light sending rays of energy throughout her body, but she wasn't afraid. She was acutely conscious and more peaceful than she had ever been in her life. The light energy formed a sphere outside her body in front of her heart. A voice in her head asked, "What do you want?" Her answer was immediate. "This," she answered, meaning the feeling she had at that moment. She felt both present and empowered. She also felt both free and connected to everything—the people she was traveling with, the land and sky, the birds and animals, even the soldiers at the fort, all life. She felt the essence from which she was born, when life was full of possibility. She realized that this essence had been available to her all along. All she had to do was push aside the conditions that cluttered her path. She felt a lightness and then her baby kicked her hard in the ribs. She laughed out loud and opened her eyes, and then looked up at the sky hoping to get a glimpse of Grey Feather's spirit even as she knew that he would always be in her heart. She reached a hand back and touched the wings of the tattoo on her back and smiled.

The Cherokee had crested a small hill and disappeared over it. She began walking to catch up and then broke into a run. She ran for her life. She ran towards freedom.

*

That evening they arrived in Tahlequah. They were greeted by other Cherokee and found the members of their Wolf clan camped along a river. Later, the clan gathered around a ceremonial fire. The night air was cool and Cory sat with a blanket around her shoulders listening to speeches she did not understand, but feeling the happiness of people who had ended their travels. They had helped her spread the word, asking if anyone had seen Lucas or Dustu, but no one had. She would begin her search in the morning, but tonight she would rest. The air reverberated with the sound of pebbles shaking in turtle shell ankle bracelets worn by men performing the Stomp Dance. She did not have to be told that the dances shared the story of suffering and hope for the future.

Someone tapped her on the shoulder and she turned slightly and glanced up. Lucas stood looking down at her with tears in his eyes unable to speak. Dustu was next to him grinning ear to ear. She cried out and jumped up to gather them in her arms. People forgave her rudeness for disrupting the dance. She was the crazy white woman who had given away all her food and had followed them around like a lost dog. It appeared she was no longer lost and some of them guessed she was not all that crazy...or all that white.

EPILOGUE

Standing Rock Reservation
Land of the Sioux Nation
near North Dakota
Winter 2017

It was freezing at Standing Rock. They had been there for a month by the Dakota Access Pipeline near the river the gas company threatened to drill underneath. It was a place of history—a land of wars, triumph and loss. Cory, Lucas, Dustu and Faith were camped with the hundred or so others led by the Sioux Nation. Over the past year, thousands had come to protest against the U.S. government's decision to let the pipeline travel through ancient burial grounds. Cory was there to support the leaders who had already utilized every legal process to stop the drilling.

She had joined a legal defense firm in Springfield, Illinois and Lucas had begun farming micro-greens in high tunnel greenhouses on her parent's farmland. They had built a modest life and Cory often saw Jill, Michael and Sam.

Amelia had been correct. Cory, Lucas, Dustu and Faith had literally blown into the future during a major tornado that hit Tulsa in 1838 and in 2017, tornadoes that caused major damage but no loss of life. So it worked. Deja vu in reverse. They had waited to try time travel until Faith was a toddler and Dustu was old enough to make the decision to go with them. He had re-connected with his family and tribe, but his adventurous spirit led him to the future.

So here they were at Standing Rock, another injustice in a modern world where the positives had still not outweighed the negatives. But Cory was committed now to Dr. King's dream of bending the arc of history toward justice.

When she started to lose hope, she always thought of angels. Not just the angel she had seen in the prairie clouds that had awakened her in 1835, but also the angels that Abraham Lincoln drew upon in 1861 when he delivered his Inaugural Address. In his speech, he appealed to the South to reconcile their differences and not break with a Union he was determined to preserve. Abolishing slavery was not his highest priority, but Frederick Douglass prevailed upon him and Lincoln did it.

He closed his Address with this poetry of hope:

"We are not enemies, but friends. We must not be enemies. Though passion may have strained, it must not break our bonds of affection. The mystic chords of memory will swell when again touched, as surely they will be, by the better angels of our nature."

***

Led by thousands of members of the Sioux Nation, over 4,000 U.S. veterans under the name "Veterans Stand" and hundreds of other protesters camped at Standing Rock in 2016 and into the winter of 2017, some chaining themselves to pipeline equipment to stop the project. On February 3, 2017, 39-year-old activist Chase Iron Eyes and more than 70 peaceably assembled protesters were arrested in a police raid ordered by the Trump administration, on charges of "inciting a riot" which is considered a felony and carries up to 5 years in prison. On February 7, 2017, President Trump authorized the Army Corps of Engineers to proceed, ending its environmental impact assessment and the associated public comment period. The pipeline was completed by April and its first oil was delivered on May 14, 2017. In May of 2020, DAPL went bankrupt.

More than 9.2 million Americans had signed a Petition against Dakota Access Pipeline (DAPL).

Acknowledgements

I am grateful for my editor at Fallen Bros. who volleys and returns what's needed with kindness and patience.

Thank you to my five siblings, making us a six-pack, and to my writer and non-writer friends and extended family who graciously read my drafts and encourage me to write from the heart.

I am thankful for my daughter and son who help me know who I am.

Much gratitude for the days Terry traveled, explored and camped with me at all of the places along the mighty Mississippi River that are described in this novel.

And thank you to the brave folks who "keep on keepin' on." People have fought enslavement and oppression since Europeans arrived in this country. Civil disobedience is not unpatriotic or lawless as our current POTUS would have us believe. Protests need to continue until systemic change happens. It requires acknowledgement and action until we rid our American culture of economic disparity and racism.

Oppression is a disease of the mind and heart, fed by greed and passed down through generations, but not impossible to cure. We have the vaccine and it is love.

About the Author

Mary Hardcastle belongs to a family of writers and teachers and became both. Starting adulthood as an actor, she gleaned experiences in theater and film in NY and LA and carried them to Baltimore where she focused on writing and teaching. Though she loves the land of the Chesapeake, she was called to set her first two novels in her home state of Illinois, land of the Miami, Winnebago, Fox and Sauk, Kickapoo, and Pottawatomie peoples. The Prairie State. Chicago Jazz. And "Land of Lincoln." She has been recognized through blogs, radio features, videos, and as writer/producer of two independent feature films, but considers her municipal job of connecting children with nature in urban parks as fundamental to building compassion and ending perceptions of "the other."